a snarky novel

The ABC's
of Dee

This novel is a work of fiction. Names, characters, places and incidents are the product of the author's imagination or are used fictitiously. Any resemblance to actual events, locales, or persons, living or dead, is coincidental.

Danielle Bannister

For information about permission to reproduce selections from this novel, write to:
daniellebannisterbooks@gmail.com

The ABC's of Dee: a snarky novel

Cover Design by CK Creations
Edited by: Rare Bird Editing
E-Formatted by: JRA Stevens

PRINT:
ISBN-13 978-1502987600
ISBN-10: 1502987600
BISAC: Fiction / Comedy/ Romance

DEDICATION

My humble thanks to my beta readers, those brave women who looked over my second draft of this book. A draft no human eye should ever see. These brave woman read the version that was not fit to print and still found a way to the last page. Their feedback, support, and suggestions have help shaped this book into what it is today. These wonder women are:

Kari Suderley,

Stephanie Philbrook

Jenn Tenney

Jeanne McCartney

Trish Davy

Cassy Bunnell

Crissy Conner

Demia Steines

Megan Stietz,

and my biggest fan, my mother, Sharon Estes.

1.

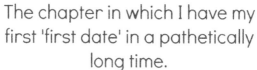

The chapter in which I have my first 'first date' in a pathetically long time.

It's ten minutes to seven and my underwear has already climbed up my ass more times than people have climbed Everest. I would love to blame Victoria's Secret for selling me faulty '3 for $25.00 panties,' but let's be honest, I'm the one trying to cram my 40-year-old fanny into underwear meant for people who don't eat food. They just looked so good on the stark white, half-butt mannequin that I thought they would totally cover the square footage of my backside. I was grossly mistaken.

As I yank the neon pink cloth from the depths no undies should go (again), I debate whether I should change them or not. On the one hand, wearing these will pretty much assure I'll be getting some because I don't intend to wear this torture device all night long for nothing. On the other hand, it is only a first date. Wearing some good old 'period panties' would guarantee that there would be no traveling South of the Elastic Band Border and my cheeks would actually be comfortably contained. Decisions, decisions.

That's it. I'm becoming a nun. Nuns don't have to deal with this shit. They don't have to question how much wedgie-control is adequate for a first date. They can just sit in silence with no judgment about who they're dating, why their legs aren't shaved, or why they haven't had sex in two years. I know. I have issues. And a lot of toys.

It's not like I've always been single. I dated a few guys in college; one was serious, but we sort of drifted apart pursuing our dreams. He was a photographer and needed to travel the world. Me? Not so much. I get air sick. Toss in a few more losers post-college (and a long bout with cancer) and you pretty much eat up my viable dating years. What I'm trying to say here is that I'm single not for lack of trying, but for lack of there being any decent, datable male humans left on the planet that would care to look my way at this late stage of my life. I'm trying not to be bitter about that.

My best friends, Gail, and Neil, both have ridiculously and annoyingly good luck at dating. Of course, they are both insanely attractive. Naturally. Some days, I think they only keep me around to show off to the world just how good they look in comparison to the common folk.

In all honesty, there is no logical reason for the three of us to be friends. It's not like we would cross paths on a typical day. Gail comes from Old Money, Neil is a designer and head of the Chicago Gay Mens' Choir, and I work in a stupid office doing stupid data entry. You couldn't find three people less likely to have things in common, but I guess that's what college does. For better or worse, you tend to bond with the people you met during that monumental time of figuring out who you are.

With Gail, we were forced together in the same dorm. Going to a State school was her way of rebelling against her parents, who wanted her to go to Yale. She lived right across the hall from my dorm room and was a bit of a needy friend. She was always knocking on my door—probably just so she could hear herself talk— but eventually, I got past her superficial 'hard-as-nails' coating and got to see her squishy, vulnerable center. She only lasted three years before her mother put her foot down and made her finish her last year at Yale under the guilt that not graduating there would throw her father into an early grave. We kept in touch during that year. Online chat rooms were just becoming a thing. God, I'm old. When she moved back to Chicago after graduation, we became inseparable.

Neil was in a class with both of us: Psychology 101. His constant whispered jokes about Freud and his dick issues made us the unlikely trio we are today. Neil is one of those people you meet in life that you know you were bound to meet. There is a rhythm that the two of us have that makes me believe we were destined to be friends. Maybe part of it is that we're all only children and found, in each other, the siblings we'd always wanted.

I should take some comfort in the fact that Gail is joining me tonight on this date, but I don't. Gail's not going for moral support, don't get the wrong idea. She's going because she wants to make sure I follow through on the bet. Ugh, the bet. Why did I agree to it? I've recalled that conversation more times than I care to admit the last couple of days.

"Dee," Gail had said over her third Long Island Iced Tea last week, "I will bet you ten thousand dollars that you can't date 100 men in a year." She downed the last of the drink, spilling a little of it down her cleavage and failing to notice.

"Gail, I'm not you," I reminded her. "There's no way I could date 100 men in a year for any sum of money. I don't have your—" I glanced down at her insane expanse of breast area, "assets." I raised my hand to get the bartender's attention.

"True, true," she said, tapping her bottom lip with her finger.

"I have my degree in writing, not fucking," I muttered.

Gail laughed. "You majored in the wrong thing, honey."

"You got that right!" I chuckled. "That degree is useless. I don't do anything even remotely related to what my degree is in.

Then again, neither do half the people I work with."

"Oh!" Gail shouted, "I have the best idea ever."

"Somehow, I doubt that."

The bartender slid another Raspberry Smirnoff my way. I twisted the cap off using the bottom of my shirt and took a swig off the bottle.

"I bet you that you can't ask out 26 men in a year." She had the grin of the Cheshire Cat.

"26." I blinked, unamused. "Why 26?"

Her grin grew as she leaned in, nearly falling off her stool. "One for each letter of the alphabet. Then you could write about it!"

I remember I shook my head at her. My writing years were long over. A college fantasy. She knew that, too. I hated that she felt the need to make that dig, so I countered her bet.

"Make it 50 grand and you have a deal," I had said, knowing she'd drop the idea. Gail may be loaded, but she's not stupid.

Well, she didn't drop it, and like a fool, I called her bluff. Now, I know I could have told her, no, but there was something about the look of doubt in her eyes when she bet me that made me want to wipe that smug, entitled grin off her face. Of course, winning the cash would be nice too. Fifty grand is chump change for Gail. She's got money coming out her wazoo. Yes, I said her wazoo. She's the Trustee of her father's oil company, so yeah, I won't feel bad taking her money. Hell, I already know what I'll use it for, but I'll never tell her. She'd just hand over the money and I do not do handouts. I earn my keep.

Not only did I have to call up this guy Adam that she said I'd be great with, she now has to see her matchmaking in action. I know I should have told her where to stick her double date, but to be honest, I really don't want to do this alone.

So now, here I am, panties in a twist (literally) as I embark on date one with the letter A. I start tugging at my bottom lip, something I do when I am nervous that Gail (and Neil) have been trying to break me of for years. I fidget when I am nervous, and right now I am officially panicking. Grabbing my cell, I hit one of my pre-sets, pacing as the phone rings on the other end.

I prepare what I'm about to say as the line connects.

"Dee, darling," Neil's bored voice echoes in my sparse apartment, "if you are calling me to talk you out of this date, you got another thing coming." I'm sure he didn't even have to look at my number to know that I would be calling. I'm apparently that predictable.

"Neeeeeeeeeeeeeil," I whine in the sing-song way that drives him nuts. "What if he's ugly?"

Neil scoffs. "Then don't give him my number."

As if Neil needs help in that department. Neil is tall, dark and bearded, which apparently makes him uber-attractive to the boys. I guess the Lumberjack look is not just a female fantasy.

"But—"

"Dee, I am hanging up now. Go. Have all the sex, it will do you some good."

The sound of him hanging up makes me curse under my breath. I want to toss the phone, but deep down I wonder if he is right. It's been eons since the Dylan 'incident'. Well, if you want to call walking in on your fiancée in bed with some big-boobed blond an incident. Honestly, it was like every clichéd movie breakup scene I had ever seen. Except this one ended with me practically ripping her fake tits off her plastic body. I may have had to take a few anger management classes after that day. Totally worth it, though. Gail, of course, had predicted that outcome from the start, claiming she could smell the sleaze on Dylan from the start. I thought it was just his Polo cologne. My bad.

Buzzzzz!

The sound of my doorbell shocks me back into the present. Gail's here. No time to change the undies from 'panty hell' now.

"Come on wedgie, let's go on a date," I mutter, as I grab my purse and head downstairs.

Pushing out of the lobby doors of my building, I find Harold,

Gail's driver, waiting for me with his hand on the door, ready to open it for me—like I'm some sort of celebrity. He shines his perfectly dimpled smile down at me, which makes me blush on command. That man is seriously hot. It's not fair. Guys shouldn't get hotter as they get older. The dude is probably older than I am but could easily date a 20-year-old without batting an eye. I'm pissed she hired him for her weekday driver. I feel like an idiot whenever he's near. I have no idea what I am supposed to say. I mean, what are the rules? Am I allowed to talk to him or is that frowned upon? Do I leave a tip? Do I thank him? Do I look him in the eye? Gah! Gail knows how frazzled I get with him, which, I am convinced, is half the reason she hired him. That, and she's kind of a sucky driver.

"Evening, Harold," I risk saying. His eyes shine down at me. God, he is pretty. He's tall, well taller than my 5'6", with dark hair that if left to grow longer would no doubt curl around his ears, and broad shoulders that every damn book gives their male leads. I now understand why. Yum. He is probably dating some buxom blond named Bambi. Guys like him always are.

I bet he didn't even need to show her his references; I bet he just smiled, and she said: mine. That's how she is. Hell, Harold probably isn't even his real name. She probably just liked the way it rolled off her tongue. Gail is … interesting in her unintended shallowness. That's probably why she doesn't have any other friends except me. It's all an act. All bark, no bite. I know she's just protecting that rock of a heart inside of her. We all do that to some extent; she just protects it with a tad more claw exposure than the rest of us.

Harold bows down a bit as I approach the car. "Ms. Harper," he says in his deep, manly voice. The kind of voice that makes your lady bits shake. Yeah, that's Gail's driver. Bitch, right?

He opens the door for me as I try to climb inside without sticking my butt right in his face. Not easy to do in spanx. The move, of course, gives me an even deeper wedgie. How is that even possible? When Harold closes the door, I begin the removal process.

"I hate everything," I spit as I try to regain my composure. Gail starts to laugh at me.

"Oh, calm down, you are going to love Adam. You'll be thanking me one of these days as you walk down the aisle."

She pulls out her designer purse, no idea who, but it's expensive, and grabs a lipstick and a compact. She glides the rose color over her Botox-padded lips.

"You've colored your hair," I note, as I click my seatbelt. Gone is the blonde from last week and in its place? A Jessica-Rabbit-Red.

She snaps her compact and runs her fingers through her short wavy locks.

"Thought it would match the dress better."

Looking down, I see that, yes, indeed, the red is a perfect match to her burnt orange sequined and very strapless dress. Suddenly, I am not feeling so good about this date. Or my choice of attire.

"Where are we going, anyway? You never told me to dress up or anything." I glance down at my very plain looking black halter-style sundress. Even the light purple sweater I threw over it at the last minute does not class me up to her level.

"Relax, Deidre, we're just going to a little French joint on Canal Street."

I roll my eyes, twice. Once, for her calling me Deidre and once for the restaurant. My guess is that the place is anything but little.

I tuck a strand of my Jennifer-Aniston-style-hairdo back inside the silver butterfly clip that I thought I'd caged it in with earlier. There is a fake violet gemstone in there that would never pass as the real thing.

"So, who is this guy you set me up with? I need more than 'his name is Adam, and he is cute as a button.'"

Gail waves her hand at me, as though she is batting away a

fly. "I showed you a picture of him."

"Yeah, wearing sunglasses. I bet he's cross-eyed. He's not cross-eyed, is he? Or worse. A uni-brow? You've set me up with someone who has a uni-brow, haven't you?"

Gail smirks at me.

"He's actually one of my drivers I use when I go visit Mother in Oak Brook. Apparently, he was born there so he knows the area well. You know him, right, Harold?" Gail says leaning forward a bit.

Harold. Shit. Kinda forgot he could hear us.

"Yes, Ma'am, Adam does areas outside of the city." The tone in Harold's voice suggests there is something not-so-great about this Adam guy, or maybe I am just really wanting to not go through with this date.

Gail looks at me as though his answer solves the problem.

I clear my throat, "Harold, I know you don't know me very well, but would you consider Adam a good match for me?"

His eyes look back at us from the rear-view mirror. Well, they go to Gail. She nods her 'permission to speak freely' smile.

"No."

That's it. No elaboration, just a flat, firm no.

Gail crosses her arms. "Oh, what does he know? He's just the driver."

"Gail!" I say affronted enough for the both of us. "That was rude."

Her cheeks flush a bit, but she quickly busies herself with the contents of her purse again.

"For reals, Gail. What's going on with you lately? It's not like you to act this high and mighty. Is your mom in town?" Gail's mother is the quintessential rich bitch and Gail tends to slide into old habits when her mom stops in for a criticism of Gail's life, I mean, visit.

She doesn't speak for a moment, so I know something big is going on, but she then lifts her head up and sighs.

"No. She's not in town, thank God. I am being bitchy, aren't I? I'm sorry," she huffs.

My eyes dart up front. "I'm not the one you should be apologizing to."

Gail sighs into her cleavage. She pouts like a child forced to tell her sibling she's sorry for yanking their hair. "Harold, I'm sorry. I'm a bitch." She pushes a button, and the glass slides up, blocking Harold from our view. Pity.

I cross my arms and frown at her. "That's not what I meant; you know?"

She sighs again and looks dramatically out of her tinted glass window. "I know. I'm just—Ugh, I feel really cranky lately and it is driving me mad."

I move my feet out of kicking area before I speak.

"Menopause?"

She shoots an evil glare at me and I cannot stop laughing.

"What? You're… of an age where that's not out of the realm of possibilities."

Instead of the onslaught of snide remarks that I have braced myself for, Gail grows quiet. She does that when she thinks. I watch her as her hands fold absently around her stomach. Almost…cradling it.

Holy Shit!

"Are you pregnant?" I ask louder than I mean to.

"Shh!" she hisses. "I don't know. Okay? I should have started a few days ago. I am like clockwork, you know that, but it's also true that I am, older and that this sort of irregularity is common for my age bracket." Her perfectly painted on face suddenly shows the lines that she so carefully tries to hide from the world.

"Gail—have you—have you taken a test?"

The solemn look she gives me confirms that she hasn't.

"Let's just go to dinner. I'll be fine. This is just PMS. Nothing more."

Her hands tremble as she pushes herself back against the window. I have never seen her act like this. Not in all the years that I've known her. She's always the calm, cool and collected one. Seeing her so scared and unsure makes me feel like the balance of the world has shifted a bit. I don't like it and I'm gonna fix it. Gail isn't the only one who can be bossy. I lean forward and hit the button to lower the glass.

"Harold," I say, "can you stop at the nearest CVS or even a White Hen?"

Gail looks at me in utter shock.

"I need to buy some feminine products." My cheeks blaze with heat as I 'take one for the team.' Harold quickly says 'of course' and I close the glass again.

"What are you doing?" she asks me.

I pull up the front of my stupid dress before my little ladies fall out then grab her hand. "We're gonna go buy a pregnancy test, and you are going pee on that stick. I need to know right now if you have the spawn of Prada growing inside you or not."

Despite her best effort to stay angry, she cracks a smile at me.

"Thank you, Dee."

I smile back. "If it's positive, I am so drinking all your wine tonight."

"Deal," she says, and her smile gets a little brighter.

For the next few blocks to the store, we hold each other's hands, neither of us saying a word. Until we find out for sure, there isn't much to say.

When Harold pulls into a spot, Gail squeezes my hand.

"We got this," I say, squeezing hers back. "I'll even buy it so you don't have to look like it's for you, okay? You just go into the restroom. I'll meet you there when I have it."

"What did I ever do to get a friend like you, Dee?"

"Hell if I know." I smile.

Harold opens the door for us, and we get out. Well, Gail gets out, I sort of bumble out. I'm full of grace.

Draping my arm over her shoulder, I lean in and ask, "If you're prego, that means I don't have to go through with this stupid bet, right?"

She laughs, "Hell no. If I am, I'll need something to amuse me for the next 9 months as I get fatter and fatter and more bitter at the world."

"You can be more bitter than you are now?"

She smiles. "You have no idea."

I snort in disbelief as we enter the store. Discreetly, she finds her way to the back where I had instructed her the public restrooms would be. I wonder how long it is been since Gail actually pissed in a public toilet.

Once she's out of sight I look around the store. The glare of fluorescent lighting and bad muzak is enough to make me nauseous. How can someone work with this all day long and not want to stab their own eyes out?

Walking as fast as I can past the rows of cheap perfumes that make me sneeze my damn head off, I find my way to the 'padded aisle of shame.' I haven't had to come down this neck of the woods in years. That's the one advantage of not having your baby making parts anymore. I remember, though, back when I did have to pick up tampons or liners, pre-cancer. I'd just search for the color of my tampons and grab them as fast as I could and then get out of there, hoping I'd gotten the right thing. Heaven forbid anyone knew I had a period every month. Yeah, I was pretty pathetic.

Since I'm not searching for light blue tampons, however, I have no idea what I am looking for. I've never had to take a pregnancy test before. Dylan was snipped, and the other four guys I've ever been with were all protected encounters. I can now understand why Gail has put this off so long. I can feel the eyes of every person in the store on me (even the eyes of the people ten aisles over). I look at the back of a test kit to read the instructions.

I'm on the second line of directions when an older lady turns her cart down my aisle and stops next to me to look at some Depends. Guess it could be worse.

"Expecting a little one, are we?" she asks as she drops a pack of the lady diapers into her cart.

"Guess we'll find out," I say, waving the package at her.

I can tell that she wants to start a conversation with me about my 'condition', and I have no interest in participating, so I turn away quickly and rush up to the front counter where there is, of course, a guy behind the register. Not a supermodel looking guy, but still, not bad on the eyes. The type of guy I could see myself dating, and here I was about to put a pregnancy test on his counter. How good a friend is Gail, really?

Since no other register is open, I wait in line behind two frat boys with a pack of beer under each arm ahead of me. I hide the test behind my purse as best as I can and pretend to have a sincere interest in the advertisement on a chewing gum display to my right. Ooh, look, this one has no sugar. I frown. No sugar, but three ingredients I can't pronounce. I'll stick with the sugar. I know that's grown from the earth and not cooked up in some chem lab.

I see a slight look of disgust on the cashier dude as he watches the frat boys depart, which makes him instantly more appealing. My eyes dart down to his left hand, as they always do when I see a non-hideous looking, potentially dateable guy. Not claimed. I smile at him. He returns the smile through a golden

The ABCs of Dee

Danielle Bannister

beard that could use some manicuring. I can't help but notice his name tag. Brian. I smile wider. His name starts with a B. The fates have spoken. Instinctively, I know my date with Adam is gonna tank, primarily because Gail set us up, and as much as I love her, she has no idea what I like in a guy. Might as well move on.

Taking a deep breath, I bat my eyes. Yup. I am pathetic.

"Looks like those guys are about to have some fun," I say nodding after the nimrods who just left.

Brian doesn't show any response. "Never been a fan of alcohol poisoning."

"Good point." I fiddle with the box in my hand.

"Can I help you find something?" he asks when I don't say anything.

Don't be a chicken. You have to do this 25 more times!

"Actually, there might be. Any chance you'd be free to go out sometime?"

The guy looks at me for a second.

"Wait, are you asking me out?"

I bite my lip and pray that no one can hear us.

"Um, yes?"

He looks down, clearly checking out my breasts before he answers. Nice.

"Cool. Sure, I guess."

My eyes light up. "Yeah? Great, awesome. Well, here's my number," I say digging into my purse and pulling out my business card. I slide it across the not so smooth glass counter. It's more brown than clear, which is frankly disturbing.

"K," he says tucking my card in his shirt pocket. "That all?"

Is that all. Is that all I needed? "Oh, I need to get this, too." I nudge the box toward him, sort of hoping he won't actually notice what it is. Brian's eyes pop up at me. So much for that.

"Oh, no! It's not for me. Promise. It's for a friend. She's actually in the bathroom now, waiting to pee on it."

I'm not sure why I think that clarification will help my situation.

"Here, just take this." I throw some money at him and rush off to the back. "Call me."

Poor Brian just stands there, holding a limp twenty, thoroughly confused by what just happened. Gail owes me big for this debacle.

By ten past 8 we are officially uber late for dinner, but giddy as school girls. Gail is not pregnant, and I got Brian checked off my list in return. We've been laughing so hard about how ridiculous the whole situation is that when Harold opens the door for us at the restaurant, I have almost forgotten why we're here. Ugh. Adam. Gail's date will be tolerable. Charles. He works at her dad's company. He's a wet noodle, but a noodle you know is better than the one you don't.

"I want a vodka martini in my hand before we sit down at that table, got it?" I hiss in her ear.

"But of course, darling."

The Maître d' greets Gail like a life-long friend, giving air kisses on both cheeks as only pure snobs know how to perform.

"Garmond, can you see that we get two Vespers before we dine with those vulgar men?" she giggles and flashes her sexy smile at him. Predictably, he does just as she orders, something Gail is quite used to.

"What the hell is a Vesper?" I whisper.

Gail glances down her elegant nose at me.

"Seriously? It is only the best martini you will ever have in your life. Trust me. They are to die for."

Our drinks arrive on a small tray held by the most uptight waiter I have ever laid eyes on. He has so much gel in his hair to slick back obvious curls, that I can almost make out my reflection in it when he lowers his tray for us in some sort of bow. Gail is oblivious to the waiter and his grandiose gestures; he is, after all, only the vehicle that brought her drink. Slick Rick, as I will forever remember him, leaves us alone. I take a huge swig from the paper-thin glass, feeling the olive brush my tongue. After I swallow, I am assaulted with the strongest martini I have ever had in my life. My throat feels like my flesh is being eaten away.

"Holy shit!" I croak, coughing a bit as my taste buds regain consciousness.

"Told you," she winks and loops her arm around mine, dragging me to my doom.

Three hours and four Vespers later, Harold is helping me to the car. I am laughing my ass off and barely able to stand up straight.

"Are you okay, Ms. Harper?" I hear him ask in some far away corner of the world.

"She's fine. She just had to endure the world's most boring date known to mankind. Remind me that I need to fire Adam. I never realized how ridiculously droll he was. My date was no better. Note to self, just because they have hair, doesn't mean they are instantly fuckable. Take us back to my place. I don't want her home alone this drunk. Knowing Dee, she'd end up dead in a puddle of her own vomit."

"Yes, Ma'am." I hear his sexy voice say.

A door shuts near my head and I smell Gail's perfume waft over me before I feel her weight shake the seat around me. It kind of makes me want to hurl. The fun stage of drunk is starting to wear off, now comes the reason I don't normally drink this much.

"Ugh, why aren't you shitfaced, too?" I moan. I try to sit up but it only makes my stomach swirl. "That was the most horrendous date I have ever been on."

"I have had worse," Gail says, looking down at her nails. It's true. She has.

I rub my hand over my forehead, which has begun to perspire. Shit. I am gonna be sick if this car keeps bouncing.

"I should not have taken your drink," I groan.

"No, what you shouldn't have done was order a third."

I grumble something I can't even comprehend as I roll down the window to feel the breeze on my face. "Adam should count as five dates, you know. That was torture."

There is something about her silence that feels off. Or maybe I am just about to pass out. We hit another damn bump. Yup. Definitely about to pass out.

***

Journal Entry: Adam is not worthy of his name. If God made man like this guy, we would have died off centuries ago.

2.
 ## The chapter in which I find out how important coffee really is to me.

I wake up to the feeling of blankets being ripped off me. My warm bubble of happiness is instantly popped. Someone is about to be killed for this atrocity.

"Shit. What's going on?" I open my eyes and squint at the light that's gouging its way into my retinas. Through the blur, I can decipher that I'm in Gail's apartment. I can tell by the color palate. Everything in her place is red, black, or white. It feels like an ad for Target or some shit. They are really loud colors for someone waking up with a hangover.

"You wake up now? I clean room." The thick accent tells me it's one of Gail's housekeepers. The frown on the woman's face tells me that she is not happy with my upsetting the natural flow of her cleaning day. Fine. I do the best I can to get out of the bed as quickly as possible. Fortunately, Gail left me in my clothes, which smell vaguely of vomit, that must also be why my morning breath is so pleasant. Note to self: Never drink Vespers again. Scratch that. Never drink again.

I duck into the attached bathroom and after a quick splash of cold water on my face and a few rounds of thunderous yawns, I stumble out of the room to the waiting staff and their buckets of cleaning product that make my stomach lurch.

I give them all a nod trying to hide the fact that I'm hung-over, but they all know. You can't hide this. I look like a donkey's left nut.

The floors are still a bit damp from the mop that must have just been run through the hall. I curse, knowing I'll catch hell for leaving footprints from one of the cleaning crew. Trying to leave as little evidence as possible, I leap across the floor. Technically, it's more of a hop than a leap. My years of leaping have long since passed. I step from one white shag throw carpet to the other, hoping that my bare feet won't get them dirty. I've never understood Gail's designs. She has white rugs, black leather furniture and blood red accent pillows around every corner of the massive apartment. Just, why? Of course, that will probably change next month when she sees a painting she loves and will redo the whole thing based around that. Guess with that much money, you can do whatever you want.

From the living room, I see that the balcony door is open. The smell of coffee floats in from outside, indicating where Gail will be. Cool misty air hits my face as I walk onto the landing.

Gail is at the railing, coffee in hand, looking out at the city skyline.

"Humph," I say before I collapse, face-down, onto her red patio couch.

"Afternoon," she says.

I lift my head up and moan. "Why did you let me drink so much?"

"One of us needed to." She takes a sip from her coffee, her eyes never leaving the horizon.

"I shouldn't have taken your drink. I am sorry. I just … he wouldn't stop talking about all the famous people he drove around. It was making me nauseous." I blanch at the memory. "Why didn't you just order another? That way we could be hung-over together right now." I rub away some of the sleep that still lingers around my eyes.

Gail doesn't answer but just continues her skyline stare-down.

"Fine, don't talk to me," I grumble. "I'm just gonna lie down here for a little bit." I flop back down on the couch and throw my hand over my face to shield me from the evil sun.

"Dee, I'm pregnant."

My grogginess is instantly lifted. I fling myself upright.

"What? But you took a test! There was only one line! One

line means not preg—you told me it only showed one line."

Gail nods, but doesn't look at me.

"There was only one line. And a second, barely there, line."

My head pounds but I try to sober my brain up. She needs me.

"Why didn't you tell me?"

She sighs and turns to face me. Her elegant frame still leans on the railing. "I wasn't ready to believe it."

"Who's the father?" I ask, careful not to say: Do you have any idea who the father is? Even hung-over I can be tactful.

Gail looks at me. The small shrug of her shoulders confirms my earlier suspicion; she has no idea. I can see she hasn't slept. Her mascara has smudged a bit down her normally perfect face.

"Okay. It's okay." I say my head spinning trying to keep my body not only upright but thinking logically. "We'll make a list. Narrow down the possibilities--"

Gail holds up her hand to stop me. "No. Don't bother. I had all night to think about this. None of them would be adequate fathers nor would I be willing to drag their names through the mud. I also know that I'm not able to parent this 'thing' on my own, so …"

"So, you're going to put it up for adoption?"

Gail makes a face. "Good God, no."

Oh.

"Wow. Abortion … I guess I always assumed—"

"Deidre Harper! You know I couldn't do that! Mother would skin me alive. She may look like a fragile old biddy, but that woman will drop you to your knees if you wrong her." Gail walks over to the couch and sits down beside me.

I rub the back of her shoulders, and she drops her head a bit.

"What's the plan then?"

Gail turns and looks me in the eye. "It's not obvious? I am going to have to find this child a father."

I wait for the punch line, but it doesn't come.

"Okay. Is there a Daddies 'R' Us I don't know about?"

She stands up and walks into the apartment again, with me right at her heels.

"It will be easy, darling. I'll just do this whole 'dating-bet' thing with you, but I won't be shopping for sex. Well, not just sex. I'll be hunting for the best dad my child could want."

I can't help myself, I burst out laughing.

"You can't be serious? This is no way to find your kid a father. Besides, we're not gonna keep doing the bet. The bet is off. We have more important things to focus on right now." I say, louder than I probably should, given the fact that 'the help' is still in the house.

Gail grabs my elbow and yanks me to the corner near the fireplace and practically hisses into my ear.

"What is more important than finding my baby a father? Hmm? Or having this child's Godmother find herself a husband she deserves?"

I stare up at Gail, dumbfounded.

"Godmother?" My eyes begin to fill with tears. I am not sure why I am moved by this since I am agnostic, but I know what a big honor the title alone is.

"Yes, dummy. If I am going through with this," she rubs the small of her belly, "then I am gonna need all the help I can get."

I give her the biggest hug my hung-over body can manage. This plan of hers is not logical nor is it explainable, but if it allows her to take comfort in her current condition, then who am I to tell her she can't at least try?

"So," Gail says, forcing a smile on her face. "It seems as though I need to find myself an A for tonight, then we'll be all caught up," Gail says walking over to a small roller desk. She takes out what I presume is her 'little black book,' although hers is red. Naturally.

"Actually, I am already up to C…"

Gail looks over her shoulder to smirk at me. "No, you're not. You're back at B. Drug-store boy called your cell while you were passed out. I took the liberty of taking the call for you. Told him you'd call back. He gave me his work number." She handed me a slip of paper.

I groan. "Fine, but that puts us both at B dates," I counter, "because let's be honest, Adam should count for both of us."

Gail smirked. "This is why I love you."

Despite the oddity of the morning, we both break down and start laughing like a bunch of twelve-year-old goobers. That's the thing with Gail and me. We always find a way to make each other laugh, and that is worth more than anything money can buy.

After we've had a full brunch, complete with eggs Benedict, a gallon of coffee (decaf for Gail), and a pile of Canadian bacon so salty I think one of my arteries caved in, Gail and I make our plan of attack. I am to call and make a date with Brian, and she will pull a B name from her book. She assures me this is not cheating since she can't remember 90% of them anyway.

While she goes into her study to make her calls, I opt for the guest room. I do not want her listening in on what is sure to be an extremely awkward conversation. The cleaning crew left mid-brunch, so I am free to go back in, but not before they witnessed me licking the bacon grease off my plate. I make no apologies.

Shutting the door behind me, I sink down onto the white goose down comforter and take out the slip of paper that Gail gave me a moment ago. It's already crumpled around the edges from my incessant fidgeting.

Painfully slow, I dial the first few numbers but stop just short of hitting the last one. Tossing the phone to the edge of the bed, I bite my bottom lip in frustration.

"Dee?" There's a knock at my door. It's Gail. "I've got a date tonight with Blaine for dinner."

"Blaine?" Who names their child Blaine?

She either doesn't hear the snide tone in my voice or she chooses to ignore it.

"See if your fellow, Bradley, wants to tag along."

I huff to myself. "His name is Brian, and I don't think he'll be interested in meeting Blaine." I feel like a teenager talking to my mother the way the words come out of my mouth, like verbal eye roll.

"Well, convince him, then. I need you there. I need someone to consume my wine."

She walks away before I can give her an earful on that. Her plan is to not let any of these 'potential' daddies know that she is with child. She doesn't want to scare them off. It's a valid point, but underhanded, nonetheless.

Annoyed with Gail for landing a date in two minutes flat, I retrieve my phone from its attempted suicide off the bed and dial the numbers as fast as I can. Like a band-aid—right off.

There's no answer after the first few rings, so I begin to prep the message that I'll leave. That is, of course, when he answers.

"This is Brian." His voice sounds deeper than from when I spoke to him last, but I was also holding a pregnancy test at the time, so my memories are not to be trusted.

"Yeah, um, this is Dee, from the other night."

"The Not-Prego-Lady. Right, right. You got my message."

I tuck a chunk of my hair behind my ear and start to pace the floor.

"Yeah, I did. So, um, listen," I pinch my eyes closed hoping to block the embarrassment from coming. Of course, it doesn't work. "Would you, maybe, wanna like, go for a drink or something sometime?"

There is an awkward silence.

"I don't drink."

Not a drinker...So they DO exist.

"How about dinner, then?" I try, still not sure how I could date a non-drinker.

He coughs lightly. "That might be tricky, 'cause I am gluten free. Not a lot of places around that offer that, I mean, they may say they are gluten free, but that stuff hides in sneaky places, so you have to be careful."

No bread either?

"How about some coffee? That's gluten free, right?"

There is a silence.

"I don't do coffee either. Caffeine is bad for you, you know?"

I hang up.

***

Journal Entry: Brian is a like a decaffeinated latte. All fluffy and tasty looking but has no real point to it.

3.
The chapter where Neil saves my ass. Literally.

Looking in the mirror, I wipe off the third shade of lipstick for the evening. "Why does every color I put on make me look like I am a two-bit whore?"

"Maybe because you're about to become one," Neil replies, batting his eyes.

Neil walks over to me and kisses me on the head. I smack him on the ass as he plops onto my unmade bed.

"What's that supposed to mean?"

Neil purses his lips. Why does he get to have the perfect-colored rose lips and lashes to die for? It's not fair.

"Dee, you are about to go on your third date in as many days. You keep this up you'll have Gail beat."

"Ha, ha." I stick my tongue out at him. "Technically, I was drunk for Adam so that wasn't really a 'date,' and I didn't actually go out with Brian, either."

"Yeah, how did you get out of that one?"

I wipe off another failed shade and opt to go with chap-stick.

The junk would probably just end up on my teeth anyway.

"Loophole." I grin at him and walk out of the bathroom and open my closet door searching for shoes that won't make me want to murder people. "The bet technically said I just had to ask the guys out. I asked Brian out."

"Ouch. He said no?" he reaches for my hand, ready to comfort me.

"Worse. He didn't drink coffee."

Neil covers his mouth in mock shock. "You dodged that bullet."

"Right?" I say, disappearing in my closet.

"So, who is this Christoph guy?" he asks. "And more importantly, is he cute?"

I walk out of the closet with my black ballet flats in my hands.

"No. Put those back. Those make you look like a soccer mom." Frowning, I turn around and look for my wedding/funeral heels. We could be here awhile. I have no idea where I stuck them.

"I work with Christoph," I say, almost bumping my head on a low hanging shelf. "He's in accounting. He's a low talker. I can hardly understand him." I come back out with the shoes in my hand. "Presuming I didn't actually misunderstand him; I am meeting him at the bar at 8. Of course, he could have said 'That was Lars I ate.'"

"Charming."

I grin and do the prerequisite fashion twirl.

"Got your big girl panties on?"

At that comment, my stomach starts to twitch with butterflies. I am about to walk into a restaurant and have dinner with a co-worker. What if this bombs? I would have to either get another job or move to Australia. One of the two.

"I can't do it. I can't go. I am gonna blow this and somehow I'll end up losing my job over telling him off next week when he doesn't return my calls, then I'll have to find someone to rent my apartment because I won't be able to find a new job and end up moving back in with my mother and her six cats! That might be preferable, actually. I mean, I work with Christoph, sure, but how do I know if we'll have anything in common?" I know I am rambling, but I ramble when I am nervous. "I am gonna end up stuck talking to him about accounting shit, aren't I? Neil, I suck at math!"

Neil comes over to me and places his hands on my shoulders. "Calm down. Breathe. You know I got your back. I'll head to the restaurant around 9:00, so if you need an out, just excuse yourself to the girl's room and I'll take you away from that big bad man."

"Really?" I jump on the bed and give him a huge hug. "I love you!"

Neil grunts from my weight and whispers, "You know I am gay, right?"

"Ha! I do. That is what makes you the perfect man."

He pushes me off and points to the door.

"Go. Shoo. Drink lots."

Now that, I could do.

Three glasses of Chardonnay in, Christoph and I are hitting it off like long lost friends. The wine must have loosened his vocal cords because I've only asked him to repeat himself twice. We've managed to talk about everything and nothing over the first course, and I realize that this dating thing might not be so bad after all. I have completely over reacted. I can't wait to tell Neil. Neil! Shit! I glance down at my cell. It's 9:20.

I almost gag on my fish when I spot him out of the corner of my eye near the restrooms. He's pursing his lips at me.

"Are you all right?" Christoph asks me. He pushes out of his chair to help.

"Um, yeah. I just need to use the restroom. I—I got something stuck in my eye. I'll be right back. Hands off my salmon," I say, laughing.

Christoph smiles and raises his hands in mock surrender. He's so cute. Balding, but cute.

Neil is tapping his foot against the tile, clearly annoyed with me by the time I get there.

"Sorry. Sorry, I forgot all about the time. Your services aren't required. Turns out he's actually great." I am beaming. Me. Beaming.

He looks down at me and places a hand on his head. "It's like I have taught you nothing in all the years we've been friends."

"Look, if you want to make fun of my clothes some more, can it wait till I get home? I kind of want to get back."

"Oh, Dee. Sweet innocent, Dee." Neil pouts. "He's gay. Well, apparently bi now." He rolls his eyes.

"No, he's not."

Neil sighs one of the most overdone sighs a person can do. He's very good at it. "Yes, honey, he is. I have slept with him, only back then, he went by the name of Kris. Trust me. Don't waste your time." He looks over my shoulder then back at me. "Itty-bitty weenie," he whispers, then turns, making sure to wave at Christoph on the way out. The color that Christoph's face turns when they lock eyes confirms what Neil just told me.

Well, fuck.

***

Journal Entry: Christoph putts from the rough.

4.
The chapter when Gail makes a not so wise call.

It's been three weeks and I have done nothing more than go to work, avoid Christoph's floor, and come home. Mercifully, Neil has not mentioned anything to Gail about that night. I couldn't take it if they both knew. It was bad enough that I have to endure Neil's pity looks every time I see him now. Hence the hiding out in my apartment. My self-confidence just slipped down about twenty notches. My gay-dar used to be so good years ago.

Tonight, is definitely a TV binge sort of night. Perhaps it's time I tried to get into the whole Dr. Who thing? It's all the girls talk about at work. I've managed to fake my interest in it so far. May as well try and see if it's worth all the fuss.

I have just flopped my pathetic butt onto the couch when there is a knock on my door.

"I am not home!" I shout. It can only be Gail or Neil and I am not up for entertaining at the moment.

"Dee, let me in. I have a surprise for you." It's Gail. Grumbling, I get up and pull my bathrobe tighter. I walk to the door and unlock it. "It's open," I say, plodding back into the kitchen. This will be her 'cheer up' visit. Neil must have told her. I'll need wine for this one. "Don't think you're getting any of my ice cream," I say from the kitchen. "Cause I am not sharing." I open the fridge to pick a white to go with my ice cream when I hear Gail enter the room with me. The tell-tale click of her heels is unmistakable.

"Um, Dee, darling. I would like you to meet someone."

My hands stop mid-grab, mere inches from liquid happiness. Slowly, I close the fridge. She better not have brought someone into my apartment while I'm in my pj's. Not if she values her life.

Clutching my fists, I turn around. There, next to Gail, is a tall, balding man wearing a tux. He smiles at me before I get my bearings.

"Dee, this is David. He's in sales. He works in Daddy's office."

"Hi," I say slowly as I shoot daggers at Gail. "What brings you to my neighborhood, Gail?" I ask as politely as a robe-wearing-train-wreck like myself can.

Gail steps forward. "I thought you and Dave could go see that new opera." She pulls out two long yellow tickets. "Surprise."

"Opera? What are you talking about?"

"Well, Mother gave me the tickets and you know I cannot stand the opera. David was in the office at the time and told me that this show was divine and shouldn't be missed. Since I didn't care to go, I thought you and Dave might enjoy it." She gives me her killer smile. She thinks she's helping me with my next letter.

I snap my fingers. "Darn it. I would have loved to have gone, but as you can see, I am in my pajamas!"

Gail doesn't miss a beat.

"Isn't she a riot? I told you she was funny." She walks over to me. "Dave will wait here while we get you dressed. Won't you, Dave?"

He smiles broader, showing off a prominent crooked front tooth. Lovely.

"But, of course," he says sitting down on my couch, next to my melting ice cream. I'm going to kill her. My dessert is ruined.

Biting my tongue, I lead Gail into my room, not caring in the least about the slam the door makes as I close it.

"What the fuck, Gail?"

She lowers her head. "I know, I know, I am sorry. I—I thought..."

"You thought that your pathetic friend can't find her own dates and figured you would fix that for her by showing up on her doorstep, unannounced." I gesture at my robe.

"No!" She looks at me, affronted. "That's not it at all. I actually was going to ask him out myself—until I saw that tooth." She shivers.

"Oh, so if he's not good enough for you, might as well toss the sucker to your friend?"

"No—Okay, so that is how it looks, but honest, I thought you might like him. We have such opposite tastes that I figured if I hated him maybe he'd be perfect for you." Intentionally or not, she rubs the small of her belly, instantly defusing my anger.

I let out a long slow breath. "Yeah, well, you figured wrong," I mumble.

Gail nods. She looks like she is about to cry. Damn it. Now I feel like a jerk.

"I'm sorry, Dee. God, please don't be mad. I don't know what I was thinking. I swear this kid is making me do crazy things. I mean look at me. I'm crying? I never cry!"

I pull her into a hug and rub her back while she gains control.

"It's okay," I whisper. "It's hormones. That's what is supposed to happen."

She sniffs a few times before she pulls away.

"Hey, I have an idea," I say. "Let's kick Dave to the curb and have a girls' night in. We can pop in a movie, maybe order a pizza, and I will, begrudgingly, share my ice cream."

That brings a smile to her lips.

"I call the soup spoon," she says quietly.

I laugh in spite of myself. "Deal."

"What do we do about toothy?" Gail asks.

"You leave him to me." I link her arm in mine and we head back out to our guest. Dave stands up the moment we come out of my room. He is a gentleman. I'll give him that.

"Dave, my friend, it looks like there has been a change of plans. Gail and I would rather stay in for the evening if that is okay with you?"

He looks at Gail, then back at me. "Oh. I see. Well. Of course." He starts fidgeting with the bottom of his sleeves. "Would you mind if I used your restroom first?"

"Sure, um, it is right behind you, just before you came into the kitchen."

Nodding, he turns and disappears into the bathroom. God only knows what sort of laundry I have lying on the ground in there. I think one of my bras might be on the towel rack. Naturally.

Gail plops on the couch, kicking her feet on top of my cluttered coffee table littered with Entertainment Weekly and The National Enquirer. Both are highly amusing in their accuracy.

"I am the worst friend in the world, aren't I?" Gail asks after a moment.

I join her on the couch and put my arm around her. "Yes. Yes, you are. But I'll keep you just the same, I suppose."

She rests her head on my shoulder. She needs more sleep. At the sound of the bathroom door opening, we both sit up higher.

"Guess we should say goodbye to Dave," I say.

Before I get up, Dave walks into the room. Naked as the day he was born.

"Dude!" I shout.

Dave smiles, resting his hands on his hips. "I know. I'm hung. I used one of your razors to tidy up. Hope you don't mind."

I gag. "Gail," I say, shielding my eyes. "Deal with this, please."

"Gladly." I can hear the enjoyment in her voice. "Dave, darling? When we told you we wanted to stay in tonight, we meant Dee and myself. It was a polite invitation for you to leave, not to disrobe and engage in a threesome."

Dave quickly covers himself with his hands and turns red. "But I thought—Oh God. You won't tell the board, will you? I'm sorry, I thought maybe she was gay," he says looking at me, "and that you were one of those rich kinky women, I—I."

"I think you should go now, Dave," Gail says calmly.

He swallows, but then turns and runs back to the bathroom, his hairy butt cheeks clenched together as he does.

"I need bleach." I gag.

"For your razor?" Gail smirks.

"For my eyes. I need to find a way to un-see that."

***

Journal Entry: Dave. No. Just, no.

5.
The chapter where I don't act my age.

I hate my alarm. I hate the reason my alarms goes off. I hate dragging my ass to work, especially today. As if Mondays don't suck enough as it is, I have a meeting in the 6th-floor conference room today which means I'll have to walk by Christoph's desk. Ugh. What a disaster that was. For about two minutes, I thought I'd met a nice, semi-attractive, straight guy. I should realize by now that those don't exist.

Coffee is the only thing left on the face of the planet that could possibly make this day get any better. Ripping my comforter off the bed, I cocoon myself in its fading warmth and shuffle out to the coffee maker, cursing at the cold tile as I walk.

When I discover the empty can of coffee, I want to cry.

"That's it," I hiss. "I'm calling in dead."

I kick out of the blanket, head back into my room, where I toss on the first thing I see and throw my hair into a sloppy bun before I get really cranky and decide to chop it all off.

Grumbling, I go to the hall and fling my feet into my shit

kickers (yes, I said shit kickers) as I rip my purse from off the wall. The jingle of the keys inside assures me I won't lock myself out again. I must have caffeine before any future progress can be made on this day. Once I slam the door shut and take in the mustiness of the apartment complex carpet, I look down and actually see what I look like. I have bright red rubber boots on, sweatpants that have bleach stains on them and a sweater that has a thread running near the boob area. Damn it. As much as I don't want to admit it, I am still vain. I can't go out like this.

Unlocking the door, I kick off the boots and find the jeans that make my ass look smaller than it is and dig out a bra that actually holds the girls upright and toss on a grungy rock band t-shirt of a group that I have never heard of but look hella cute in and slip on my knee high leather boots. Ah. Much better. If I'm calling in dead, I don't need to look like it, too.

Outside, I yank the elastic out of my hair and let the wind do its thing. My left eye has begun to twitch from lack of caffeine. Focus, woman. The nearest Starbucks is a good four blocks away, which isn't many, but when your eye is twitching, four blocks is too far to go. So, reluctantly, I swallow my coffee snobbery and enter the questionable diner on the corner of my building. Picture a greasy spoon sort of diner. Got it? Now spit on the diner. That is where I am forced to get my coffee this fine Fall morning. Just once, once, I would love for the cliché I have in my mind not be the reality. But no. The air is thick with burning hash browns, overcooked eggs, and cheap-ass cologne. I vomit a bit in my mouth and almost turn around and leave when a waitress walks by with my liquid love.

Following after the waitress, I slide into a stool. I do my best to ignore the duct tape holding the leather seat together.

Without even having to order, a woman in a dingy apron fishes out a mug from under the counter and pours me a cup.

"What can I get ya?" She pulls a pad out from one of the pockets of the apron, licking the tip of the pencil with her tongue. I shiver.

"Just a coffee. To go."

She frowns at me and shoves her pencil behind her ear, where it is immediately engulfed by the mass of bright orange, hair-sprayed curls. Reaching below her again, she retrieves a paper cup and unceremoniously dumps the coffee she just poured into the paper one then digs out her pencil again to scribble on her pad.

"That'll be two dollars." She rips a green sheet off and slaps it on the counter before she walks away.

"Oh, um, where do I pay?"

Without turning around, she says, "At the front."

"Of course," I mutter to myself.

I take a swig of the coffee before I get up, though and let the warmth of it run down my throat.

"This is better than sex," I sigh.

"You're doing it wrong then," a voice beside me says.

Flushing, I turn and look into the eyes of a twenty-something hotty-McHotterton. He's wearing a blue DePaul University sweatshirt. I roll my eyes in my mind.

"Says the college kid who's never been laid."

I get his predictable snicker.

"Why don't you let me show you just how wrong you are?" he whispers, then I feel his hand grab my ass.

"Whoa, easy fella," I say, smacking his hand away. "I could have given birth to you." Okay, so maybe not literally since the ovarian cancer took away all the working bits many moons ago, but mathematically, it is a possibility.

He just shrugs. "So? You're a MILF, I don't discriminate."

"Ha!" I got to admit, the kid has balls. "How nice for you. But I must be off now. I have adult, grown up things to focus on."

I walk up to the counter to pay for my caffeine.

"At least, let me pay for your coffee," the guy says behind me.

I turn around and see him smirking at me again. "Mrs. …?"

I shake my head and look at the ground instead of his cute

ass dimples. God, I am a sucker for dimples.

"It's Ms. Ms. Harper." I can't help it, I offer to shake his hand.

His large hand engulfs my own. "Nice to meet you, Ms. Harper. I am Eli. Eli Watts."

Eli.

E.

Ah, fuck.

Just for the record, I don't feel bad for tiptoeing out of Eli's dorm room, not that I needed to be quiet. The kid is dead to the world. We went at it like animals the whole freaking day! I am gonna be sore for weeks while he probably won't even remember my name when he wakes up. And that's okay. We both knew going into this that it was a one-night stand. God. I haven't had one of those in years! So long ago, in fact, that I had forgotten what the whole 'Walk of Shame' feels like.

I did the best I could to clean myself up before I left his room, but sex hair is not something easily hidden, no matter how much detangling you try to do with your fingers, and I was not about to shower in the communal dorm bathrooms. Been there. Done that. Never again. So, all I could do was pull the hair back with a rubber band I found in his room, straighten my clothes, and get the girls back in their cage before stepping out of his dorm room.

Mercifully, the hall is quiet. There is the loud thump of bass coming from down the hall and the ever-present smell of incense covering the blatant use of pot in just about every room I pass.

The only knowing look I get is from the front-desk work study chick who tells me I need to sign out.

"No. I don't." I say pleasantly. "I never signed in." I smile and push out of the door. Like I am gonna let some 20 something tell me what to do. Well, not again I think, blushing over the orders Eli whispered hotly into my ear not a few hours ago.

By the time I make it home, 6 hours later, I realize I never called in to work and I still haven't had my coffee. The high of hot sex has worn off and now the headache that is severe caffeine withdrawal has come crashing down.

Digging out my phone, I call Gail. She will come to my rescue. Work will have to deal. I'll make something up.

"Darling, I know you hate your job, so please quit so you don't have to keep calling and complaining about how your cubby-buddy smells like tuna fish again," Gail says once the phone picks up.

"Gail," I whine. "I need coffee."

Her snort is unavoidable. "I need a daddy for my baby, wanna trade problems?"

"I am serious. I need coffee and you. I played hooky from

work today and I may have a letter to check off my list I wanna tell you all about…" I tease.

"Why, you little vixen. Starbucks and I will be over soon."

Hanging up, I can't help but smile. Great sex and coffee being delivered to me... does life get any better than this?

I've only been home a mere twenty minutes when I hear a familiar honk. Running to the window, I see Gail's car pull up to the curb. Harold gets out and opens the door for her. I see her gold stiletto emerge first, followed by the drink tray which she hands off to Harold. When she finally steps out of the car, she is dressed to the nines, as usual. Although, instead of her normal tight-fitting dress, she wears a high belted sort of empire waistline, blue chiffon number. The hemline is way higher than I would ever wear, but with legs like hers, who can blame her?

She points Harold to the front of my apartment building, which means she is making him lug up the drinks. Damn it. My place is a dump. The second they disappear from my view, I begin rushing about trying to get rid my apartment of empty chip bags, dirty clothes, and bottles of wine coolers (Yes, I drink wine coolers. Don't judge me—they're delicious.)

I throw a towel over the dirty dishes in the sink and scoop off crumbs on the counter into the trash. I do a quick survey of the visible parts of my apartment and frown. It will have to do.

Gail doesn't bother to knock, but rather moseys in, knowing I never lock my door until I get into my pajamas.

"This had better be good," she says. "I was in the middle of not doing anything when you called."

I have managed to fling myself into my overstuffed chair, trying to look casual, but Gail's not fooled.

"Well, well, well," Gail says, smirking and crossing her arms. "Someone has just had sex." My cheeks flood with color as Harold looks to the ground, probably equally mortified. She rubs my head, "And not just sex, rough sex, look at you, girl!"

"Oh, my god, shut up," I glare at her and motion to poor Harold.

She turns and looks at him and takes the coffee tray from him. "You're worried about Harold overhearing?" She frowns back at me. "Darling, he's the help, he could care less who you're fucking, nor would he be allowed to tell anyone even if he did."

My mouth hangs open. From the corner of my eye, I see Harold's lips press into a hard line.

Gail offers me my coffee, but I refuse it, get up and walk over to him instead.

"I am so sorry about Gail. Apparently pregnancy has turned her into the Wicked Witch of the West."

"Dee! That was a secret!" Gail shrieks.

"Gee, Gail, he's just the help, he doesn't care, nor could he repeat it if he did." I throw back at her.

She gives me a warning snarl. "You can go now, Harold. There seems to be a stick shoved up Dee's ass that I need to yank out."

"Of course. I'll just be outside," he says, a slight grin on his face. Glad we could be so amusing.

When the door closes, I start in on her.

"Gail. You have got to stop treating people that work for you like they are second class citizens. It's rude, cruel and not a characteristic I want in a best friend!"

"I am a rich bitch. What do you expect? Harold is a big boy; he's used to how I treat him. If he didn't like it, he'd quit. The bigger question is why the fuck you thought it necessary to tell my driver that I was pregnant?"

"What the hell does it matter if he—shit. Is he the father?"

"No! Dee, Jesus, I don't sleep with the help." The way her face screws up at the thought confirms she is telling the truth.

"Right. Sorry. What was I thinking?" I bump past her and back to my chair.

Gail does not say anything for a moment. "Wow. I forgot what a bitch you turn into without caffeine."

I look down at the floor, ashamed of myself. It's not caffeine withdrawal. I know where this anger is coming from and it's not a pretty place.

"I'm sorry, Gail. I don't know what came over me. Unlike you, I can't blame my bitchiness on pregnancy." I hate how much that stings.

She laughs and walks around the couch to sit. The overstuffed pleather practically swallows her whole. "I know exactly what's going on." She blinks knowingly at me.

No, she doesn't. "Oh really?"

"You have a thing for my driver."

"What? No! That is so not what this is about."

"The lady doth protest too much," she grins.

I grind my teeth. "I protest the proper amount. That's not the reason I was upset."

"Mm-hmm." She pulls the lid off her latte and takes a deep sip.

"Gail, this isn't about Harold, okay? I was just—jealous, I guess." Fuck. Did I just say that out loud?

"Jealous? Of what? My help? You hate rich people, me excluded. Well, on most days, anyway."

I let out a deep breath. "Your—pregnancy." The last word is all but whispered.

"Oh, darling." She puts her drink down and comes over to

me. "I am so sorry. I didn't even think--"

"No, it's okay. I thought I'd come to terms with it." I give a weak laugh. "Guess not." I run my hands through my hair. "After my hysterectomy, my mom kept telling me that adopted grandkids are just as good as biological. Hell, everyone kept saying that. 'You can still adopt.' God. If they only knew how much that comment hurt. You can't just adopt. It's not as easy as the made for TV movies make it out to be." I shut my mouth before Gail gets any ideas to try and buy me a kid. "This isn't so much about wanting a kid, I guess. It's more of: what the hell have I done with my life? I mean, I got my clean bill of health seven years ago. There was still time then. Time to land the great job. Time to find the perfect husband, buy the new house, adopt a zillion kids if we wanted to—but I wasted it, Gail. I wasted all that time, and I have nothing to show for it."

That's when the tears start. Tears I have held inside for so long. Gail just holds me and lets me mourn the life I thought I would have one day. She doesn't speak. She doesn't try to get me to stop, she doesn't try to make me feel better, she just holds me. There isn't anything that she could say that would change things anyway so she knows that this will have to be enough.

She lets go of me, only long enough to grab a box of tissues. After the tenth round of nose blowing, I look up at Gail, all puffy-eyed and blotchy faced. "Can I have my coffee now?"

Her bottom lip quivers. "Of course you can, honey."

***

Journal Entry: Best friends and caffeine are the best things ever. Yes, even better than sex with college boys, but only just barely.

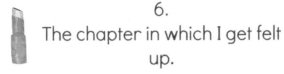

6.
The chapter in which I get felt up.

Gail ended up staying over. She sent Harold home, and we sat on the couch and threw ourselves a grand pity party over the injustices of our lives. First world problems, for sure.

Tuesday morning rolled around, and I cursed because I had to actually show up for work (since I apparently did not die yesterday as previously believed.) I was able to shower, start the dishwasher and make myself a Pop-tart without Gail waking up. That chick can sleep like the dead.

Ticked that she got to sleep in (per usual), I toy with the idea of tossing ice water on her, you know, just for fun, but I don't have time. I still didn't have coffee in my apartment and would therefore have to venture out into the world a whole ten minutes before I had to. I know.

I make a point to walk on the opposite side of the street from the greasy spoon diner where Eli was yesterday. Not that he'd be there today, but just in case, I do not want to have that conversation. He was fun, don't get me wrong, but *way* too immature to take seriously.

Several minutes later, I have my Starbucks firmly in hand. I grab the L and pretend to be engaged in the non-existent message on my phone. Heaven forbid I make eye contact with anyone. The rattle of the cars as they head underground always tries its best to lull me to sleep. One of these days it's going to succeed, and I am going to wake up in Oak Park with no idea how I got there.

My stop is coming. It's the suckiest stop ever; 90% of the passengers get off at Lake Shore Drive. Today's rush of working folk leaves me holding my latte for dear life. I just love feeling like an orange being juiced to a useless pulp before 9 am.

As I walk down the stairs I get an e-mail reminder from work that yesterday's meeting would be happening today instead. Well, shit. I didn't even get out of avoiding Christoph.

Following the swarm out of the station, I start thinking about what I'll say if I bump into him. Odds are, he won't even be at his station when I walk to the conference room, still—I never actually said goodnight that night. I kind of panicked when I heard about the whole gay thing and left on the spot. Poor guy probably has no clue why I left. Then again, he did see Neil, so maybe he will be the one avoiding me? One can only hope.

When the elevators open, I glue my eyes onto the floor. If I don't see him, I don't have to talk to him. Yes, I am a child. My antics pay off, though, 'cause I slip into the conference room without seeing him (or anyone else for that matter). I allow myself a monstrous victory sip of my caramel deliciousness. I ignore that it is also the last swig and is kind of cold and nasty, but that would diminish the success story.

The trip back to my cubicle is easy because I make sure to walk inside the cluster going up to the 8th floor. No guy ever talks to a woman in a gaggle of girls. I think I might see him too, from the corner of my eye, and make a point to be really interested in the conversation the group is having though I have no idea what it actually is about.

Once in the safety of my purposefully unadorned cubical, I shrug out of my coat and flick my computer on. Thirty-seven e-mails greet me. Awesome. That's what I get for calling in yesterday. Yawning, I grab a notepad and my pencil with a pink haired troll on it (What? I said I was a child) and start making notes of the things I need to do. That's when I notice one from Christoph. Shit. I glance over my shoulder to make sure no one is spying on my inbox and open it.

Dee,

Sorry about the other night. I can only assume that the reason you left dinner the other night was Neil. I did not realize you two were friends. While it is true that Neil and I had a short relationship, I was hopeful that you might be open to try new things. Clearly, I was mistaken. I would hope this incident remains between the two of us.

Sincerely, Christoph.

Well. There goes that problem. Breathing a sigh of relief, I stretch back in my chair and just about jump in the air when my hands hit something, or rather someone. Something hot and brown goes flying all over my outfit. My cream-colored outfit.

"Fuck!" I shout, jumping up and trying to get the hot liquid off my chest. Frank, the HR person, starts blabbering his apologies about his coffee, how he should have been holding it better, as he reaches for some tissue to help clean up the mess. I focus on making sure my nipples don't get burned. Fuck, this is hot!

When his tissues start dabbing against my chest he stops.

"Oh, ah—," he says, his hands frozen on my boobs.

"Frank. Can you take your hands off my girls?"

His eyes blink in rapid succession as drops of sweat form at his temples. I can already bet that he is thinking of all the actions I can file against him. The fact that his hands are still on my chest as he contemplates is not helping his case.

"Frank. Hands. Chest. Off."

That seems to wake him out of his stupor. His tiny little face flushes. He pushes up the rim of his glasses and tries to straighten his already straight tie. The guy is wound so tight. I bet this is the most action he's gotten in years.

He finally moves his hands but is now practically shaking. "I am—I am sorry, I did not mean to—I was just coming to see how you were feeling since you were ill yesterday, and then my coffee and I—"

"It's okay, Frank. It's no big deal. I'm more upset about looking like I just took a dump all over myself than you feeling me up."

At that, he goes white. I feel bad for the guy. He's always so stressed. Poor Frank. Poor Frank's wife.

That's when a bad idea hits me.

"Hey, Frank, Frank, look at me." His eyes are on his shoes like he's afraid to even try to make eye contact now. "Why don't you just buy me lunch and we call it even?"

Okay, yes, this is probably cheating on the whole asking the guy out thing, but I am covered in coffee. I deserve this.

"L-lunch?" I can see the wheels spinning in his little balding head: What do the implications of buying a co-worker lunch mean? Is that Sexual Harassment?

I can't help but laugh. "Yeah. That new Indian place just opened up, and I have been dying to try it. I totally spaced on bringing my lunch, so you'd be doing me a favor. You buy me lunch, and no one needs to know about this gross sexual assault," I whisper.

Stuttering, he agrees and rushes out of the cubicle.

"Happy free lunch Tuesday to me."

I finish mopping up the last puddles of coffee and dig around in my desk and find a scarf that was given to me by a co-worker some years ago (that I never wore). Draped around my neck, it covers most of the disaster. For the rest of the morning, I get compliments on my attire, which only means one thing: the scarf is fugly—just as I suspected. People only go out of their way to say how nice you look if they secretly want to make fun of you.

Right at noon, I flip off my monitor and pat my stomach. "Come on, tummy, let's get some grub."

Frank begrudgingly takes me to the India House, where he proceeds to order the first thing on the menu. He's in a rush to get this date over with. Poor guy has no idea what he is getting into. A four-flame dish is probably not the smartest choice for someone who clearly doesn't eat Indian food. I played it safe and got chicken pakoras. No farts-of-fire for me tonight.

"So, Frank," I say between bites. "How long have you been

in HR?"

Frank takes his napkin from off his lap and dabs the corners of his mouth. "Ms. Harper, I feel I need to get this out into the air."

I put my fork down and give him my full attention. This ought to be good.

"Please, be frank, Frank." He frowns at my pun.

"Although you are a very attractive woman, I am a happily married man, and I have no interest in having sex with you."

Now, there are two ways I can react to this. I desperately want to guffaw and tell him just how wrong he is about this whole thing. I opt for the kinder version. Don't ask me why. Consider it my one good deed of the year.

"Wow. Thank you for being so forward. Your wife is a very lucky woman."

He nods. "Yes, she is."

After that, we finish our lunch in blissful silence. Frank may be my best date so far.

We part ways after lunch, and I waddle my way back to my desk. I shouldn't have had that last bite. I feel like I am about to burst, but I wanted to get my free lunch's worth, you know since I was denied all the sex from Frank. Ha!

My monitor comes back to life. I crack my hands a few times

getting ready for yet another day of monotonous data entry. God, I hate my job.

"So, you and Frank, huh?" I hear from behind me. Turning, I see Steph. She's holding her tell-tale can of Coke.

"Ew," I say.

She walks in and sits on my two-drawer file cabinet.

"I saw you two sneak off to lunch."

I stop my assault on the keyboard and spin around to face her.

"How long have we known each other, Steph?"

She cocks her head, thinking. "Eleven years?"

"Twelve. We've worked together for twelve years. Ignoring how pathetic that statement is, in all of that time, have you ever known me to date the likes of someone like Frank?"

Sighing, she says, "No."

"There's your answer."

Steph runs a hand through her super short do. No, she's not a lesbian. She's just really lazy in the morning and doesn't like to spend time getting ready for work. The woman is brilliant for that discovery alone.

"You were out yesterday. I had to eat lunch with Elaine." Steph shivers.

"Yeah, sorry about that, but I was... busy. Getting busy."

Steph chokes on her soda. I get a sick amount of joy from that. I turn around and start plucking away on my keyboard while she composes herself.

"Okay, you need to tell me everything, and you have to do it in six minutes before my break is over.

Truth be told, I have been dying to tell Steph about my stupid bet with Gail. As I explain how the whole situation went down around the bet and the dates that followed, I notice how Steph's contorts with each date. She goes from horror to jealousy. Ending with Eli would have been ideal, but then, she needed to know about Frank. There had to be no confusion over that.

"Dee, I'm not sure if I should call you insane, or my hero."

I laugh. "I'll let you know at the end of this."

Steph chuckles with me until she glances at her phone. "Damn. Shit. I have to go. You have to keep me filled in, though."

"Go. Do all the work. If you hurry, you can still feed that Coke addiction at the machine before you get back," I say without skipping a beat.

"Truth."

She stands up and starts to leave, but then turns back. "As you so kindly reminded me, Dee, we've known each other a long time. You claim this bet is only to stick it to Gail, but I think there's something else. Something you want that money for."

I start to answer but find myself mute.

"I hope you get what you're searching for," Steph says, raising her can at me.

With that, she heads back to her cubicle.

I sit in silence for a moment, soaking in the truth of her words. Slowly, I open my side drawer and dig out the adoption brochure I picked up over a year ago now. I flip to the inner page where it lists the typical attorney fees. Those in of themselves aren't too horrid, maybe a few thousand. It's the medical expenses for a birth mom, that's where the numbers skyrocket. There is no way to gauge how much a pregnancy would cost. If there were any complications—I only have four thousand in my savings, and I worked hard for two years to scrape that together. If I am going to do this, it has to be sooner rather than later. I'm not exactly a spring chicken. Winning this bet would make becoming a mom a reality. I hug the paper and tuck it back in my drawer, hiding it under my package of pads for safe keeping. No one can know about this. If I failed to be given a child, I wanted no one to know about it.

***

Journal Entry: It's time to step up my dating game and find whatever the hell it is I'm searching for.

7.
The chapter in which Gail orders me to dinner.

It's been three date-free months for me. Yeah. So much for stepping up my game. I suck. It's just, I couldn't get myself motivated to do it. I got sucked into baby prep with Gail. Shopping, painting, putting together the crib, by myself, thank you very much. The time flew by without me even really thinking about it. Gail, however, has not slowed down on the dating front one bit. She's already at J. Johnson. That's it. That's the guy's name. He's apparently the male version of Madonna. At this rate, she's gonna beat me to the end in no time or find the perfect man to 'become' her baby's father. Either way is a victory for her.

Maybe she's actually found one that's a keeper. That could be why she made me cancel all my plans (like I had any), get Neil and meet her downtown at Davanti Enoteca (that's fancy for pasta joint) at 8:00 sharp. Ever the good friend, I entertain her demand, mostly because their fettuccine alfredo is to die for. Neil gladly agrees to a Gail invite. He's always game for one of her invites. Since money is no object, Neil always orders the very best of everything the place has to offer, while I still look for the cheapest thing on the menu, not wanting to seem greedy.

After showering myself into a functioning human state, I run into my room, shivering my ass off. I need to remember to bring my damn clothes into the shower and change in there instead of doing this insane polar bear run every damn day. I think of it the second I'm in the shower, but not before. That's how my brain works. No forethought. Maybe this whole adoption thing isn't such a great idea after all.

I'm polishing off a pre-dinner glass of red when the door knocks. I know it is Neil from his patter of knocks that circle the peephole.

"Come on in," I say pouring a second glass for Neil.

"Please, tell me you have beer," he says, walking in with his dark blue suit that really brings out the deep blue of his eyes. The full (yet manicured) beard he's been rocking lately makes him absolutely gorgeous. No fair.

"Beer?" I ask. "Since when do you like beer?"

"God, I know." He reaches up and touches his mouth lightly.

I hand him the glass and hop up onto my counter. A story is coming. Might as well get comfortable.

Neil takes a tentative sip of his wine and frowns. "Fuck. What has he done to me?"

"Chad?" Neil's boyfriend is even manlier than Neil.

He nods. "The bastard has me hooked on Goose Island. Beer! Me!"

The two of them have been going out for a few months on and off. Chad works for a brewery, so naturally, beer is his life. He doesn't actually brew the beer, mind you. Oh no, his job is far more sophisticated. He is one of their tasters. His job is to drive to places that sell their beer on tap and taste it for quality. I shit you not.

"Well, you stick with me, kid. I'll get ya back on the good stuff."

He reaches out and takes my shoulder. "Thank you. You're a good friend."

"I am. Now, drink the wine."

After we've cleansed our palates, we snag a cab chatting about the 'much too long' hem of my dress. Apparently, I need to show off a little chooch to attract the boys.

Mercifully, it's a short ride. I'm not sure how many more snide remarks I can handle before I start punching him in his boy parts.

When the hostess shows us to our table, we are shocked to see that Gail is already there. She's never the first to arrive. She likes to make an entrance. She's staring at the candle in the center of the table. I shoot Neil a look.

"Uh, oh," he whispers.

Gail doesn't move when we sit down or even acknowledge that we're here. After the waitress has left to get our drink order, I snap my fingers in front of Gail.

"Wake up," I say.

Gail blinks. "What? Oh, sorry. Hey, guys. I was lost in thought."

"No joke," Neil scoffs.

She doesn't say anything, which means she is decision making. Neil and I know better than to try and pull her out of it. She'll just keep drifting back into thought. It's easier to just wait for her to come to a decision. It's quirky, for sure, but we love her anyway.

"So, Dee, until Gail decides to join us, tell me about how the alphabet is going," Neil asks, unfolding his napkin.

I grunt as the waitress arrives with our drinks. I take a nice long sip from my chocolate martini. I'll need strength for this.

"Well, you know about Adam, Brad, and Christoph,"

"Sadly, I do."

Another sip.

"Then Gail tried to set me up with a guy at her work named Dave. He seemed to think she was inviting him to a threesome,"

I wait for his laughter to die down before I continue. "Then there was Eli. A twenty-year-old with abs to die for and a thrust like no one's business."

"Damn!"

"I know. Trust me. Then there was my HR person from work, Frank. He accidentally felt me up so I made him take me to dinner as compensation."

"How do you accidentally—you know what? Never mind. I don't want to know."

I down my martini (I know, I am a lush) and signal the waiter for another.

"I take one trip to Canada with Chad, and all the fun stuff happens!"

I laugh. "Eli was the only fun one. The rest all make me question the existence of datable men in the universe."

"Profound," Neil said, taking a swig of his beer. Ugh.

"I'm up to 'G,' but haven't felt much like dating, so I'm just kind of vegging."

"H," Gail says, causing both of us to turn and look at her.

"Well, hello there. Welcome to the conversation," Neil says.

Gail ignores him and looks at me. "You're on 'H'. Not 'G.'"

I look from her to Neil. "Clarify, please."

"I asked you to dinner, yes?" Gail says.

"Um, yes..."

"And you said yes..."

"Kinda why I am here."

"So, you are now on a date with me. I am 'G.'"

I sigh. "It doesn't count. For that to work I would need to ask you out—Oh man, is that what this is all about? Is this a pity date now? We've passed the setting updates, and have moved on to a pity date?"

"Consider it my apology for Dave."

I shiver. "I may need H as well, for that one."

"Agreed." Gail nods. "I'll arrange to have Harold pick you up tomorrow at 8:00. He works early on Wednesdays so don't keep him out too late. It's the one day of the week I actually have to be in the office to meet with that awful board of directors." She picks up her menu and starts to scan it.

"Gail, I don't need your driver to bring me on my dates," I say, opening my own menu with more force than required.

"Don't be daft, Dee. I don't mean that. I mean that Harold will be your date. You need to catch up with me, the K's are positively dreadful."

Neil does a low whistle. He knows when I am about to blow my top. I think steam actually jets out of my ears or something.

Fortunately for Gail, our waitress comes back over. "What

can I get you all this evening?" she asks in her rehearsed polite tone. Her job must suck big, hairy balls. Having to suck up to jerks like us all evening must make her want to poke her eyes out with her pen. I'm leaving her a good tip. Well, I'll make sure Gail leaves her a good tip.

"I'll have the roast duck, the seasoned pilaf, and asparagus," Gail says without looking at her.

"And for you, sir?"

"I'll have the Angus, medium-rare, mashed potato with the sweet carrots, please."

I glare at him. "Steak, really? Who are you?" Neil used to be a vegetarian before meeting Chad.

"I know!" He buries his hands into his hair.

The waitress turns to me. I haven't even looked at the menu, so I just order the same thing I always do. Their pasta is da-bomb.

She leaves, taking with her the oversized menus the rich people so seem to love.

Gail starts digging around in her purse for something, so I wait for her full attention to ream her out for interfering, yet again, with my dating life. She pulls out a phone and starts texting a message. A minute later she slips it back inside, clasps her hands together and beams at the two of us.

"There. Your date is all set. Now, where were we?"

There is something off with her that I cannot put my finger on. It won't spare her from my lecture, though. I mirror her perfect posture and blink my eyes. "Well, I was about to read you the riot act for butting into my life again."

"I am having twins," Gail says.

My rant loses its steam.

"Oh, where did you meet them?" Neil squeals. "Twin sex is the best." He grins, completely unaware of his faux pas.

"Babies, you idiot. She's having twin babies." I slide out of my chair and rush over to Gail, who has gone completely white, to hold her upright.

"Babies? Wait. What? You're pregnant?" Neil practically shouts.

I motion for him to keep his voice down.

"How did Dee know about this and not me?" he pouts.

"Really, you're gonna play the 'I feel left out' card, now?" I ask, stroking Gail's hair. I don't think she even heard his comment, she's so lost in thought.

Neil frowns. "Who's the father?"

I just shrug.

Neil rubs his hands over his face. "This doesn't make any sense. If she's pregnant, why the hell has she been on more dates than Paris Hilton?"

I just look at him and wait for it to register.

"No. She is not daddy shopping..." The look of horror when I don't correct his assumptions leaves me feeling like I've betrayed Gail in some way.

The waiter arrives with a basket of assorted bread and a vat of fresh butter. She notices our stricken faces but doesn't say a word. She quickly leaves once the bread is placed. Yup. Good tip for that one.

"This is crazy," Neil says.

"I know. But she needs us to be here for her, and not judge her. Got it?"

He raises his hands in surrender, then goes for the bread. He opens the black cloth napkin up and the smell of the yeast is heavenly. I look from the bread to Gail. She's got that vacant expression. Damn. She could be like that for hours. The sound of the bread crackling as Neil slides soft butter over his slice does me in.

"Oh, fuck it. Gail can wait. My stomach can't," I say, grabbing a thick slice for myself. I slather it with butter and am about to take a bite when Gail comes back to life.

"I know that the two of you aren't eating all that bread. I know that you are saving the largest slice for the fatty that has to squeeze out two fatherless children soon. Right?"

"I was getting this ready for you, darling." Grumpy, I hand her my perfectly buttered slice.

She takes it and shoves a bite, unceremoniously, into her mouth. Even Neil looks taken aback.

"Damn, girl."

I reach over and smack him on the arm. "Don't poke the bear," I hiss, and go back to my seat and take the butt end of the bread.

"What am I going to do?"

I look back and see Gail, bread still hanging from her bottom lip, tears welling in her eyes.

Neil answers before I get a chance to form a solution.

"Simple. You are gonna have some babies. That's what you're gonna do. And we are going to spoil the bonkers out of them. Aren't we, Thing 1 and Thing 2?" he says to Gail's stomach.

Instead of smacking him over the head, like I expect her too, Gail starts blubbering. "You guys won't leave me, will you? Once I'm one of those angry, sleep deprived moms? I can't do this alone."

The two of us bombard her with hugs and assurances.

After dinner, Gail invites us back to her place for a nightcap. She forced our hand by saying that someone needed to drink the $500 bottle of scotch she had gotten from her Uncle before she dumped it. Well, being the good friends we are, we couldn't let that happen to the poor scotch. Before I went over, though, I decided I was going to rent a movie and there was one joint in town that just might have what she was needed to lift her spirits. You know the one with Danny DeVito and Arnold Swartz-his-butt, <u>Twins</u>. I am such a good friend.

***

Journal Entry: In the event that I don't make any more entries, you will know that Gail has killed me for my twisted sense humor.

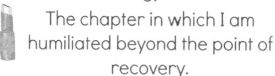

8.
The chapter in which I am humiliated beyond the point of recovery.

So, in all of the twin talk and celebrating/crying until well past two, then going to work, slightly hung over, I have forgotten all about the date that Gail set me up with tonight with Harold. That is until I open the door and see him standing in my hall, holding a batch of lupines. Lupines. I fucking love lupines. How the hell did he know that I loved lupines? They're not even in season.

"Harold. Um. Hi." I say, trying to forget the fact that I am in my I heart zombie sweatpants, that my hair is in the messiest ponytail known to mankind and also currently bra-less. I am going to kill Gail.

Harold shifts uncomfortably. "I was told to come get you at 8:00."

"Right. Yes. Um. Ha." The words are failing me.

"Did I get the wrong day?" The poor boy is all flustered now, which does nothing but fluster me even more.

"No. Um, right day. Wrong brain." I laugh. I hear the elevator ding with potentially nosy neighbors with it. "You know what? Come in."

"You sure? I can always—"

I grab his jacket and pull him in and close the door. "Nope. We're good. Um, why don't you have a seat and I'll actually go put a bra on so I can talk to you without the full nipple salute." Please tell me I did not say that out loud. Judging by the color red in his cheeks, I totally did.

"Excuse me," I say and practically throw myself into my bedroom.

I half hope that by the time I come out, he will have made the right choice and bolted, but alas, when I emerge with my hair down, ass-showing-off jeans on and push-up bra firmly in place, he is still there, looking as delicious as ever, even out of his work attire: Dark, loose fitting jeans, a light brown sweater and 5 o'clock shadow—he is an L.L. Bean model. I would so like to order one of him. 'Yes, I'll take him in a size large, please.' I smirk at my perverted thoughts.

"Something funny?" he asks.

I walk over and sit on the chair furthest away from him.

"Besides my life?" I snort. Yup. I snorted. What is wrong with me?

"What's funny about your life?"

I scratch the back of my head. "Cliff's Note version?"

"Sure, why not."

"I need a drink for this. Can I get you anything?" I ask. Please don't say you don't drink; please don't say you don't drink.

"Um, wine if you have it."

I beam at him. "If I have it. Ha. You, sir, clearly do not know me." I walk over to my kitchen and open what looks like a pantry door. Inside, however, are about thirty bottles of wine. "I have white and blush in the fridge if you prefer, but you strike me as a red sort of guy."

"I think I love you," he says standing up to admire the collection. I ignore the thrill the joke he made gives me. "Whatever you're having is fine," he says, picking up a bottle and practically caressing it. "You have Malbec?"

I walk over and look at the bottle. "Apparently I do. I am part of the Wine of the Month club." He looks up from the label. "Don't judge me," I say taking the bottle from him, "or there shall be no wine for you."

Harold clears his throat. "So, tell me more about this wonderful club you've joined."

"Smart boy." I pull open the silverware drawer for the corkscrew and remove the cork in record time. I may be a bit of a lush.

As I pour, I feel his eyes on me and it makes me spill some of the wine. Dumbass.

I hand him the glass as I take the flowers from off the counter and put them in a water pitcher, further proving how non-domesticated I am. Who doesn't own a vase? The girl who has never been sent flowers, that's who.

"Cute place. Do you have a view of the lake?" he asks craning his neck to look out my window.

"I do," I say walking to the window and pointing. "Or will, once I tear down that building right there."

He laughs. Well, at least, he gets my sense of humor. It is an acquired taste. Much like many of the wines on the wine of the month list. This one is actually yummy. Or maybe it's just the company.

"Look, about tonight," I begin.

"Yeah, about that. Ms. Morgan was adamant in her text that I 'show you a good time'." He blushes. "Mind explaining why?"

"Ha, if only I could in a way that you didn't think I was insane after," I sigh, taking a huge drink.

He stands up and walks over to my couch and pats the space beside him. "Try me. I have known quite a few lunatics, and I highly doubt you fall into that category."

"Ye of little faith," I say, taking the seat offered, but making sure to leave a good amount of space between us. Things can't get weird between us. We see each other too much for this to go beyond whatever this night is.

"Now, I am intrigued," he grins. Gah. He has a really cute smile. He has one dimple over his left cheek. Not two, just the one. It looks so damn adorkable. "Okay, but don't say you weren't warned." I clear my throat and sit up a little higher. "You, sir, are part of Gail's sick sense of humor."

"Gonna need a bit more than that, I am afraid," he says, leaning back into the couch.

"Okay." I grin. "You are my H."

I wait for him to register the statement.

"Your H."

"Yup." I down my glass. "I am getting the bottle." I walk back into the kitchen, grab the wine and pour an extra full glass before I sit back down. "You sure you want to hear this?"

"As your 'H', I feel it is my duty." He places his hand over his heart.

I laugh. Here goes nothing.

I curl my legs up and let out a breath. "I am assuming you don't know about the bet Gail and I have going on?"

He cocks his head. "No, I do not. Ms. Morgan doesn't share personal information with her drivers." The tone in his voice confirms that Gail does treat him like a second-class citizen, which makes me pissy.

"Gail has a 'rich brain,'" I say, trying to apologize for her. "She was taught how to treat people by a very cold and callous woman. I've been trying for years to unteach her."

He grins again. "I appreciate the effort."

I ignore the blush seeping in and carry on with my story. "Anyway, Gail and I had a night of drunken foolishness as we bemoaned the state of our lives." Harold looks at me and scoffs. "I know, Gail has no idea how good she has it." I take a slow sip of the wine, trying to find the right words to explain the bet. "Gail was moaning about how dull her life was, and I was saying how empty mine was, and well... Gail turned that into a bet."

Harold nods, waiting for me to continue.

"She bet me fifty grand that I couldn't date 26 guys in a year."

Harold frowns. "That's hardly a bet for an attractive woman like you."

I do my best to ignore the compliment. It was just the polite thing to say, nothing more.

"I wasn't finished. I have to do it in alphabetical order."

"Ah, hence the 26."

I nod, waiting for the judgment to come.

"And I am the 'H'," he says slowly.

"Apparently. Gail arranged this date on her own. I didn't know anything about it until yesterday. I can get my own dates."

He doesn't say anything, just stares at the floor, which makes me think I've hurt his feelings. It's not that I wouldn't have asked him out—he's just way out of my datable reach. He's on the ten scale and I'm hanging back with the 5's. We can multiply, sure, but we don't add up. Okay, I'm done with the puns—for now.

"What would you do with the money?"

I stand up and walk to the window and my non-lake view. "Um, that's kinda personal." I look down at the people down on the street against the streetlights. "My reasons stay in the vault."

"The vault?"

I nod, "A place only I have the key to," I say, my voice above a whisper. There were a lot of wishes put in 'the vault' during the years with cancer. Painful wishes that rarely were granted. When the ovaries had to be removed as well, I learned to stop wishing.

Harold, seeming to understand when to drop a subject, puts his glass down.

"So, I am to be used, am I?" he asks.

I blink and turn back to him. "What? Oh, no, it is not like that."

He gives me a sad sort of smile. "Isn't it, though?"

I find myself at a loss. When he puts it that way, all cruel and emotionless, I see myself for the jerk that I am.

He walks over to me and tips my chin up, so I'll look at him. "Thanks for the wine."

Here it is. He's leaving. Fuck, how did I fuck this up so fast? I try to think of something to make this better, but I just don't come up with a single word, so I just nod.

A second later, his lips are on mine, confusing my poor wine-soaked brain. I want to make sense of it all, but he is so soft and warm, I start to bring my hand up to grab his hair, but then he pulls away. Like a fool, I realize why he just kissed me.

"I don't have to kiss them, just go out with them," I say, wiping my lip and dropping my eyes.

"Sorry. I didn't know the fine print," he says. "Look, I'm sure a lot of guys would love the chance to be used by you, but me— I'm just not built that way." He squeezes my hand. I look up at him, expecting to see judgment there. Instead, there is just, what? Sadness. "I hope you find what you're looking for, Dee."

The sound of his footsteps down my hall echo in my shallow stupid head. When the door closes, so too does the tiny bit of my heart that had dared to open.

***

Journal Entry: Harold is not good for the old ticker. Avoid him like the plague.

9.
The chapter in which I fuck up.
Yes, again.

For a good hour, I ust stare at the door from whence Harold left. I feel dirty. Unclean. Cheap. I am an awful human being. I try to convince myself that if I had told Harold why I wanted the money that would have made it all different, but honestly, even knowing—what does that say about my character?

When I finally move, it's only to polish off the bottle of red (because that's how pathetic I am). After ¾ of the bottle is gone, I have a little change of heart.

"What the hell does that fucking driver know anyway? He does not know me. He doesn't know anything at all about me. I'm a good person. Fucker."

I pull myself off the floor without spilling the wine, adjust the girls, and look in the mirror.

"Hey, you. Yeah, you," I say to my reflection. "Wanna go on a date? Yeah? Cool, let's go."

I turn around and find my purse. "I am going out on a date with me, myself and I. Hey, that the next letter! I. I'm zipping through my list." I put the bottle down and rake a brush through my hair, not even feeling the hairs being ripped out. "Uh, my eyes." I start digging in my makeup bag. "Got ya." I pull out the green tube and stick out my tongue to get it open. Now, trying to apply mascara while buzzed might not be the best move, but I don't give a fuck. I'm gonna go out and have some fun. I don't need Harold. I don't need anyone but myself. "You and I were getting along just fine before he stuck his big fat nose into everything," I tell the mirror.

Once I find a bar within walking distance that's not blaring country music, I consider calling Gail to get her ass down here and join me. Then I remember she can't drink and that I am on a date with myself. I don't think it's too early to call this 'the worst date ever.'

Inside, the air is thick. Smoke lingers, even though it's a smoke-free place. It wafts in from the doors leading to smoking sections. Strobe lights flash in the corner of the bar illuminating a small wooden dance floor packed with college-age kids. The bar is mostly empty since there are lots of tables still open. I grab the first stool I see and try to flag the bartender down. Next to me, a dirty blonde in a leather jacket, looking all Dukes of Hazard, walks up and orders a beer. This night just got a whole lot better.

"Oh, that sounds good," I lie. I loathe beer. "Make that two,"

I say to the bartender.

The guy turns around and smiles. "I am impressed. Most women don't like Guinness."

I smile like I know what the hell a Guinness actually tastes like. "Well, I am not like most women," I say, overtly flirting. That is so not me. I must be pretty buzzed.

"Really? Well, I guess I should find out a little more about you then." He gives me a slow, hungry smile, which I should see for the red flag it is, but I'm depressed and dumb at the moment, so I ignore those warning bells and have a few drinks with blondie.

Okay, maybe more than a few drinks. We spend the rest of the night laughing, talking, and dancing, essentially closing out the bar. He works in TV. I should have guessed with the way he looks so plastic. Probably all fake, but right now I could care less. He is talking to me. Interested in me, and not judging the piss out of me.

When the last call bell sounds he leans over and whispers in my ear. "Wanna come back to my place, sugar?" he asks. Derek. That's his name. Derek. Derek. Derek. Why can't I remember that?

"That would be wonderful, Derek." Yes! Got it right.

He flags down the barkeep and pays what must be a very

expensive tab with everything we've had. I slide off the bar stool and almost fall on my ass.

"Whoa, you okay there?" He catches my arm and holds me steady,

"I am more than okay." I step on my tip toes and pull on his jacket to whisper in his ear. "I am exceptional." I lower myself down and lick my lips. Yup. Officially drunk now.

Stumbling out of the bar, we hail a cab. Well, he does. I just stand there shivering, not wanting my buzz to leave. If I sobered up, I might not go through with this, and right now, I don't know what is worse. Going home with him or going home alone.

"814 W. Agatite," Derek says to the cabby, pulling me close to him.

My brain tries to process the address. Where the hell is Agatite?

While I think, his hands slide up my leg, reaching high thigh. I shove his hand to the side.

"Wait. Agatite? Isn't that in Uptown?" I ask.

"It is." He slides back over to me, kissing my neck and trying to get under my shirt.

I try to talk between his kisses.

"Uptown. That's—" *Oh, okay, hi there tongue.* "that's kind of a sketchy part of the city, isn't it?"

"So?" He starts to kiss my ear. The loud smacking makes me cringe. I hate having my ears touched, let alone kissed.

"I thought you worked in TV."

His hand slides around my neck and practically sucks my bottom lip off. *Ow.*

"I never said I was very good at it."

Well fuck.

"Right." I tell myself where he lives doesn't matter, because it doesn't. Money is so not a thing for me. What matters was the rich life picture he tried to paint for himself, probably just to get me into bed. Now I feel a little slutty. Maybe this isn't such a good idea after all.

His hand breaches my shirt. His fingers are now digging their way under my bra. "Living there saves me money," he says, as he plants another sloppy kiss on me. Then he grabs my boob so hard it feels like it's gonna pop.

"Ouch! Okay, buddy, let's take it down a notch."

He ignores me and grabs my other breast, just as hard. *Jesus that hurts.*

"Okay, seriously stop. My mammogram isn't until next year." I push him off me where he looks down at me, clearly pissed.

"So much for your being exceptional."

Nice. The true asshole is unmasked.

"Can you pull over here?" I say to the cabbie.

Derek just laughs as the car pulls over.

"I didn't want your old, washed-up body anyway. Get the fuck out of the car."

The cab comes to a halt. I flare my nostrils. "Gladly."

I slam the door and watch as it pulls away.

"Asshole!" I shout at the taillights.

The night air takes a hold of my bear arms, causing them to goosebump. Looking around, I realize I have no clue where I am. It's dark, I'm drunk, and I'm scared.

I spy a bus stop a few yards away and walk over to it. There will be a map there. I should be able to figure out where I am. I'm sure I can find a place to fill my metro card somewhere since I never have cash or try to hail a cab on this deserted and ghetto looking street. As I walk toward the streetlight, I call Gail, because that's all I can think to do.

By the time she picks up, I am a blubbering mess.

"Gail, you have to help me. I don't know where I am," I sob.

"Dee? What's going on, it's like 2 in the morning?" she says, her voice thick with sleep.

I sob some more. I am a very emotional drunk. "I just want to go home."

There is shuffling on the line. "Okay, calm down. Where's Harold?"

"Harold?"

"He didn't pick you up tonight? That's it. He's fired," Gail shouts.

"No, wait, no. Don't do that. This is my fault. I fucked up. I went out after and got piss faced and got in a cab with some ass-munch and now I don't know where I am—and my boobs hurt," I say massaging the left one.

I hear her sigh on the other side like my mother used to when I wanted to come home during a sleepover because I wasn't having any fun. "It's okay, Dee, we'll get you home. Where are you?"

"I don't know. At a bus stop. Nine, it looks like. Clark and Ashland. Fuck, Gail, they don't start again until 7 am. What the fuck am I'm gonna do?

I hear her pushing buttons on her phone.

"Okay, I have it down. Hold tight, Dee. Sit right there at that bus stop. Stay under the light. Less chance you'll get mugged under the light. I'll get you home."

The line goes dead.

"Gail!" God damn it. The least she could have stayed on the line with me until she got here. Christ. Now I have to sit here in the cold praying that I am not dead by the time she finds me.

I pull my knees into my chest and get angry with myself for crying. These tears aren't about Derek; he is just the excuse to cry. This is about me, and what a pathetic waste of space I have become, which, of course, only makes me cry harder.

My head starts to throb. And this, Dee, is why you should never drink.

Feeling drained and just plain sleepy, I lie down on the bench to wait for Gail. As I drift off, I make a note of how falling asleep alone in the middle of the city may not be a bright idea, but then I forget the thought as I succumb to the darkness.

I drift off. I have no idea how long I have been asleep, but the slamming of a car door wakes me up. In fact, I bolt up, as though I've been shot. The way my heart is racing, I could have been.

"Gail?" I ask the night. My face feels crusty. Mascara must be glued down the sides of my face. No wonder no one bothered me, I must look like shit.

"Dee? Jesus Christ, what the hell happened?"

Even drunk I know that is not Gail's voice. I open an eye, ignoring the glare from the headlights. I groan. It's Harold.

I turn away from him and curl in on myself. "Go away. Gail's coming for me."

"No, she's not. She sent me to get you." I feel him sit at the edge of the bench near my knees. "Come on, let's get you off the street."

I raise my head to glare at him.

"In the non-hooker sense."

As funny as that be, I am not budging. "Screw you. I'm not going anywhere with you. Just go away and leave my sorry ass here."

I hear his sigh even from my cozied-up position on the bench. After a minute or so, he gets up, and I hear a car door open. "Good. Go. I don't need you," I say as I hold back the tears that want to come again. Jesus, why do I drink?

I wait for the door to close and for the car to take off when I feel arms close around me, lifting me off the bench. Naturally, I fight.

"Let go of me," I shout.

"Dee, stop it," Harold says, trying to keep my arms pinned, probably so I don't hit him upside the head, which I really want to do. "I am not leaving you out here in the cold all alone, now stop hitting me."

Undeterred, I struggle to break free, but this fucker is strong. "Let me go!" I cry, but he just tightens his grip.

"I am not leaving without you," he says, then picks my ass

up and throws me over his shoulder, like a fucking Neanderthal! I have to tell myself, several times, that this isn't the least bit sexy. Not. One. Bit.

"Put me down," I shout, pounding against his back. He doesn't waiver and the next thing I know, I am being shoved into the car.

My back lands hard against the seat as Harold hovers above me, "Enough. You need to relax."

I laugh. "You don't have a clue what I need."

He releases his grip on my wrists and his face grows serious. The pad of his thumb traces the side of my face. "Yes. I do."

My heart flies up into my throat and I suddenly can't breathe. He pulls away and climbs out of the back seat. The sound of the door slamming reminds me of his earlier rejection. A moment later, the car starts, and we pull away. Just like that, a new flood of tears begins, but only on the inside this time where he can't see.

***

Journal Entry: As predicted. Worst. Date. Ever. I can't even date myself with success.

10.
The chapter in which I debate giving up coffee.

It's quiet. Much too quiet. There should be more noise if there's sunlight on my face. Doors slamming, talking in the halls, the elevator dinging away my sanity, horns honking from 6 flights down, but all I can hear is silence. I open an eyelid and raise a hand to shield myself from the devil sun rays, and I notice instantly that I'm not in my own bed.

Panic starts to flood my mind. Who did I sleep with? That's my first thought. God, I'm classy. I look around the room trying to stir up some clue as to where I am, but nothing is ringing a bell. My head starts to throb now that I'm upright. Booze. There was booze. I remember that. So much booze, and that fuckhead, the boob pincher, Derek. Shit. Am I at his house? I look around for evidence of another body but the pillow beside me is flat, the sheets not disturbed. I am alone. So far so good. I slowly peel back the covers and sigh in relief when I find I'm still dressed. Only my shoes are missing.

I sit in the silence, straining to find out if anyone else is here.

A faint sound of someone snoring comes from outside of the bedroom, so I carefully tip-toe across the hardwood floor, freezing every time the floor creaks. The wooden door of the bedroom has one of those wobbling looking metal doorknobs that will surely make a ruckus, so I pull against the door itself instead. A tiny squeak of protest sounds but the snoring rages on. I'm safe. For now.

When I step onto the hall, I notice a bathroom next to me and a kitchen further down the hall. To my right looks like the living room, and the source of the snoring. Holding my breath, I make my way there. I have to know where I am.

Once I reach the end of the hall, I notice that the living area is small. Dark gray walls mismatched end tables and a huge, overstuffed recliner that has seen a lot of love. There is a body on the couch, a blanket is thrown over them so I can't make out who the sleeper is. Out of the corner of my eye, I notice that there is a set of keys, some loose change, and a wallet on the coffee table.

I creep over to the wallet, moving slower than I've ever moved before and carefully flip it open. The picture on the driver's license makes my memories click. It's Harold. Fuck. The bus stop. The yelling. The caveman carrying. All of it comes rushing back. I made a complete and total jackass of myself.

Beside me, Harold stirs and rolls over. The brown throw that once covered him now exposes his very naked chest. Of course, he has to have the body type I find super hot. He's lean, but not skinny. Just enough build to wonder what it would be like to be held in those arms. Damn it. I stand there, transfixed—both wanting to run out of there and never leave this spot again. A very dangerous place for the heart to be in. There's only one logical choice. Leave. Before he wakes up and never, ever, see him again.

It takes some serious effort, but I divert my eyes from his chest and turn around looking for the door. I see what looks like a promising exit when I am caught by my own reflection in a large mirror hanging in his living room. Dear God, I look like a dying raccoon. Mascara has literally run down to my neck. My neck! My eyes are still puffy and red, and my clothes are wrinkled beyond even dry-cleaning hope. I do my best to wipe away the caked-on black dotting my face using the hem of my shirt and my spit; yes, I know, gross. It makes little difference. I still look like a public service announcement against smoking crack.

Frustrated with my current level of stupidity, I find a pencil on a table near the door and use it to secure a very messy bun that hides most of the pathetic-ness of my night. He will wake to find his sunglasses missing, but it has to be done for the sake of the children passing by me. Can't go giving them nightmares. My purse is sitting next to the mirror with my phone inside, almost dead, of course. I tuck my shirt into my jeans in an attempt to hide the wrinkles and look around for where he put my fucking shoes. They're most likely back in his room, but I am not gonna risk going back for them. I'd get caught for sure on that stupid creaking floor.

I'll go barefoot. Fuck it.

Determined, I walk to the door at a turtle's pace. When my hand hits the handle, I breathe a little sigh of relief. This could have ended so much worse.

"You might need these," a deep voice from behind me says.

I freeze. Shit. Fuck. Piss. Damn!

Turning painfully slow, I see Harold sitting up, still bare-chested, I might add, with my apartment keys dangling off his finger. That little fucker took my keys.

"Right," I say. "Those might be helpful with the whole unlocking thing." *The whole unlocking thing? What the hell are you saying, Dee?*

"Trying to escape before I got up?" he says, scratching the back of his head, which makes the blanket sink down to the ground, revealing not only more delicious chest but also a half-dollar sized tattoo of a heart just below his left pec. It has the name Claire written on it. *Claire.* I hate that I feel like I was just hit in the gut. Of course, he has a girlfriend. He was *paid* to take me out, after all. Gail probably would have fired him if he refused. I feel sick suddenly. I have to get out of here before my embarrassment consumes me. I glance up and notice that he saw me staring at his chest, because apparently I'm not subtle.

"Claire was my sister. She died eight years ago. Breast Cancer." The hurt of the memory is written on his face, even after all that time. He touched the small letters with the pad of his thumb. "This was, I don't know, a way to make sure I didn't forget her, I guess."

"Oh, wow." Is the brilliant reply I come up with.

"Most people say, 'I am sorry,'" he says, a slight grin on his lips.

I shake my head at his words. "I don't say sorry. I always hated that when people said it to me. What good does being sorry do? It doesn't take the cancer away."

He sits up straighter. "You had breast cancer?"

I walk further into the room, resting my hands on the back of one of his chairs. "No. Um, ovarian. I am kind of hollowed out down there now, but the cancer is gone."

"Oh, wow," he says.

I can't help it. I laugh. "See? That's better."

"So, you're in remission?" He stands up, taking a few dangerous steps towards me. I swallow and take a step back to counter his closeness.

I nod. "It's been three years cancer free."

"That's great."

I shrug, and cross my arms over my chest, something I do when talking about my cancer years. It's like a security blanket or something. "I guess. I mean, they took away the cancer, but they also took away my ability to ever be a mom. Which is stupid really, because I had never even considered being a parent until they took that option away. It's hard to understand, I guess."

He doesn't say anything for a while, which takes the pressure off me. I have to gather my wits before I can speak again. This is not the sort of post-hangover conversation one plans on having.

"No, no. I get it. My sister had a similar sort of thing happen when they wanted to remove her breasts. She wanted to be able to breastfeed her kids one day, so she refused the surgery. The docs kept telling her the likelihood of the cancer coming back if she didn't have a double mastectomy, but she wouldn't budge. They kept saying she can just feed her kids formula. They didn't get it, though. I didn't either, for a while. They wanted to remove part of her womanhood—"

"Exactly," I whisper.

We're quiet for a while. Harold rubs his eyes. "I wanted nothing more than to be able to shove pictures of my sister nursing one of her kids in that doctor's face, but—the cancer got aggressive. She was gone within six months."

I hate the pain that's sinking into his eyes, so I try to take off some of the heat.

"You know, I wanted to punch every single person who told me I could 'just adopt.' It's not that easy. First you have to manage to get over the massive amount of head shit that you have to work through. You have to convince yourself that you aren't broken and that not having kids isn't really part of God's plan, but then there is the reality of it all. I mean the sheer cost of adoption is insanity. Just because you want a kid doesn't mean your wallet can buy you one."

"You researched it?"

"Um, a little," I say, trying to sound casual. "It's like 60 grand or so if you try for a baby that's still in utero. I don't make that much in a year, so--"

"So that's why you took the bet," he says.

Shit. Did I just let him into the vault? I swallow down the lump in my throat.

"I, um—I need to go to work." I hold out my hand for my keys.

I don't look at him, but I feel his eyes burrowing into me—I won't let him in. I can't. He places the keys in my hand, and I fold my fingers over the cool metal. I can't look at him or the pity I know that will linger in his eyes.

I turn around and walk to the door. My hand hovers on the doorknob. Without turning around, I say, "Please don't mention this to Gail. I don't want her offering to buy me a kid."

With that, I leave his apartment, bare footed and a bit more broken than I was the day before.

I try to shake out of it once I'm outside in the Chicago wind. I refuse to feel sorry for myself. The tears dry up against the wind, and the reality of being outside (without shoes) is starting to make itself known. Damn, the concrete is cold. And covered with gum. Great. How did I not notice the myriad black circles dotting just about every inch of the sidewalk before now?

Once again, I am stuck and don't know where I am, but at least, this time, it's daylight. Barely. I pull out my phone. The battery has reached orange status. It's only 6:16. My head hurts so much. I need to get home, showered, and inhale the biggest cup of coffee known to man if I am going to make it into work today. And I can't call in sick again. I need to save those days for when I actually get sick. Which, if I catch pneumonia due to bare feet, will be soon.

Curling my toes, I walk to the curb and look for any taxis that may be lurking, but of course, there is nothing. I opt to walk further down the block to see if I'll have better luck hailing a cab there.

I'm just about to round the corner when I hear Harold's voice calling after me. I stop and look over my shoulder. He's running down the sidewalk with my shoes in his hand and a sexy motherfucking leather jacket on his back. Let me be clear, he is wearing a brown leather jacket over his bare chest. Can we just enjoy that visual for a moment?

As much as I want to keep walking, I also really want my shoes, so I stay put.

He catches up to me, panting a bit. Disheveled looks good on him and I hate that I notice it.

"Thanks," I say, taking my shoes from him. I try to put them on quickly, but if you've ever worn any shoe with a heel, is not the easiest thing to do.

Harold holds out a hand for me to balance on, and my clumsy ass is forced to take it, but just long enough to put them on. No lingering. No hand holding allowed.

"Again. Thank you."

"Look, about earlier—"

"Can we just forget about that?" I shift my weight in the heels that still don't manage to bring me to his eye level.

"No. I was a jerk before, about the bet, I mean. I didn't

know."

"You weren't supposed to know. You broke into the vault," I say.

"Ah."

We both stand there, shuffling our feet, unsure what to do now.

"Look, I gotta go." I finally say. "I have a date with my 'J'."

He looks up at me, almost hurt, which is somehow pleasantly surprising.

"Joe." I clarify although I'm not sure why I feel the need to. "As in 'Java Joe's.'" Kind of rocking a major hangover inside my head right now and if I have any chance of making it to work today, I need to be filled with caffeine. My GPS says there is one a few blocks over."

His face brightens, and I hate that it makes me feel good.

"In that case, mind if I join you? I could use some coffee, too. That is if you think Joe wouldn't mind."

I look at him, confused.

"You want to join me. On my date. With Joe?"

He gives me a wonderful half-grin, then walks up so close that he is practically nose to nose.

"I would very much like to join you."

Hmm. I know that I can be daft a lot of times, but this is not one of those times. He is legitimately hitting on me. Me.

"Doesn't Gail need you this morning? I was given clear instructions not to keep you up late—" I stop. "Guess I blew that, too."

He lifts my chin up. "You didn't blow anything. I don't need to get her until 7:45. Eons of time. Let's not keep Joe waiting."

"I love Joe."

Harold frowns. "Guess I have my work cut out for me, then," he says.

I start to speak but stop. Wherever this is headed, it's not going to end well, but you can't stop a train wreck already in motion. All I can do now is enjoy the last few moments before the crash. And it will crash. They always do.

At the coffee shop, we find a booth in the corner with soft lighting, which does my head a world of good. I massage the rounds of my temples in an attempt to make the pain vanish.

"So, while I was getting our coffee, I noticed something," Harold says, a big smirk on his lips.

"That it's far too early in the morning for humans to walk upright?" I reply, taking a huge sip, not caring at all that the liquid below the foam is hotter than Hades. The burn feels good.

"I already knew that. What I noticed was the barista up front."

My heart does a little squeeze that it has no right to.

"She cute?" I ask, focusing really hard on my latte.

He surprises me by laughing. "He's not really my type."

"Good to know," I say, slowly. "So, what did you notice about this clearly not-your-type-but-if-he-grew-boobs-might-work barista?"

"You're snarky," Harold says, smiling at me.

"Aw, you're so sweet." I take another liquid magma gulp of my coffee.

With a chuckle, he says, "I noticed...that his name was Kevin.

My eyes grow wide. "You can read! I finally found one that can read, Ma!"

His laugh is infectious. "Yes, I can read, but I can also alphabetize, and you're gonna need a K next, because this totally counts as your J-date."

"Oh." It's barely audible and does nothing to hide the overt disappointment in my voice. A big hard awkward rock forms in my gut. He wants to get me another date.

Harold reaches over the table and takes my hand.

"Hey, look at me. I like you, Dee Harper. A lot."

Oh-My-Bob. I'm getting the 'it's not you it's me speech,' aren't I?

"Mmm," I say. I can't look at him. I feel like such a child.

"And I think you'll be a great mom." I can't believe it. I'm getting the brush off. Now that he knows I want kids; he wants to bolt. Fine. Whatever. I'll put him out of his misery.

"You can stop talking now. I'm a big girl, don't worry about me, okay?" I start to scoot out of the booth when he puts his hand on my wrist.

"Whoa. Where are you going?"

"You're pretty, but not that bright, are you?" I sigh. "I'm leaving. Although I am a blonde, I do understand what you're saying."

"You do?"

I let out a breath. "Yes. You think I'm a swell girl and all, but you don't wanna be my baby's daddy," I say in my best hick voice. "Well, I don't want you to be either, okay? Now, if you'll let go of my hand, we can both live our lives. Separately."

His hand doesn't move.

"Dee, you're wrong. That's not what I'm trying to say at all."

I plop back down in the booth. *Oh, this ought to be good.* "Fine. What are you trying to say?'

"Um, that I want to hang out with you more."

I gape at him. Trust me, gaping isn't a good look, I know this, but a gape is still what I give.

"And I also think you need to finish that bet."

I just blink at him, for several seconds. "That, sir, is an oxymoron."

"No. It's not. You need the money for a really good reason."

I glare at him. "Is there a point to this?"

He leans back and takes a long drink. "I recall you telling me that you didn't have to kiss them in order to check them off the list, just go on the date, right?"

"Yeah...I have to ask them out. If they say yes, I go out on the date. Trust me, planning on a lot of rejections."

He frowns at my self-deprecation. "Then it's easy. You ask out the rest of the alphabet but come back to me." It's his turn to look down. "I don't mean, literally to my place, unless you want to...because you'd be welcome to come over but, we just met, so I'm guessing you wouldn't want to do that—" He stops talking and covers his face with his hands "Well. I just botched this up nicely."

I sit there, staring at him, trying to convince myself that he really just said what he said.

"Why?" I ask. "Why would you want to do that?"

He reaches over and takes my hand. It feels like he's done it a thousand times. My hand doesn't feel the least bit uncomfortable cradled in his, it just feels—at home. "I like you, Dee."

I shake my head. "No, you said that, but I still don't understand the why part?"

"Dee, I've wanted to ask you out from the first day I met you," he says, looking down at his cup. "But you never once looked my way. When I got the text from Ms. Morgan about our date, I guess I was kind of hoping it was your idea."

"My idea? Why would I be stupid enough to ask you out?"

"Stupid?" he asks, confused.

"Well, yeah. I mean there are rules about dating up. You can't do it!"

"Dating up?" I can see he has no idea what I'm talking about.

I let out a breath. "Yes. It's not done. I can date down, but not up! I mean the whole survival of the planet depends on this rule!" I have a point; I just don't know what it is. Clearly.

"Dee, what are you talking about?"

I find myself getting all flustered over having to actually tell him I'm too ugly for him.

"Ugh! People like you don't date people like me. It's not done. It's not good for the species as a whole!"

"The species?"

I sigh. Apparently, I will have to explain. "Look at you," I say. He looks down at himself. "Now look at me." He does but smiles when he does it. Damn him. "Stop smiling. I'm not smile-worthy for someone like you."

"Dee, what are you talking about?"

My hands fly up to my face in frustration. "You're too hot for me!" The table next to us glances over. I can see from their expression that I'm speaking the truth. "Am I right?" I ask the onlookers. They turn back to their tables. Cowards. "Look. Tens have to date tens. The lowly fives and below, they can intermingle, but the tens never date down, unless there is money involved, and let me tell you now, I'm fucking broke." The sound of my voice has reached a dangerously loud level of panic, but Harold doesn't flinch. He just looks up at me with those damn chocolate eyes and smiles.

"Dee, when was the last time you looked at yourself? Like really looked at yourself. You're beautiful."

I sigh. That's what men are trained to say. Trust me, I don't believe it for a second. "Harold, I'm going to give this to you straight. I'm a 40-year-old washed-up nothing."

"Nope." He leans back and crosses his arms. "You're like the fiery version of Drew Barrymore and Halle Berry all rolled into one. The fact that you can't even see that just makes you sexy as hell."

I bite my lip and fight off tears that prick in the corners of my eyes. "I don't know why you're saying that. It's cruel, and you need to stop. I know what I am, and what I'm not. There is a reason that I'm still single at 40, Harold, and sooner or later you're gonna figure that out too." I stand up. "Run Harold. Run far, far away, while there's still time."

I rush out of the booth and out of the coffee house. I ignore the sound of his calls after me. It's better this way. If nothing else, my life has taught me not to get too attached to something. It hurts too much when you lose it.

***

Journal Entry: I had to dump my coffee after I got out of the coffee shop. It just—hurt too much to think about who I got it from.

11.
The chapter in which I sink to a new low.

I try not to allow myself to think when I get home. I just jump in the shower and focus on getting dressed and off to work. I don't even care what color the fucking pantsuit is. They all look the same, boring, and dull, just like me.

Enough. Get your ass to work and out of your head.

The train in is crowded with the buzz of conversation, which is just want I need. I listen in on other people's issues as I push away a reality that will hit me soon enough, but for now, this is what I need. Just stay numb to anything but the road ahead.

At work, I go out of my way not to talk to people, which isn't as hard as you might think. Apparently, I don't have a ton of friends. Shocker. I stay in my cubicle for lunch, ignoring the e-mails from Steph to fill her in on my dates. Instead, I turn off my monitor and hide in the corner of my cubicle and eat a stale bag of salt & vinegar chips from the vending machine. After lunch, I don't even open any social media. I'm not in the mood. I need to bury my brain in the mundane and just focus on the numbers. Tape after tape, I enter client data. Mountains of useless information keyed into the system that will never be needed has somehow become my legacy.

Once I've burned through the pile of dictation tapes on my desk I keep the Dictaphone headphones on, long after the last tape has run out. I just stare at the screen and wait for five o'clock to roll around.

When the day is over, I pull out my junk drawer to grab my purse. I am about to shut it when a bent corner of the adoption brochure catches my eye. I take out the brochure and stare at it. This is what I need to be focusing on. I need to forget the blip that was—him—and get my eyes back on the prize. This is what I want. This is what I need to be putting all of my energy into. Nothing else matters now. Nothing is as important as this goal is. Being a mom is so much more important than a dark-eyed boy who would only rip me in two after he was through with me anyway.

Slamming the drawer shut, I stand up straight with a renewed purpose. I am going to get through this damn alphabet if it kills me. Well, not literally, cause then I would kind of suck at the whole 'mom' thing.

I head home, determined. I'll plot the rest of this list out in my journal. Hell, I'll join a dating service, have Gail help again, anything to get this thing done. And I know just where to start.

I wear an evil sort of knowing grin as I skip my normal route home and I double back to the coffee shop from this morning. Sure enough, 'Kevin' is still at the counter, though, by the looks of it, the changing of the guard is about to happen. Somehow, dating Kevin is going to get Harold right out of my mind. Somehow.

I watch from outside as Kevin takes off his green apron from over his massive frame. The guy has to be 6' 8" easy. He's probably in his mid-thirties, which makes you wonder what's wrong with him that he is still working at a coffee shop at his age. I push the door open and stand in the obscenely long line.

I hear him saying his goodnights to co-workers as I pretend to read the overhead board of the day's specials. Kevin opens the half-door to let himself out of the counter area and walks over to a display stand of mugs and cookies. One of the mugs is apparently askew because he starts repositioning them. I like that. He has attention to detail or OCD.

Okay, Dee. It's now or never.

Stepping out of line, I head over to where he is and am about to say hello when I see him pocket about four of the fancy packaged cookies.

My eyes grow wide. Kevin is a kleptomaniac.

Before he can notice, I turn around and pretend to pick something off my shirt, so he doesn't pick up that I caught him red handed. From behind me, the jingle of the door signals his departure. The girls at the counter mutter a few half-hearted good-nights to the unsuspecting thief.

Fuck. What do I do? The responsible thing would be to rat him out, but I'm not about to let a perfectly good K escape on me, so do the next logical thing: I go after him. Outside, I follow after him, surprised by how far he's gotten. Either he has a wicked gait or a guilty conscience. I literally have to run to catch up with him.

"Hey, Kevin!" I shout.

He stops in mid-stride, as though he was expecting to be caught, then turns around, hands shoved firmly in his pockets, no doubt hiding his stash. When he sees that I am the one calling his name, he frowns.

"Who are you?" His voice is deep. Scary deep, like serial killer sort of sound. Remember why you're doing this, woman.

"I'm Dee. You made me coffee this morning."

He waits for me to continue, thus far not charmed by my gift for sentence making.

"I thought we could go out sometime?" Wow. I just blurted that out, didn't I?

Kevin looks over my shoulder, then around him. "This some

124

kind of joke or something? If so, I am not interested. I'm tired. I've had a shitty day and I want to go home and relax."

He doesn't wait for my reply, just turns around and starts to walk away.

"Eager to get home and enjoy those cookies?"

He stops walking. His head turns slowly over his shoulder to glare at me.

"Have a nice night, Kevin," I say waving, as I turn and walk in the other direction, pleased with myself. I only had to ask him out. If he didn't say yes, it still counted. A loophole to be sure, but I'm still checking K off my list.

Content with my latest victory, I hop on the train and I take out my cell to text Gail.

I am up to 'L'. What about you?

The car starts moving, so I adjust myself in such a way as to not actually have to touch the germ-laden bars and yet remain upright. It's a learned skill that comes with many years of practice.

Gail texts me back a second later.

'Bullshit. Come to my place for dinner. I'll be the judge of where you are. And bring ice cream. And a Slim Jim. Say anything but 'yes dear' to this request, and I will cut you.'

Guess I'm not going home after all. Just as well. I could use a friendly face tonight. I get off at the next stop to transfer to the red line to head back downtown.

Twenty minutes later I arrive at Gail's condo. As much as I hate the idea of condos, this one has a great convenience shop on the first floor for guests and tenants only. I'm in here so much that I think they assume I actually live here.

The shop is small, with only about four aisles. One back wall is entirely devoted to alcohol. That's usually where you'll find me. They have a decent amount of junk food, considering the tenants. But then, maybe the rich like their junk food just as much as the common folk do. The ice cream department is a bit of a letdown, though. There are several empty spaces where the good stuff is usually kept. Perhaps Gail has already raided the store today? Wouldn't surprise me. All they have left is pineapple, gag, and caramel coconut—two flavors that should not go together. Scowling, I grab the caramel coconut and discover a hidden carton of chocolate mint. Score! I head up to the front and grab a handful of Slim Jims instead of just one, 'cause I know I am just gonna have to haul my ass back down here if I don't.

After I pay, I head to the elevator. Good old Renaldo is there, manning the buttons. I swear the guy is like 100, but he's as tough as nails. If he doesn't know you, you don't get upstairs. Fortunately for me, Renaldo and I are like old pals.

"Evening Renaldo,"

"Good Evening, Ms. Harper. Delighted to see you. Here to see Ms. Morgan?"

"Yup. And to do her bidding," I laugh, shifting the bags. When I do, one of the Slim Jim's falls out of the bag.

"Damn it—I mean, Darn it. Sorry, Renaldo."

He laughs but bends down to get the dehydrated sodium stick before I have a chance to.

"I remember these," he chuckles. "Back when I had teeth," he sighs. "My wife used to get these every time she was with child, too," he winks.

My face reddens. "Oh, I am not pregnant," I say.

"I know that, dear. I wasn't born yesterday. I know a baby bump when I see one. Not to mention she has been a tad…on edge…lately."

Oh, crap. How many people has he told?

"She hasn't really told a lot of people yet," I blurt out.

He nods. "What is observed in this elevator stays in this elevator."

The carriage dings to a stop. He gestures the way out. I rest the bag on my hip and fish out a five spot.

"Thanks, Renaldo."

"Of course," he says as the golden doors close on him.

I walk down the hall to her door. I put the bag down and fish out the key. I do not want to risk dropping the ice cream; that would just be the best end to a shitty day. Better to be safe than without ice cream. Inside, I walk down her entryway which is about as large as my entire apartment and into the formal dining room. Yes, there is an informal dining room too, but this one is closer, and my hands are cold.

"Gail! Where are you?" She doesn't answer me. Maroon 5 is playing in the background, so I know she's here somewhere. I grab the bag and head for the kitchen, dumping the ice cream in the freezer and the meat sticks in the bowl of fruit sitting on the counter and hunt around for Gail.

"I have ice cream," I sing.

A head pokes out from Gail's room. It's her cook. The one who doesn't speak the best English. Rosetta. Great. She hates me.

"Ms. Morgan is no feeling good." She mimes puking, an action no one should have to mime.

"Guess she is not gonna want the ice cream I brought her," I say.

"Or the dinner I make," she says.

128

I nod. "Why don't you take the rest of the night off? I'll make her some soup later if she feels up to it. There is an awful flu going around," I lie, knowing full well Gail hasn't told her help about her pregnancy.

She purses her lips, "Flu. Si." She knows. She gives me a small nod and makes her way to the door.

Slumping my shoulders, I enter Gail's room. The sound of her vomiting echoes into the room from her enormous porcelain bathroom beyond. Ugh. I hate vomit. Not wanting to actually witness the event, I sit on her bed and run my hands over the black satin duvet.

"How ya doing, hot stuff?" I ask when the sounds die down.

"I hate everything," she moans.

"Cool." I lie down on the bed and cuddle up in her mound of pillows. "I sent the cook home. I assumed you didn't want whatever spicy dish she made up for you."

I get a dry heave in response. Lovely.

"I thought morning sickness only happened in the morning," Gail pants.

"Pretty sure that is a lie." I know I'm not being very helpful, but I don't do well around up-chucked food. I've had a lifetime of throw up thanks to chemo, and if I never have to do it or see it again, I am okay with that. I've paid my hurling dues.

Gail enters the room. She's as pale as my butt cheeks in summer. "Oh, God. Not again." She places a hand over her mouth, then runs.

I plug my ears and start singing Happy Birthday, really loud. I really hate the sound of hurling. It's a trigger for me, a trigger of a not so great time, so I have to drown it out somehow. "Happy birthday to you, happy birthday to you, happy birthday dear vomit, happy birthday to you!"

Gail comes out of the bathroom again. Her hair is all disheveled and she looks clammy in her cream silk nightgown. "Are you done?" she says, glaring at me.

"Are you?"

She collapses onto the bed beside me and curls up in a tight ball, shivering. "I don't think there is anything left to come out." I shimmy off the bed to pull the covers over her.

"Rest, peanut."

"Don't leave me," Gail whines.

"I'm not. I'll crash here just to make sure you survive the night." I pat the top of her head. "I'm gonna go raid your kitchen for some saltines or soup or something to calm your stomach."

"Mmm. You would've been such a good fucking mom," Gail says.

I push back the unintended sting of her comment and sit on

the bed. "Quick tip. Now might be a good time to stop swearing like a cheap whore."

She laughs, then grows silent. "I am gonna fu—screw this up, aren't I?"

I rub the small of her back. "Probably."

She lifts her head off the pillow, giving me the death glare,

"What I mean, is that all parents screw up their kids. It's part of being a parent. You make it up as you go along, or so I hear."

"But, twins, Dee…"

"More to practice on." I smile. "Stop worrying. You'll know what to do when the time comes."

She gives me a small smile and squeezes my hand.

"And if not, at least you can afford their years of therapy."

***

Journal Entry: I totally deserved that pillow to the face.

12.

The chapter in which Gail and I date the same guy and it's out of this world.

When I wake up the next morning in 'my room' at Gail's, it is to the smell of coffee. Coffee that I didn't make, which is the best kind. So much for giving it up. Following the scent, I find Gail in the kitchen humming and cooking something.

Let me repeat that. Gail is humming. While cooking something. Even uncaffeinated, I know a glitch in the matrix when I see it.

"Gail, honey," I say slowly as though approaching a time bomb. "Are you okay?"

She turns from her pan and "Of course I am, why shouldn't I be?" She turns back to the pan. I take a tentative step and peek inside.

"Well, you're cooking. What is that, by the way?"

"Eggs." She smiles.

"They're brown."

"They're not supposed to be brown?"

I take the spatula away from her and turn off the flame. "No, eggs are not supposed to be brown."

Gail frowns. "The shells were brown, so I thought that was, like a hint."

I bite my tongue. It's too easy. I must contain my snark.

"Why are you making eggs? Where is Rosetta?"

"I let her go."

Gail walks past me and out into the kitchen.

I watch her leave, stupefied. Following after, I ask the obvious question, broaching it to her as though I would a crazy person: "Gail, munchkin. Smoopie pie… how are you going to eat without out Rosetta? You don't know how to cook, unless, of course, you like brown eggs?"

She doesn't answer me and walks into the screening room. (Yes. She has a screening room.) Inside the lights are out, save for the projector's beam. It illuminates a paused black and white home movie. Gail walks to the center of the room and sits in one of the large, overstuffed chairs next to the projector. She hits a button, and the past comes to life. There is a man and a woman, middle aged. I assume it's Gail's parents, although her mom looks nothing like that now. I walk to the other chair beside her and sit, watching her face and not the movie. It's clear from the emotion etched there, that it is, in fact, a video of her parents. A young girl enters the shot. That has to be Gail. I would recognize that devilish grin anywhere. She's dressed in a cute little dress that rests well above the knee. Guess that's always been her thing. Her hair is in ponytails. Large, perfectly tied bows are in place that dangle low toward her chin. She is skipping in between her parents who seem to not notice her weaving in and out of their stoic stance. Their attention is on something off the camera. Just then a woman in white, a nurse, walks over carrying a baby and gives it to Gail's mother.

Who the hell is that? Gail is an only child.

I look back at Gail, whose face has grown somber.

The nurse walks out of the shot as forced smiles become locked on both her folks.

Her father puts his arm around his wife and does the 'aren't we a perfect family' sort of pose, and then the nurse takes the baby back away. The film strip stops.

"Who is that?" I ask.

She doesn't look at me when she answers. It's as though her eyes are glued to the image that used to be there.

"That was my brother, Charles, Jr."

I am rendered speechless. "I never knew you had a brother."

"Not many did. He was placed in a home for boys not long after this video was shot."

"What? Why?"

Gail rubs her temples. "He had Down's." She gives a sad laugh. "Not exactly what they had in mind when they decided to get pregnant with him. He was their last-ditch attempt at a male heir." She turns off the projector. "Guess that's what people did back then; either gave them up or put them in homes."

"Gail… I-I had no idea."

"That day is the only time I ever saw him. Mother never mentions him, not even after she found out he had died. She didn't even flinch at the news. There isn't one single photo of him in her house. Hell, if she knew I had this footage, she'd probably burn it. I found it after daddy died in one of his shoe boxes."

I don't know what to say.

"I had actually forgotten about him completely until I went in for my check-up. God, how sick is that to forget you had a brother?" She scoffs and wipes a tear away. "But yesterday, they asked about family history. I had a brother with Down's, Dee. That means that I have a much higher risk of giving birth to a Down's child, not just because my brother or my age, but also because of my parent's genetic mix. They were second cousins. Bet you didn't know that, either."

I deflate further into the chair. "Um. No."

"Apparently, there is a test they can do, you know, to see if they have it. I told them I didn't want to know. I didn't want to know if—because if I knew—I'm not entirely sure I could go through with it." Gail gets up from her chair and walks a few feet before she stops, needing to rest on a nearby chair. "God, I hated them, Dee. For so long, I hated them for doing what they did to Charles. I was five. I didn't understand why he couldn't come home. I didn't understand when they said he was sick. He wasn't sick, Dee. He just wasn't perfect, so they got rid of him! What if I end up being just like them?"

"Gail, you aren't like them, okay? You don't even know if they have it. I'm sure the risk is actually very small."

"With all my risk factors? It's about 65%, Dee." A small laugh escapes her lips and I see how tired she looks. "65 fucking percent chance that one or both of my kids will be born with Down's Syndrome."

"Okay, but there is also a 35% chance that they won't be. And even if they do have it, it's not the end of the world. We know so much more about it now than we did when your parents were young. It will be okay, Gail. I'll be here. I'll help you, no matter what."

Gail gives me a small smile then wobbles a bit, steadying herself along the wall.

I rush after her. "Are you okay?" I ask, rubbing her back.

"Yeah, just got a whiff of those eggs. I'll be fine in a sec."

Her skin has grown pale.

"Gail, did you get any sleep last night?"

She shakes her head. "Can't sleep since that appointment. My brain won't stop running."

"Okay, that is it. Come on. You're gonna, at least, lie down. I am going to make you some tea and we are gonna binge watch something on Netflix or Hulu or whatever. Your choice, just please, God, nothing with Zac Efron again. I know you lust after his pubescent body, but my eyes are still bleeding from that last film that you made me watch with him in it."

She laughs despite her glum mood. "If one of them is a boy, I'm gonna name him Zac just to piss you off."

"That's my girl," I say, leading her to her room. I make a note to call in sick again. Who needs a pesky paycheck anyway? Food is highly overrated.

As my arm supports her, I feel the ribs along her waist. She hasn't been eating enough. She should be showing much more than she is at 12 weeks. Even a single birth should be showing more than her by now. I can't help but wonder if this is intentional on her part since she hasn't found the kid a father. I decide not to bring it up now but will. Soon. She needs to start thinking about the health of these babies or there won't be a need to find them a daddy.

Once I've gotten Gail settled on the bed, I head into the kitchen to make her some tea. A quick Google search on my phone tells me what type of tea will be safe given her condition. It would be just like me to give her a tea loaded with caffeine that will give them each six heads. I'm hoping to find one that might have little sleep help with it, too.

Gail has every tea known to man. I swear. There is one walk-in closet sized pantry filled from top to bottom with tea. Loose leaf tea, bagged tea, tea leaves, if it has to do with tea, she has it. She barely drinks it, though. The stash is for her mother's visits. I shudder. That woman is shudder worthy.

As I steep a tea that claims to 'calm and soothe', I think about the film we just saw. There is a huge part of Gail's life that I don't know anything about. I never met her father, but her mother... Ugh. I could totally see her giving up an imperfect child.

When the tea is done, I fix her a tray with some gourmet rice cracker things (who doesn't have saltines in their cupboards?). I fish out a bagel from the fridge and hold it in my teeth as I balance the tray and carry it to her bed.

I set the tray down, careful to not slosh the hot water everywhere.

"Okay, so what are we watching?" I ask, taking a bite of my bagel breakfast.

"Not so fast," Gail says, taking her teacup. "You are trying to get me to forget why you were beckoned to me in the first-place last night. Give me all the dirt on your alphabet soup."

I groan at her pun. "Yeah, well, you yacking your guts over everything sort of put a damper on that conversation."

She glares at me from across her teacup. "Smart ass."

I grab my cup and bring it to my lips. It's hot as fuck. Why the hell is tea so hot? In my shrieking, I end up spilling half of it onto myself, which is just as freaking hot.

"Damn it! Why don't I ever remember to blow first?" I fume.

"Honey if you did that, you'd already be married, and you wouldn't have to go through this dating thing."

"Now who is the smart ass?" I ask.

Gail smiles. "Seriously, spill, and for God's sake, not the tea again," Gail says.

I sigh. "I told you on the phone. I am up to 'L.'"

"What happened with Harold?" Gail asks.

"I don't want to talk about that if you don't mind. For real, Gail, not talking about it."

Gail sips her tea in such a way as I know she won't let this drop for long. "Fine. I knew about Energetic Eli. What about F? G was me, you're welcome, by the way. H was Harold, again, you're welcome. That leaves I, J, K … Four dates you haven't told me a thing about." She sounds exasperated.

"Look who's talking! You never tell me anything about your dates!"

She waves her hand at me. "They're all the same. Boring, rich, and no good in bed. I want to hear about yours."

I groan.

"Come on, help a sick, pregnant lady find some joy in the world."

"It's not nearly as interesting as you would hope. 'F' was a guy at work that was happily married. He spilled coffee on my jugs, and I asked him to take me out to lunch to make up for it. The letter 'F' done in a single afternoon, and before you ask, there was no afternoon delight."

Gail frowns. "Boring."

I ignore her and ramble on. "The letter 'I' was, cough, me, as in me, myself, and I."

"Come again?" Gail asks, batting her eyelashes.

"What? I asked myself if I wanted to have a drink, and I said yes."

"That is totally cheating."

"You're gonna love 'J' then. We went to a place called Joe's for coffee and I totally called that a date, too."

Gail cocks her head. "We?"

Ah, fuck. "Yes. Harold and I. We—he …" I bumble.

She puts down her tea and settles in. "Go on."

"Gah. Fine. You sent Harold to get me, thanks for that, by the way. I wanted you to come and get me."

Gail laughs. "You must have been drunk. I don't drive anymore."

"I thought you might make an exception for your best friend."

"Well, clearly you were mistaken," she says with no hint of remorse.

"Clearly." I huff. "He picked me up, I was drunk. He brought me to his place since I passed out in his car and he couldn't remember where I lived. In the morning we had coffee. That's it. That's where it ended. Period."

"Why did it end there? What happened?" There is a softness in her voice, the kind someone gives when talking to a child that no one likes to play with, which hits home harder than I should let it.

"No chemistry," I lie. To Gail, that is a stake in the heart. There has to be a raw animalistic thirst for her to go out on a second date with a guy, so I knew this would make her drop the subject.

"Ah. Well, can't do anything about that. Nothing worse than

being with a guy with no chemistry. Just know, I would never let you get away with dating someone with no chemistry. Friends don't let friends have vile sex lives."

"So noted," I say.

"Moving on. What about 'K?'"

"Ah, Kevin. He was the pimple laden, giant barista at the coffee house. I asked him out, he said no. It was heavenly."

Gail rolls her eyes. "Which brings you to 'L,'" Gail says, grabbing the remote.

"Right."

"Well then," she searches for something with the remote, makes a choice, then smiles, hitting play.

I frown this time. "<u>Star Wars?</u> Really?"

"Luke, baby. It's all about our getting our 'L' on tonight."

"Now, that is cheating."

"Not in my book, and it's my checkbook that makes the rules," she giggles and rests back against her pillow. It was cheating, and not just in the bet. I cheated on Luke, too. He's too whiny for me. I'm Team Han all the way, baby.

By dinner time, we are Star Wars-ed out and Gail actually seems to be hungry for something other than rice crackers. Since she fired the cook, I order us pizza. Grease works for a hung-over belly, why not a prego one? I wanted to go out. I've been cooped up in this apartment too long. I needed air, but Gail was afraid she would vom again and wanted to be close to her own toilet.

When Renaldo rings to ask if we ordered a pizza delivery, I almost shout with glee. Without Rosetta to cook, I have eaten nothing but bagels and apples. I need my meat group since Gail went all grizzly bear on me when I hinted that I was gonna steal one of her Slim Jim's.

The smell of the meats (yes, meats plural) wafts up the elevator shaft. I stand at the doors, cash in hand (mine, of course, since Gail doesn't actually use cash—too dirty) and rip the box out of his hand with my right hand and toss him the cash with the other.

"Keep the change," I say, opening the box and inhaling the aroma like one might with a fine wine. Closing the lid securely, I head into the 'entertainment' room and plop the box on the glass table and fish out a slice.

"You better hurry, Gail, if you want any of this." I left her to shower and put on something other than her pajamas. It was 7 o'clock at night, after all.

I am halfway through my second slice when I shout for her again.

"I am totally serious, woman! Get your pregnant ass in here before I get as fat as you."

Chewing, I hear her feet sliding across the floor as though she is dragging herself out of her bed to endure the common folk food.

"Oh, come on, it's not that bad," I say, wiping a line of grease onto my jeans.

"Dee," she says.

"Yeah?" I pull my attention off the crisp pepperoni that almost fell onto her white carpet. That would have been a disaster. When I meet her eyes, my skin runs cold. She's pale. Way too pale. The slice falls from my hands. "Gail?"

She holds up a white towel from her guest room. It's covered in red.

"I'm bleeding."

***

Journal Entry: Fuck.

13.
The chapter in which I hold my breath.

Gail spent that night in the hospital. Since I wasn't "family", I wasn't allowed in to see her. I knew I'd have to call her mother soon, but I wanted to have some news to tell her first. I pace in the darkened waiting room, feeling cold and alone even in the crowd of other pacers. I've tried calling Neil about a hundred times, but he didn't pick up his phone. He never answers if he's with Chad; he thinks it's rude. That leaves me here, alone and freaking out. I need someone to hug. Someone to tell me that she is going to be ok, that everything is going to be okay.

I fish out my phone from my back pocket to dial Neil again, but my fingers betray me and dial another number instead.

"Hello?" Harold's voice is groggy with sleep.

"Harold, it is Dee…" My brain tries to form complete sentences but fails miserably.

"Dee? What's going on? Are you okay?"

My bottom lip starts to quiver. "I know it's late, or, well, early now but, Gail's in the hospital."

"What?"

"She started hemorrhaging ... she might lose the babies," I say as tears start forming.

There is the sound of shuffling. "Babies? She's having twins?"

"Um, yeah. Guess she didn't really want anyone to know yet." I tug at the bottom of my shirt. "I don't know what to do. I am scared. I've tried calling my friend, Neil, but--"

"I'm on my way," he says.

"Thank you." I end the call and stare blankly at the floor.

I don't know why I called him. I shouldn't have called him, I know, I just—I just need him here. I can't explain it. People do weird things under duress. This is my weird thing.

I've managed to down two cold coffees and walk a few hundred laps in the waiting room floor in the time it takes Harold to get here. When I see him enter the room, I can't stop my feet from rushing to him, or stop the rest of me from refusing the hug that he welcomes me with. Just the feel of his arms around me, holding me upright, is enough for now. He doesn't say anything or even try to pull away as I sob into his chest. He just lets me find my way back out of the darkness. I'm the one who eventually pulls back.

"How is she?" he asks. His dark eyes are filled with concern though it feels like it is more concern for me than for his employer, which feels odd, but then again, Gail does treat him like shit all the time.

"I don't know," I whimper. "No one has come in here in hours. I heard them say that she was going into labor. She's only 12 weeks along. They aren't big enough, they'll die." I fall back into his arms again and for the first time realize that I shouldn't be this upset. These aren't my babies after all, so why am I so afraid for them? Concern, of course, but not this body-numbing ache that has taken root. This feeling is irrational for me to be having.

Harold strokes my hair gently as I try to pull myself together. Again.

"She wasn't feeling well this morning, but that was sort of the new norm. We lay in bed all day with Luke and tea—."

"Luke?" He asks. I quite enjoy the hint of jealousy I hear in his question.

"As in Skywalker. We had a Lucas binge since we were both on L."

He pulls back to look at me.

"You're both doing the bet?"

I tuck my hair behind my ear and walk over to the chair I have claimed as my own. "She joined in after she found out she was pregnant. I guess she wanted to try and find a father for her kids before they were born. Not of a word of this to Gail," I say, suddenly realizing the stuff I'm saying. What is about Harold that makes me lose my filter?

"What about the real father?"

I give him a sad smile. "If she only knew."

"Wow." Harold sits beside me. We sit in silence for a few moments. "I don't even know what a 12-week-old baby would look like," he says in a whisper.

"About this big," I say opening my fingers a small bit.

"That's not very big."

I sniff. "No. No, it's not."

Somehow, I end up falling asleep in Harold's lap. The last thing I remember was his fingers running absently through my hair. It must have soothed my spinning brain into the rest it so desperately needed. I wake only when he whispers that a doctor is coming. I'm surprised at how fast I become alert.

"How is she?" I ask, getting up to meet the woman who has walked toward us. She removes her head cap and tucks it into the pocket of her scrub. Her tight curls are unaffected by the cap.

"Gail is in stable condition for the moment. We were able to get her contractions under control."

"Oh, thank God," I say, looking up at Harold. "And the

twins?" I ask.

That's when she blinks. A bit too long.

"It was touch and go with one of them. We think, with time, the fetus will get stronger, but we can't be sure."

There is suddenly a loud rush of sound in my ears, practically drowning her next words out.

"The other fetus seems to be fairly strong. Vital signs look good."

The doctor takes her mask off. "I am going to keep mom here for a few days. She is going to need to take medicine and strict bed rest. The doc on call tomorrow will have the final say, but that is my strong recommendation. Is the dad around to help if this happens?" she looks at Harold.

"There is no dad," I say, clutching onto Harold.

"Family?" The doc asks.

"Um, she has a mother, but she doesn't know about her pregnancy, yet." I clarify. "And me. She has me. I'm her best friend."

She nods. "Okay. Well, she's going to need a lot of support in the coming months. For now, we've got your information. We'll call you if things change, but for now, go home. Get some rest. She's going to need you strong for her."

I swallow hard, but nod.

"Thank you, Dr…?"

"Dr. Lemay. I'm going to insist on no visitors until tomorrow afternoon. Family only. She needs her rest. Understood?"

I want to protest, but she holds up her hand. "Take my advice. Rest. Pray. Repeat." She gives us a small smile, then walks out of the waiting room.

I dig my hands into my hair and hunch over as though trying to summon my own strength.

"She's right. I need to be strong so that I can focus on Gail and those growing babies." My resolve is firm.

"Do you need a lift home?" Harold asks.

"Oh, um, yeah. Thanks. I kinda came here in an ambulance."

He laughs softly. "I don't think they will take it kindly if you ask for a ride back then." Harold stands and holds out his hand to help me up, which I accept.

"Thank you, for coming tonight. I just—I didn't know who else to call or what to do. I was kinda losing it and I guess I just needed to see a friendly face."

"Well, you found one." He smiles and tugs my hand toward the door, but doesn't let go, and I don't drop it after I should have. I know. I know. I'm a moron.

"Let's get you home."

It would have been nice and romantic to just smile and sigh

at my savior, but instead, my stomach lets out a rockin' roar even a T-rex would be proud of.

"Hungry?" Harold asks with a smirk.

"What gave it away?" I groan.

"Come on, I'll take you out to grab a bite before I take you home. Can't go to bed on an empty stomach. It's bad luck."

"It is?" I blink.

"No, but it sure makes it hard to fall asleep."

"Damn straight. But, I am paying my own way, deal?"

His face darkens for a flash but then says, "Deal."

About a block from my place, he pulls over and kills the engine. He stretches his arms over his head. His fingers brush against the top of the car. After a monstrous yawn, he asks, "There's sushi bar two blocks down there or a greasy spoon burger place three or four blocks behind us. Your call."

"Greasy spoon. Hands down. I don't eat uncooked fish." I make a gagging sound.

"Ha, thank God. I hate it too."

I turn to look at him. "Then why did you suggest it?"

He shrugs. "Chicks seem to dig it."

I frown. "So, you'll eat raw fish—risk death mind you, just to get in a girls' pants?"

"No! I don't do that," he says, thoroughly insulted by my

insinuation. "I would never do something like that. I'd order vegetarian." He grins.

I laugh quietly, but then feel guilty about it. "It feels wrong to be joking around. It feels wrong to be thinking about food…"

"Becoming an angry anorexic won't help Gail—or her babies. You heard the doctor. She'll need your help. She'll need you to lift her spirits. To make her strong. She's going to have a hard road ahead. She needs a rock, not a twig. Eat you must. Laughter you make. Friend grow big and strong," he says in a very bad Yoda attempt.

I roll my eyes. "Fine. Let's get me fat then."

"Atta girl."

He gets out of the car as I dig in the back for my purse. Before I can put my hand on the door, he has it open and ready for me, his own hand extended out to help me. Chauffeurs. Guess it is ingrained.

"You don't have to do that you know; I am not tipping ya."

He laughs. It's a deep, sincere laugh. "Well, that's too bad. I am gonna be out of a job for a few days it seems. I could really use the money."

I reach out and grab his arm, full of concern. "I'm sure Gail will still pay you for the week."

He grins, showing off that wonderfully crooked smile. "I

know she will. That was a joke."

"Oh. Sorry. I blame my hunger on that momentary lack of humor."

He takes my hand again, and like a fool, I let him. This is not a good idea, which is of course why I'm doing it. We start walking toward the restaurant. Now that the sun is down, the chill has sunk into the air and I shrink down into the collar of my jacket to fend off the wind. I know Chicago got its nickname because of politicians, but the grid structure of the city doesn't make the wind cut through you any less.

"So, since Ms. Morgan won't need me to drive her tomorrow, you think I could join you when you go see her?"

"God don't call her Ms. Morgan. Makes me think about her mother." I shudder. "And why would you want to come with me? Wouldn't you rather stay at home watching TV and eating pizza?"

"Nope."

"Why not? That sounds like heaven to me," I say as we cross the street to reach the diner.

"Perhaps," he says, holding the door open, "but then, you wouldn't be there."

Despite my desire not to, I blush and burrow my head even further down my jacket.

***

Journal Entry: Let's see how I fuck this up, shall we?

14.
The chapter in which the past rears its stupid head.

The next morning Harold picks me up at noon to go visit Gail. I took her doctor's advice and got as much sleep as I could once I got back from dinner. I had a surprisingly good time; despite the day I would have had if Harold hadn't showed up. He tried to keep the conversation light and mostly on the food. Smart boy.

I told him to just honk when he got here and I'd come down, but no, he insisted on coming up to get me. "It's how I was raised," he said.

"Where you born in Chicago?" I ask, inviting him in, so I can finish tying my shoes. I'm the type of person who could trip over my own laces and plummet the meager 5 feet to my death. My ability to stumble over air is a gift.

"Nope. California, actually."

"Really? Why the hell would you move here?" I say double knotting my first shoe.

Harold walks into the living room to wait for me. As he

walks, he looks at the picture frames I have scattered about the walls. It's my mini museum of memories. No rhyme or reason to how the pictures were placed. I just hung them as I pulled them out of the boxes when I moved in. Currently, he is looking at one of the many that I have posted from my hairless years. I flinch a bit. Cancer was far from glamorous, but I keep the pictures up to help reminded me of how short life is. Inspiring? Sure. Flattering? Not so much.

I focus back on my shoes to let him look in peace. I have to remind myself that he knows what cancer looks like because of his sister. He can absorb these pictures better than most could.

"We moved here when I was little," he says after a moment. "My step-father was transferred here when I was like ten. My mom had just gotten pregnant with Claire. Lot of changes. It sucked. My mom didn't want to leave the reservation. She really hates the cold."

"Reservation?"

He's looking intently at one of me back in college. God, I'm old. He takes it off the wall to look at it closer.

"Um, yeah. My mom is full blooded Choctaw. Dad is white. He's in sales. That's how they met, he was trying to sell his crap insurance to the reservation. She told him off for trying to take advantage of her people, and it bloomed from there," he says, distracted. I look up at him, he's staring at a college picture of me.

"That was me, 20 years ago. Jamie took that." A sting of pain shoots through me. "An ex. He was a photography major. He was always taking my picture, bugged the shit out of me. That's the only one he took of me that I kept after we broke up." I finish up with my other shoe. "I don't know why I keep it."

"I do," he says, looking up at me.

I frown. "You do?"

He smiles, holding up the picture to me. "Look at you. Look at that level of contented concentration. Can you remember what you were writing about in that journal that was making you so happy?"

"Sure, I do," I say. I walk past him, stand on my tip toes, and scan the top shelf of one of my many bookcases. They are each lined with numbered spiral bound notebooks. My fingers pull out a muted green one. The wire is all bent out of shape and the cover is barely hanging on. "I was an English major. I used to write. A lot. Short stories mostly. The occasional poem or two." I smile at the memory. I open the journal and flip through the pages, each one filled to capacity with the thoughts that used to flood my mind.

He looks at the journal in my hands.

"I was writing about a kiss." I blush.

"It must have been one hell of a kiss. With Jamie?"

I close the book and feel a heaviness set in. "Nah. It's fiction. Kisses like that one don't exist in real life."

"Will you read something to me?" He asks out of the blue.

I clutch the journal to my chest. "Oh, these aren't finished or anything. They are more ideas, really…" I am stalling and tripping over my words. I haven't looked at these in a good ten years.

"Still, I'd like to hear something, if you would be okay with that."

I swallow. "Um. Well." I open the journal a fraction, then close it. "It's just—I haven't written anything recently. This was kid stuff, back when I thought I knew what I was gonna be when I grew up. Ha." The laugh is weak. Forced.

He sits down on the couch and crosses his legs. "I won't judge you. I am just really curious about what you used to write about."

I bite my lip. The whole sharing-your-words-with-others thing is half of the reason I gave up writing. Reading your own stuff out loud is like standing up on a stage, stark naked. Every little flaw about who you are is hidden on the page within the words. If we speak it, we risk them discovering the truth. I'm getting all sweaty even now, just thinking about it.

I think Harold can sense this because he resorts to begging.

"Please, just a few lines."

"I'm not…" I hedge.

"Please."

I let out a great breath of air and crack the journal open. I flip the pages, noticing the scribbled-out words, doodles in the corners and dog-eared pages. About halfway through the journal, I found the 'kiss' page. I still recall writing this. I was so full of hope and stupidity back then that a sort of kiss like this could exist that I've almost torn this page out a hundred times. I clear my throat. "I can't believe I'm doing this," I whisper.

"With one single kiss, her world slipped away. She had let go of reality and succumbed to his touch, eager to step outside of the shell she'd so carefully constructed. She should have held on tighter, refused to lose her grip, but his warmth was so addicting that she knew she'd never need that wall again."

I close the journal. Probably faster than I should have.

"Wow," is all he says.

"And this is why I stopped writing," I say walking back over to the shelf and put the journal back.

"What do you mean?

"That whole passage, God! It's kid stuff. Melodrama on steroids. I can't believe you got me to read from that."

Harold shakes his head, "I thought that was really good. Is there more?"

"No. I stopped writing that, and all my other stories when I got sick. Didn't really see the point, ya know?" I see a look of sorrow in his eyes which makes me uneasy. "Hey, it's okay. I've come to terms with it. Besides, fluffy words don't pay the hospital bills." I smile. "Speaking of which, I make the last payment next month." I do a fist pump. "Yet another thing I wouldn't let Gail help pay for me, no matter how hard she begged." Harold isn't as amused as I thought he'd be. He walks over to me, pulls the journal back out and tosses it onto my dining room table.

"So next month then. Next month, you start writing again."

I shake my head.

"Dee, you have a gift."

I roll my eyes and head for the door. His hand catches my elbow, drawing me around.

"When you just read to me, I saw more spark in your whole being than in all the time that I've known you. You need to do this. You owe it to yourself."

"The only thing I need to do right now, is to go see my friend." I know it's mean, but I pull out of his grasp and head for the door. I haven't thought about writing in so long that I almost forgot it used to be my entire world. Of course, when you get cancer, any dreams you ever had got flushed down the toilet—at least for a while. Priorities shift. Suddenly, it doesn't matter if you got that in that 500 words before you went to bed. Trying to make it through the day without vomiting becomes your new goal. It was a reality I had a hard time letting go of. Even after they declared me in full remission, I didn't dare move forward. Didn't dare to believe it was true. For about a year, I stagnated. I didn't want to move forward and risk having to lose anything. If it hadn't had been for Gail and Neil, I may not have come out of that funk. I kept waiting for that other shoe to drop; waiting for the hospital to call me up and tell me that they'd made a mistake, that the cancer was still inside of me, killing me off cell by cell. Then one day, I found myself writing a note inside a calendar for a full 3 months away and not batting an eye over it.

Behind me, I hear Harold start following me. He shuts my apartment door for me, but I keep walking down the narrow hall toward the stairwell. I try to use the stairs as often as I can and ignore the shaky elevator. Elevators should not shake. Not even in L.A., I try to think of it as a blessing. Most days, these stairs are the only exercise my body gets. I should probably work on that if I'm going to try and become a mom. Gone are the days that I could eat a gallon of ice cream with no lasting evidence.

Since turning forty, I see the very obvious signs of my aging:

pants that never before required the lie-down and cram method have now become the norm; skin that used to be soft and bouncy now feels more like dried out fruit leather. The wrinkles came in during in my mid-thirties and I've come to terms with them, so long as they stop. Like right now. I won't mention the gray hairs that have started to appear faster than I can yank them out. *Bastards*. And my poor breasts... I swear they have sunk another good inch since last year alone. Pretty soon, they'll be able to double as knee pads. And I wonder why I'm still single.

On the car ride over to the hospital, I'm pretty quiet. I have a lot on my mind. Too many things to process lately.

"What are you so deep in thought on over there? You haven't said a word the entire ride."

I pull on my bottom lip as I watch the buildings pass by, contemplating.

"Honestly? I was thinking about how stupid it's for someone my age to try and adopt a child. If I were the adoption agency, I would laugh my own application right into the trash can." I rub the palms of my hands over my face, trying to push away the negativity.

"You're not too old to make a difference in the life of a child that needs a loving home," he tries. "Trust me. My step-father adopted me in his 40's. I learned more from him in that short twenty-year span than I could ever ask for. Sure, my time with him was short, but we made what little time we had together matter. Was it always ideal? No. We had our issues, trust me, but at the end of the day, he helped shape me into the man I am today."

"How old were you when you were adopted?"

Harold's face darkens, just a touch. "Thirteen. Old enough to foolishly mourn for a biological father that would never return for his family."

I can tell he doesn't feel comfortable with the subject, so I try to shift gears.

"I never would have pegged you as Native American."

He smiles, "Because I don't have a tan or long black hair?"

"Or the war paint," I say, weakly. "Shit. That was insensitive."

Harold just smiles. "It's all good. I'm used to it. My mom was pretty pale, so I guess I favored her. When we moved off the reservation, my stepdad made every attempt to whiten us up with our clothes and haircuts and such so people wouldn't make fun of us. I guess I kind of outgrew my heritage. He never actually said it, but I think he was really just ashamed of the Native part of us." He frowns. "Wow, that's a downer."

I laugh lightly. "Do you have any memories of your father?"

"The one who adopted me, yes. Of the man who left us

behind, not ones I care to hold onto. That's all I care to say about him right now. Lot of stuff kicking around in the memories vault, as you call it, that I would prefer just stay put if you know what I mean?"

"Of course. I—I shouldn't have asked you all of those personal things anyway. I do that when I'm nervous. I ask things I have no right to know, been that way since I was a kid. Kind of a foolish sort of tic to have, don't you think?"

He shrugs. "Could be worse."

"Very true."

We've managed to talk away the rest of the drive to see Gail. When he pulls into the parking garage, I had almost forgotten why we were here. Talking with Harold is much too easy. I need to establish some boundaries if my plan to get him out of my system will work.

After he is parked, he turns off the engine and squeezes my hand for a moment, and I melt a little inside.

"Let's do this," I say. He smiles and lets go of my hand to get out of the car, and I tell myself to be okay with not holding his hand. When he opens my door and offers me his hand again, I take it willingly.

***

Journal Entry: Tomorrow. I'll establish boundaries tomorrow.

15.
The chapter in which Gail loses her mind.

As we head toward the parking garage elevators, the click of our shoes bounces wildly off the damp concrete walls. Inside the garage, it smells like a wet mitten that has been bathed in exhaust and powdered with cigarette ash. Ah, city life.

"Do you think she'll be up?" I ask, fidgeting with the hem of my shirt.

He opens the door for me and pushes the button for the elevator.

"If she's still sleeping, we can wait or come back," he says calmly. I wish I were that calm. I'm a nervous wreck. What if something happened during the night? What if she got worse and no one thought to call me?

"Dee, calm down," Harold says, draping an arm over me. "If something had changed, they would have called you. No news is good news with doctors." I know that all too well; still, I'm on edge.

The elevator doors open, and we walk in. As they close, I

curse.

"I should have brought her some clothes, or a magazine or something, shouldn't I have? Maybe the gift shop is open. I could get her something there, but what would she want? Should I ask her first or just show up with a bunch of stuff to surprise her?"

"Dee," Harold hums.

"Mm," I say, only half listening. I'm too busy stressing. It's my hidden talent.

"I know you're nervous but try not to worry. If Gail asks for a change of clothes, we can go back and grab her some. If she wants a magazine we can get one in the gift store. You don't have to be able to read her mind in order to be a good friend."

"Edward could read minds." Yup. I went there. I Twilight-ed the poor boy and he has no clue what I am talking about.

He cocks his head. "Even Edward couldn't read the mind of the woman closest to him. Perhaps you and Gail are the same."

I whip around to look at him, shocked he got the reference.

"What?" he says. "I have dated other women, you know. I've had to endure my fair share of that book to be an expert on all things sparkly."

"Did you read them?" I ask, taken aback.

"Now, let's not go crazy. I still have my man card intact, thank you."

I laugh. At least he has a sense of humor about how grown woman seem to have collectively lost their minds all at the same time over such a ridiculous thing. I have held some sense of dignity in the whole madness by being Team Jasper. Can't fault a girl for that pick. Ain't nothing wrong with that boy's crooked smile. Not. One. Thing. (Except his hair in the second movie.)

When the elevator doors open to the hospital, I'm struck like a slap in the face by the smell: Bleach, disinfectant and wilting flowers. It's the smell of impending death. Without my consent, memories of my cancer years, ones I thought I'd overcome years ago, nearly knock me to my knees. The last time I came off this particular elevator was for my hysterectomy. The day the dream of having kids died—instead of me.

It's suddenly hard to breathe. The air is thick, making it hard to swallow. My mouth has gone dry. My vision blurs a little. I sway a bit against the rush of sensory overload.

"Whoa," Harold says grabbing my shoulders before I pass out. "What's going on, are you okay?" He walks me over to a bench and tries to signal a nurse.

"Stop," I say, pulling at his hand. "I'm okay. I just—need to catch my breath. The smell—it, it just brought me back to—well, a not-so-great time."

His face contorts with concern. "Oh. Shit. I didn't even think.

What do you need me to do?"

I shake my head. "Nothing. I'll be fine in a second," I say with a firmness that hopefully conveys that I have no intention of discussing my time in the hospital right now.

"How about some water? Can I grab you some water?" He's a guy. He needs to try and fix the problem. I get it. There isn't any way to fix this, though. I thought time would, but I guess not.

I shake my head. "I am fine. I just need a minute."

"I am gonna get you some water," he says and walks toward the gift shop. I sigh and lie back onto the bench to take some deep breaths. I close my eyes against the hum of the overhead fluorescents. The sounds of people walking and chatting in the hall thunder in my head. A high-pitched sound of laughter bounces from the corners of the room. I open one eye to see where it's coming from. A little boy, maybe two, is chasing after a 'Get Well Soon' balloon that dances just out of his grasp in his mother's hand. He skips down the hall determined to touch the balloon, as though it held the secret to all happiness. I fight the smile that wants to spread across my lips because it hurts too much. I'll never have moments like this. It's too late for you, Dee.

I watch as the boy gets swallowed up in the sea of people roaming the hall, but the balloon stays in sight. I watch after it, as though I was watching my own dreams float away. I look away, disgusted with myself.

After drinking a full bottle of water, at Harold's insistence, I tell him I feel better. And I do. Those memories are locked away, for the moment anyway. Together we head to a nurses' station to find Gail's room. They have moved her out of the ICU unit, which is a good sign. I think.

The nurses told us that she was having a rough morning. The doctors insisted that she not get out of bed except to use the restroom, which didn't go over well with her apparently. They instructed me that if she didn't stop calling them names they were going to stick a catheter in her and secure her to the bed until she's released. Great. Gail's in rare form. Help us all.

Carefully opening the door, so as not to scare the beast, I put on my bravest face, but have to crack a smile at what I see. She's sitting upright in bed and has the remote control in her hand, pointing it at the screen as though she were trying to shoot the thing.

"What did that TV ever do to you?" I ask.

Gail turns to look at me, while Harold hangs back, probably unsure of where he fits in this picture.

"Oh, thank god, Dee! You didn't forget about your best friend and her desperate need to get out of this ridiculous hospital. Will you please let them know that I have a doctor on my staff who will take care of anything they can do here?"

"I will make sure to do that the first chance I get," I lie. "How are you feeling? Or is that a question that I shouldn't ask you with a very lethal looking remote control still in your hand?"

"You have to get me out of here. They won't let me move! This is like jail! Or what I assume jail must feel like." Gail flops onto her pillow, melodramatic as all get out.

"It's for the babies' safety, honey, they're not trying to be mean to you."

Gail moans. "I know. I must seem like a big old baby right now, but I don't like hospitals."

I laugh. "I'm not a big fan either."

Gail turns to look at me and goes a little pale.

"Oh, I'm such a jackass. I didn't even think. See how self-absorbed I am? How can you stand to be friends with me?"

I shake my head at her drama. She's in good mental health, self-deprecating as ever. "I brought Harold with me," I say wanting to get her out of her own head. "I told him that you would still be paying him for today even though he's not driving you anywhere. After all, it's not his fault that you're in here."

Gail glares at me. "Dee, what sort of cheapskate do you take me for? Of course, I am going to pay the man." Gail looks at Harold. "Did you put her up to this?"

I roll my eyes. "No. He didn't, now stop being high and mighty. He's actually carted my ass around more these last few days than he probably does yours in a week, so he might actually deserve a raise." I look back over my shoulder to Harold and wink at him.

Harold's eyes grow wide. "What? No, I'm okay. I don't need a raise and I don't need to be paid for the time you're in the hospital. I was happy to be able to help out Ms. Harper." Harold says, stepping closer into the room. "Is there anything I can get for you while you are in the hospital? Anything you'd like me to have delivered to the house or here?"

Gail smiles. "Isn't he sweet?" She looks at me and motions for me to come closer.

"Too bad there's no chemistry between you two," she whispers.

"Just because you're in a hospital, don't think that I won't murder you," I hiss back.

She just leans back and gives me her knowing grin. I hate that grin.

"Harold," she says, still looking at me, "could you be a doll, and go check with one of the nurses to see when a doctor might be in to tell me finally what the hell is going on? Apparently, I am to be the last one to know!"

A monitor goes off beside her bed, my eyes widen, but Gail waves me off.

"It's fine. They're monitoring my blood pressure. Damn things have been going off every few minutes. I told them if I knew when they were going to release me, I might be a little less bitchy," she yells toward the door, probably hoping the nurses will hear. "Maybe your charm, Harold, will get me an answer." She bats her eyelashes at him.

"Of course, Ms. Morgan." He shoots me a glance, then leaves the room. I sit on the edge of Gail's bed and take her hand.

"Okay, he's gone. You can drop the act. How are you? Really?" I ask.

The bitchy mask she was wearing a moment ago crumbles. "I am terrified. I went into labor, Dee." She brings her hand to her stomach. I grab her other hand but don't speak, it feels like she's working up the courage to say something hard. "Dee, when I saw all that blood, I—" she pinches her eyes closed.

"You got scared," I finish for her. "I did, too."

Gail looks at me, her eyes are sad. "No. I wasn't scared, Dee. I was—relieved." She looks down at the blankets. "It could have been a way out of this nightmare. God's way of confirming what a bad idea this was."

I force myself not to say anything, to not pass judgment. Just because I wanted kids, doesn't mean the rest of the world wants them.

"You think I am a horrible person, don't you?" she whispers. Her hands are playing with the edge of the hospital sheet. Her face is devoid of her normal layer of makeup, so she looks more real— vulnerable, not like the ice princess she pretends to be.

"No. I don't think that at all. I think that you were, are, scared. You're afraid that you're not gonna be a good mom." Her sniff confirms my assumption. "Spoiler alert. You're gonna mess up, Gail. A lot."

"Gee, thanks."

I laugh. "But that's what all moms do. Nobody is ever really ready for this. The only way to be a good mom is to make mistakes. That's how we learn. Just don't drop one of them and you'll be fine."

"Oh, hell. I didn't even think of that? What if I drop one of them!" Gail's manic face returns, setting off her blood pressure and I frown.

"Chill, girl. I hear they're bouncy when they're little," I say patting her hand. We sit for a moment as I wait for her heart rate level out.

"It changed you know?" she says eventually.

"What did?"

She shifts in the bed with slow and careful movements. "What I want."

I look down at her and raise an eyebrow.

She rubs her baby bump and smiles. "I want this," she says. "Them. I want both of them." Gail starts to cry and damn it all, I join in. I can't help it. It's an unwritten pact woman have. No one cries alone.

Of course, it's while we are in the midst of our happy cry that Harold comes in with a doctor.

"What's wrong?" Harold asks, his body tensed.

I stand up and wipe my eyes. "Nothing, we're just happy everyone is healthy. They are all healthy, right, Doctor—?" I ask, trying to find a name tag.

The doctor comes forward to shake my hand. "Dr. Greene," he says. He has a thick accent that I can't place. UK-ish. "The babies appear to be in good condition at this point. Although," we all watch the doctor, "I am going to insist on bed rest from here on out. I'm also going to give you some medication that you'll need to take every 4 hours, even during the night, to stop the premature contractions." He looks at me. "She'll need to set a timer. Every four hours. It's important that we keep these premature contractions at bay. You'll help her remember?"

I nod emphatically.

Gail grabs for my hand. "Doctor, could you be a dear and define what you mean by bed rest?"

The doctor chuckles. "I know it seems overwhelming, but I am told you have your own medical staff?" He raises his eyebrows.

"I can hire them by the dozens, that's not the issue. The issue is this bed rest thing. I can still get out of bed, right? Right? You just mean, take it easy."

The doctor turns to look at Harold and me as though for support.

"Bed rest is just as it sounds. You are to be in bed. Resting. For the duration of your pregnancy, you'll need to stay in bed, or sitting down, preferably with your legs reclined. You are to only get up to use the bathroom and take short showers. That's it."

Gail's eyes grow wide. The doctor walks closer to Gail and sits on the edge of her bed. His voice is soft and kind when he speaks.

"We need your body to be a low-impact zone. We need these babies to stay put. We can get you a wheelchair to increase mobility, but again, only for short periods. You'll need help, Ms. Morgan. Around the clock help. And you have to ask for it; now is not the time to be independent. Not if you want them to make it to term. Understood?"

Gail nods, though her eyes are welling with tears. This will not be easy for her.

"Do you have friends or family that can stay with you for the rest of your pregnancy?"

Gail's eyes drop. "I have my staff. I'll be fine."

"She has friends that will make sure her prego butt stays put," I say more for Gail's ears than the doctors.

Dr. Greene smiles. "That's good. Friends are better than staff." He stands up. "I'll have the nurse get your discharge order ready. You'll be resting at home tonight, with a giant list of things that are off limits for a bit."

Gail moans.

"I know it sounds daunting, but it's the best way we can keep you all safe. Letting go of control will be hard, but it's time for you to lean on the support of those who love you." He gives a soft smile then leaves us in peace.

Gail sniffs and her lower lip trembles a bit.

"I'm just gonna be out in the hall," Harold says, sensing our need for privacy.

"You don't have to go," I say, more to be polite than anything.

"You two need to catch up and I have a level of Candy Crush to obliterate," he says, wiggling his phone at me.

I shake my head.

After he is gone, Gail grabs my hand. "I have to ask you something. Something you're going to say no to, but I am going to ask it anyway because I am an incredibly shallow person."

I laugh at her honesty. I'm glad to see that spark is returning.

"Ask away."

She swallows and starts fiddling with the sheets again. "I—I need you, Dee. You are the closest thing I have to family. My mother doesn't count as a human being, let alone my mother. You and Neil are like the siblings I was never allowed to have." I hear the sting in her statement.

I nod my head because I feel the same way. My mom, though still alive, lives in New Hampshire. She hates to travel since Dad's passing, and it's not like I'm a great daughter and visit often, so basically, it's been the three of us my adult life.

"I can't ask this of Neil because he absolutely loves his job, the fool, but you—well you have, can I say it? A shitty job?"

The look on her face is one I've never seen. She's trying really hard not to insult me.

"What's your point? Not everyone can love their jobs or have billionaire daddies." That was a dig. Not a nice one either. "I'm sorry. That was uncalled for. True, but uncalled for."

"My point, smart ass, is that, yes. I have staff. But they aren't who I want with me when I am feeling nauseous, bitchy, or fat.

And let's face it, I'm all those things now, but they will, presumably, become worse."

"I'll be there to visit you, silly. You're being put on bed rest, not quarantine." I clarify.

Gail picks up the remote beside her and I flinch instinctively, afraid she's gonna smack me with it. Instead, she just flicks off the television and the mind-numbing sounds of QVC are silenced.

"Dee, honestly. I thought you were smarter than this."

"Kinda not the best thing to say someone that you are asking a favor of," I say, smirking at her.

Gail lets out a deep, exasperated breath. "I can't believe you are actually going to make me ask," she huffs, looking indignant.

"Ask me what?" I say a bit exasperated myself. "Just spit it out woman, I don't have all day to lie around and watch the boob tube." I snicker. "Some of us need to go to work. I've already used all my sick time, and I doubt Frank is gonna give me any more time off after his run-in with Indian food." I glance at the clock. It's already one. If I leave now, I could get a few hours in. God, I am gonna be so fucked this paycheck.

"Fine. I'll spit it out," Gail says, crossing her arms. "Quit your job and come be my live-in helper." Her words rush out of her lips like a machine gun, forced out so fast that they can't be reconsidered mid-sentence.

I stare at her for a good twenty seconds before I start laughing. Clearly, I misheard her. She can't really be serious.

She ignores my guffaws and raises her hand up to stop me. "Believe it or not, I have given this a lot of thought. I am aware that you can't just up and leave your job. You have bills to pay. I do know what those are, you know." I raise my eyebrow at her. "What I am suggesting, is that I pay you for your services, double what you were making in that god-awful cubby hell. You practically live with me anyway. Why not save your money live there full-time? You heard the doctor. I'm going to need round-the-clock supervision..."

"Gail," I say carefully. "I can't just quit my job to come take care of you."

"Why not?" she asks with a completely straight face. "You hate your job; you say it all the time."

"Okay, for starters: once you have these babies and can walk again, I'll need to find another job! And as sucky as my current employment may be, trying to find a new one in a few months is not something I'm interested in doing! Working at a job I know in my sleep is much better than starting from the bottom again." I stand up and walk the floor a bit, just flabbergasted by her lack of ability to see past her own needs.

"Who said I planned on letting you go after they are born?"

I look over at Gail who has a look of intense vulnerability there. "I can't do this alone, and I don't want some strange Nanny taking care of my kids like I was raised. I know I need to be there for them, but I also know I'll need help." A tear runs down her cheek. "Now that I'm on bed rest, it's not like I'm gonna be able to shop for a father anymore either. Please, Dee, you have to help me. I don't know how else I'm going to get through this unless you're with me."

I wait for some sort of punch line, but nothing comes. She's dead serious.

I pinch at the base of my nose. "You want me to be your live-in nanny once the twins are born?" I ask, hardly believing what she is proposing.

"Yes."

I open my mouth, but I can't find the words. She hasn't thought this through. Has she? "Gail, no offense, but I don't want to be one of your staff. You treat them like second-class citizens, and I want no part of that. Besides, I don't want to feel like I am always at your beck and call when you feel like taking time off from your responsibility of being their mom," I say, trying to make her understand why this wouldn't work.

She nods slowly, staring at the blank TV instead of looking at me. "You're right. I have been awful to my staff. Just awful. I do not know why, either. Some days I hate being rich."

I glare at her.

"I didn't say there were a lot of them," she retorts.

I rub my hands through my hair, trying to clear my thoughts. After a moment, I look up at a waiting Gail.

"Please, Dee. I'll do anything you want, just please don't make me do this alone."

I sigh. Fuck. I hate seeing her like this. I hate even more that it actually sounds doable.

"All right. Here's the deal. I'll do it—"

Gail squeals with delight.

I hold my hand up to stop her. "I'll do it under certain circumstances," I say, cutting off her jubilation.

"Name your terms." She's got her business hat on now.

I start pacing in the small space of her room and start ticking off fingers. "First, I want to set my own schedule, which will not exceed 40 hours. I shall be paid no more than I currently make—"

At that Gail tries to butt in.

"Let me finish. I shall be paid the same rate as I currently make. I shall move out of my apartment and live with you. The money saved on rent will be enough to additionally compensate me."

Gail holds her hands up in surrender.

"Anything else?" she asks crossing her hands over her belly.

"Yes. I will be treated no different than currently am," I say. "And that I don't have to treat you any different than I do now. I don't want our friendship fucked up here."

"Of course," she agrees willingly.

I hold up a final finger, "And you will stop talking down to your staff. Agreed?"

What the hell was I saying? I can't quit my job...can I? Could it really be that easy to leave the place I have worked for twelve years to help take care of Gail's children?

"Now hold on," Gail says. "I have a few conditions of my own first."

Baffled, I look up at her. "You have conditions on my working for you? Bear in mind, you just begged me to do this."

"There are only two."

"Oh, I am dying to hear these."

She clears her throat.

"First: And this is not negotiable. You start writing again."

I scoff.

"I'm serious," she says. "You've moaned for years that your job left you too drained to be creative, but this should change that. I miss your stories, Dee. I loved reading your work. I loved how you were when you were writing. You were... blissful."

"I was never blissful," I snort.

"Yes, you were." Her voice is undeniably sad.

I shake my head. "I was twenty. What was there to be glum about?"

Gail ignores me. "And second: You finish our bet."

"What? No. Gail, the bet is over. We have way more important things to worry about now."

She shakes her head vehemently. "No. I need this bet. For me, Dee. I was sort of joking about needing something to keep me amused while pregnant, but now, I don't know what I'm gonna do with my days. I need something to focus on, Dee. Something to keep my thoughts off losing my babies."

I look at her for a moment and see the desperation in her eyes. I get it. She needs something to still feel normal. I needed the same thing after chemo started. I clung to my journals. I wrote down everything. What time I took my naps, how long they were, what I was able to keep down, what I wasn't. It didn't matter what I wrote, it was just the practice of having something to do. Some sense that there was a reason for you being alive that day.

"Fine," I say with a sigh. "I'll take your money, I'm almost done, anyway." I'm only half-joking. If this didn't work out—if I ended up wanting to strangle Gail by the end of this, at least, I would have fifty grand as a starting-over fund.

"You won't regret this," Gail sings.

I laugh. "That's what they all say in the movies just before the dumb schmuck regrets what they've done."

Gail gives me a small smile. "You're a good friend, Dee."

"Yeah, yeah, yeah."

***

Journal Entry: How does she keep talking me into these things?

16.
The chapter in which I begin a new journal.

The ride back to my apartment is completely silent. Harold doesn't even try to pry information out of me. I must look that deep in thought. I am. Typical mid-life change of job sort of panic. It's an odd feeling. The change feels urgent, suffocating and hopeful all at the same time. In that hospital room, I was at crossroads and didn't even realize it until just now. Either I continued down the same vanilla path I've been on since I finished college, or I jumped off the track and took the next phase of my life onto a part of the map that hasn't been printed yet. Scary and invigorating all at the same time. I always assumed I would be the plain, predictable, single friend that you could go to for a laugh or shoulder to cry on, but never the friend that stuff actually happened to. Now, here I am, leaving that life behind and diving in with both feet without the mind-consuming terror that I assumed would feel. Instead, there is a sense of calm. It is almost like fate. Now, I don't believe in that horseshit, trust me, but that's the only way I can describe what it feels like. It is as though a door opened that I have absolutely no doubt I need to walk through.

There is, of course, a ton to think about now that I made this leap. How will I tell work? When will I tell them? How am I gonna move all my stuff into Gail's place? Do I want to bring it all over there or do I just ditch it all and start new? So many questions. It is maddening. I need to write things out. I have to create a list of all the things I need to do so my head doesn't explode.

"Stop the car," I hear myself say.

Harold turns to look at me. "Mind if I pull over first?"

"I need to buy a notebook."

"Um, okay. There's a CVS up here," he says, turning down Lake Shore Drive.

I barely wait for the car to stop before I am out the door and running towards the store. Flashes flood back to the last time I came into a drug store. No pregnancy tests or date-making tonight. This is far more important than that.

Pushing through the glass doors, I scan the aisle headers for what I want. Bee-lining for Home/Office, I don't even stop to gag at the cornucopia of scents from the perfume counter. I am a focused woman.

When I get there, I run my eyeballs up and down the racks

for what I want: a five-subject, college ruled, 5 Star notebook. Purple, if possible, but today I would be happy with yellow—shiver. I'm desperate. I see one-subject and three-subject notebooks all around and start to panic that I'll have to change up my traditional writing habits—Huh. I have writing habits. That never dawned on me until just now. Even after I stopped 'writing,' I still journaled. Every day.

Frustrated with the selection, I pick up five one-subject journals and contemplate whether there is a way I can make them into one somehow, when wonder of wonders, I find a five-subject (navy blue) notebook hidden behind all of those stupid one-subjects. Sold.

I grab the first blue pen I can find and take them up to the counter. I have barely finished paying when I yank out the pen from its wrapper, nearly knocking over Harold (who has just walked inside) in the process.

"Whoa, slow down crazy lady. What's going on?" he asks me, standing near a display of cheesy looking Christmas mugs. I gag internally. It's not even October yet, people!

"Turn around," I say.

"Excuse me?" He laughs.

"Turn around, I need to use your back for a second."

He gives me an awkward expression that makes him look

ridiculously adorkable, but he complies. I open the first page of the journal and click the pen.

I jot down: Today, I begin my new life. Today begins The ABC's of Me.

I frown and cross out a word: Today begins The ABC's of Dee.

Hugging the journal close to my chest, I smile. Things are about to change.

"Harold, we need to talk."

He turns around to look at me with those deep chocolate eyes. "Okay, but can we move away from the mugs first? They're kind of creeping me out."

I glance around him towards the grinning faces painted onto tree-shaped coffee cups. Some of them are cross-eyed (not intentionally) and are smiling in such a way that it looks an awful lot like they might be masturbating under those fake branches.

"Good call," I say "How about some lunch? Soup Box?"

"Sure. My treat, though," he says, holding the door open. I nod, only because my mind is in think mode. I don't make good choices when thinking.

When we get inside the Soup Box, which isn't much bigger than an actual box, I order the tomato basil with half a tuna on wheat. Harold gets beef stew and a hunk of French bread so large it would satisfy a hungry Hagrid all on its own. Hungry Hagrid. He, he.

"Okay, what's up?" he asks after our initial lip burning sips. You'd think as adults we would learn not to sip hot fluids right away, but nope; we dive in and curse like hell each and every time. I don't know how the human race has survived for as long as it has.

"You were right," I say, putting my spoon down to avoid the temptation of trying the soup again too soon.

Harold looks pleased with himself. "I find that I quite often that I am, but what, specifically, am I right about this time?"

I can't help but grin at his arrogant smile. I know it's just a show, that's why it's funny. Otherwise, I would punch him in the balls.

"I should probably back up first." I pick up my spoon and start to fiddle with it. "While you were out in the hall after the doctor left, Gail sort of asked me to quit my job and come live with her as her in-house helper for now, and a nanny after the babies come." I take a breath. "And I said yes." For some reason, I am afraid of his response, so I put my spoon down and stuff my mouth with tuna salad. Glamorous, to be sure.

"Wow. That's..." He's just as stupefied as I was.

I swallow down much too large chunks of tuna so I can

speak. "I know! I was fully prepared to tell her that she couldn't buy my services and expect me to do her bidding, but then," I wipe mayo off the side of my lip that I managed to smear on myself in mid chew. I'm so lady-like. "Then, I realized that I hate my job. I've hated every single day of it. I spend a ton on an apartment that I am hardly ever in because I'm usually at her place, and I don't have a thing to show for it."

Harold lifts his bread and uses it to point it at me. "That's not true," he says before dunking it into his stew.

"You have nothing to base that on, sir, so hush. This is my story."

He bites of his bread with vigor in silent protest. It's cute, but I don't smile. I am trying to be mature. It sucks.

I pick up my spoon and risk a taste. Ah, perfect sipping temperature. I take a few hearty sips, forgetting that I'm in the middle of telling a story.

"Take your time, I'm sure you'll get to the point eventually," Harold quips.

I cock my head to the side and swallow. "The soup has reached ideal drinking hotness. To ignore that would be a disservice to soups across the world, and I'm annoyed that you're not enjoying the perfection with me and are instead, choosing to judge me." I blink knowingly at him.

Frowning, he takes a sip of his own. "Mmm, you're right."

"You'll find I usually am." I grin.

Together we sip our soup, loudly, each trying to out slurp the other. I have to admit, the boy has some skill in the sucking department. Wait, did I just think those words? I need help. Clearly.

"As I was saying," I take my napkin and daintily dab the corners of my mouth, "if I moved into Gail's guest room, which really is my room, let's be honest, I would be saving $1,100 a month just on rent. Not to mention utilities. I could save that money up—"

"And add it to the adoption pot."

I dig at my empty bowl with my spoon. "Or something."

Harold pushes his bowl away and leans forward.

"What something? Do you not want to adopt anymore?"

"No, I do. Very much. It's just… I have a lot of strikes against me, so I just thought it was time to build a start-over fund. Just in case. In case this doesn't work and I need to forget myself for a while."

"If what doesn't work? Us? Or Gail?" Harold says, without a trace of belittlement.

I just shrug at my soup.

"Putting the 'us' discussion on hold for a second, let me just say that I think you're making the right choice, for what it is worth. Frankly, you're getting the better end of the deal. I do have a question, though."

"Just one?" I say, downing the last corner of my sandwich.

"Well, you started this conversation, some time ago, I might add, by saying I was right about something. Were you planning on circling back to that topic or am I supposed to assume what I was right about?"

"Smart ass."

"Graduated Magna Cum Laude," he says without missing a beat.

I push my bowl next to his. "You were right, about my needing to finish the bet."

He looks at me, a bit taken aback.

"I was?"

I nod. "Gail wants me to finish too, only so I can amuse her during her bed-rest stint, but I think I need to do this... for me. As miserable as these dates have been—" Harold coughs, trying to get my attention. I'm sure he wants to object to his date being miserable, but I ignore him. "I have learned that going out with these guys is actually teaching me a lot, about myself. A real Lifetime movie collection of moments."

"That's deep."

"I know," I say folding my disposable napkin in half. "But, I was wondering, if after the bet is done, and I haven't met the love of my life, would you want to maybe grab some coffee? I know this great place."

Harold leans back in his chair. "That's a very tempting offer." He smiles, but it's a fleeting smile. "But, I am going to have to turn it down. We need to talk."

I hear the words as he speaks them, but it feels like it's in slow motion. Suddenly the background noise of the restaurant is deafening. The ladies to our left are laughing about some asinine thing, but I watch as their heads roll back, and their eye pinch closed with giddiness. The guy closest to Harold is on his cell, shouting something obscene into his cell. Each table has their own drama unfolding, but none so big as the one happening here.

He's ending—whatever this is—in a public place, so I don't freak out on him. My throat begins to tighten, heat rises along my neck. I shouldn't be surprised. This happens all the time to me. I can never seem to read the signs until the crash is already in progress.

"Talk. Right. I—um..." I fiddle with the edge of the table. "Actually, now isn't good. I have to go. Um, thanks for lunch." I rip my jacket off the edge of the chair, nearly toppling it over. The guy on his cell looks up from his phone long enough to notice my tears then forgets about me and turns back to his phone. I try to close my head to the sound of Harold's voice calling after me.

The gust of wind outside drowns him out. I don't stop to think what direction I go, I just turn right. I'll catch the first train or bus I can. The sooner I'm buried under my covers, the better.

How could I be so stupid? How could I let something like this happen again?

"Dee!" Harold shouts. I push against the pavement harder to get as far away from him as my short little legs will take me. I try not to listen as his footsteps follow after me. He must be running. As much as I want to run too, I know that his gait would outstrip mine in a heartbeat.

I whip around and throw my hand at him. "Stop following me! I got your message, Harold. No need to rub salt in the wound." I try to turn away, but he grabs my arm.

"God damn it, Dee. Stop shouting for a second and look at me."

I stop, but I refuse to look at him. I can feel the eyes of people passing by, assessing the spat. We've become a spectacle. Great.

"Please, Dee. Look at me." I hate the strain in his voice. What I hate more, is that I obey.

"What?" I ask, crossing my arms over my chest and curl my toes inside my boots to anchor myself in place.

His lips are on mine before I can even process what he's doing. As much as I want to smack him across the face, I can't. My body refuses to do anything but engage. I feel my hands unlock themselves from my own body to curl around his waist, pulling him closer. My feet once planted to the ground, now lift me up to meet his lips. Neither of us flinch as people's bags crash into us or even as catcalls are shouted. We just stand there, in the middle of a crowded lunch time sidewalk, lip locked.

When he pulls away, the look on his face is one of pain, as though breaking the kiss was the hardest thing he is ever had to do.

I dig my hands into my pockets, hardening my heart again.

"So, this would normally be a point in which I would make some sort of snarky remark about what just happened, but I got nothing. Why did you kiss me?" I ask.

"I think the more important question is why did you kiss me back?" he retorts, his bottom lip juts out just a touch with satisfaction.

I glare at him. "I asked first."

Harold sighs, then digs his hands into his jeans pockets, mirroring me. The wind has picked up, reminding us all that winter is just around the corner. "Mind if we have this chat in the car? I am kind of freezing my balls off out here."

"Classy," I say, trying to hide my smirk. This last few minutes has my brain in a blender. I don't know if I should be laughing or crying. "Fine. We can talk in the car." I catch the bitchiness in my tone. It's as though my subconscious is keeping the walls up. Thank god someone is paying attention.

When we reach the car, which he has parked a good three blocks away, he tries to open the door for me.

"I got it. Go warm your nuts up," I say, climbing into the car. Beside me Harold climbs in and starts the car, maxing out the heat.

For a minute, neither of us talk as we adjust ourselves in our seats.

"So?" I finally ask. "What was that shit?"

His face darkens. "You thought the kiss was shit?"

"That's not what I'm talking about, and you know it," I say, pulling my hands out from my pockets. I rub them in front of the tiny traces of heat coming from the vents.

The frown turns into a leer. "So, you did like it?"

I smack him on the shoulder. "I didn't say that either. Now tell me what the hell is going on."

Harold regains his composure. "Right. Sorry." He clears his throat. "Well, back at the restaurant, you asked me if I'd like to grab coffee sometime after you'd finished the bet."

"Which you politely turned down. Yes I know, I was there," I say through gritted teeth. "The question is, given that refusal, why did you chase me down the street and stick your tongue down my throat? Did you think I was gonna wig out over being rejected? Like, I would go postal on people or something and you thought kissing me would somehow soften the blow? Cause trust me, sir, you are not the first guy to turn me down." I'm not sure why I am bragging about this. Confrontation brings out the moron in me.

Instead of laughing at me, which he should because I'm being ridiculous, he shrugs. "The answer to your question is simple. I turned your offer down because I didn't want to wait to get coffee with you until after the bet."

I open my mouth to say something defensive, but that wasn't the explanation I thought he was going to come back with.

"Say what?"

He reaches out and takes my hand in his. "Dee, I told you this before, the last time we had coffee. I said I'd wait to hang out with you until after the bet, but I would rather take this journey with you."

I open my mouth, then close it. "You understand that in order to win the bet, I need to go on dates? With men. Men that aren't you?"

He nods.

"And this doesn't bother you?"

"Of course it does, but that's my shit to deal with. But clearly it bothers you more."

I shift to look at him head on. "There can be no—whatever this is—until the bet is over. I know how jealousy works. What you are suggesting isn't healthy. I know all about unhealthy relationships. I guess I'm just trying to do this one right," I say, more to myself than to him.

Harold is quiet as what I say sinks in. As much as it will hurt losing him now, it would hurt so much more down the line when he got jealous or frustrated with how long I was taking to finish. It's much better to cut the cord now and tend to the superficial wounds.

"Okay. All right." He says. "So, from here on out, we're just friends?"

I nod. "If you're still around when I finish the bet..."

"Then we'll have coffee." A sad little smile touches the corners of his mouth.

"We can still talk, right?" I say, not sure what this really means.

"Absolutely. You can tell me about all your dates," he sees my frown, "or not." He laughs.

I just sit there, staring at him. "What if I meet someone I like?"

"Someone better than me, you mean?"

He's trying to play it cool, but I swear there is a hint of worry in his brow. Of course, I could just be making that up.

"Yeah, what if, I end up with, um—Zac Efron as my last date and he swoops me off my feet?"

"Then the two of you would make beautiful babies together." He smiles, then stops. "Shit, I am sorry, I cannot believe I just said that."

"It's all right. I forget sometimes too," I lie.

Harold growls at himself. (Yes, growls.) "See? This is why you need to finish the bet. You need to be a mom. You need that cash. If I had it, I would offer it up to you myself just to not finish the bet, but I also know this is a personal demon you need to thwart."

I lower my head. He's right. The bet is some sort of mental battle with myself. It is the most stupid, illogical, and most idiotic fight I have ever tried to win.

"I know it doesn't make sense to you," I say. "It doesn't really make sense to me, it's just... all of my life I've never really followed through with anything. I have a degree in writing, but I spend all day crunching numbers. I got engaged then unengaged.

Granted, I was completely in the right there, but you get the point. Hell, I once tried to get a perm, but it stung so bad I had to have them wash it out before it could set. I have such great plans to start things, but I always fall short of actually finishing them. The only thing in my life that I have managed to be consistent with is staying in neutral. Never moving forward, just sort of hanging out where it's comfortable." Even as I say the words, the truth of them sinks into my gut. "I guess I'm afraid of failure."

"I think you're more afraid to succeed."

I blink up at him. Damn. He may be right.

"Now is the time to see what the finish line looks like, Dee. Finish what you've started. When you cross that line, I'll still be here waiting. I won't get in the way. I'll let you do this, on your own, just like you need to. It will suck, but I'm willing to wait if that's what it's gonna take."

I glance up at him, a bit shell shocked. "That's not fair for you. I can't ask you to wait around for me."

He smiles. "You aren't. I'm offering to be your friend." He holds up a finger. "For now."

"You'll regret it," I say to the floor.

"We'll see about that," he smiles.

***

Journal Entry: And with a flip of a page in my journal, so begins the next phase of my life.

17.
The chapter in which I tackle
online dating.

The past few weeks have been a big old hurricane of activity. I haven't had time to think about the bet since that day with Harold. We haven't spoken much since then either. I'm just too dang busy trying to start my life over here. It's not to say that we haven't seen each other. He helped bring Gail home from the hospital and helped lug some of my stuff from my apartment to hers. We spoke, laughed, but it was different than it has been before. He never said anything that could be construed as flirtatious, just professional. Maybe it was because Gail was with us, or maybe it's just the way he feels he needs to act while the bet is still on. Maybe he's started dating someone … or, I'm reading into our brief dialogue exchanges way too much.

Neil and Chad have been over almost every day since Gail got released from the hospital. Neil kept apologizing over and over again about not getting to see Gail sooner. He vowed to remove his 'do not disturb' function from his phone until the babies came. He hates that he wasn't there for the two of us when we really needed him. Neil is a lot like me. He hates to let people down.

As a way to try and make it up to us, they volunteered to provide much of the manpower in getting my shit from my apartment to Gail's. I still remember the day they showed up at my apartment. Neil was sporting a clearly brand-new tool belt and Chad was wearing a bright yellow hard hat. From the twinkle in Neil's eye, I could tell those items would be used later that night.

In his guilt, he has even arranged to have my wine stash smuggled into my room where Gail couldn't see it. He made me a cube-shaped foot stool to hide it in. When you lift the hidden cover, it reveals wine storage underneath. I could have kissed him. The whole not-drinking-thing was proving to be almost harder than the staying-in-bed-thing these days for Gail. I want to be supportive of her, I really do, but I also need my wine. I'm not prego, I can damage my liver all I want. Besides, if I were going to continue with these dates, I would need every bottle in there, and then some.

Gail has hired back Rosetta, thank god. Pizza every night was getting old—I know, I can't believe I am saying that either. She also had a new adjustable lounge chair placed in the living room. She has a wheelchair that she has to use if she wants to get around the house. Doctor's orders. Thank God her apartment is all on the same floor.

Now that dust has settled and my new address established, I am ready to begin 'dating' again. Time to get this bet over and done with. Last night, I went through my list of single men that I knew and came up depressingly short. Meeting men in a bar isn't really something I want to try again after my last drunken nightmare. I pat my girls gently at the memory. Since I'm no longer going to work, that takes away anyone in that gene pool. It's not like I go anywhere either. I'm pretty much a hermit. That leaves one choice: online dating. I know. I know.

Tonight, is my first try with it. I'll admit it. I have sunk to a new low, but time is passing faster than I thought. It's already the last week of October. Somehow almost four months of my year has slipped away, and I still have 14 letters to go! I know I'll lose a lot of that remaining time as Gail gets closer to giving birth, and the time immediately following their birth is going to be shot all to hell, so really I have maybe a 3–4-month window of actual dating time, which isn't really a lot for someone as noncommittal as me.

So, it is with this sense of dread that I hop online and manage sign up for no less than four dating sites. There was no research into these before signing up. Those were the first four sites that popped up when I typed in desperate, single, white female needs a date. For each one, I set up my profile to say that I was only interested in dating men whose real names started with the letter M. Once M is checked off, I'll change the profile to N names only. See? Brilliant. I had to make it clear that their real name must start with M since it looked like no one came close to even listing what their real name was. Seriously, you want me to date someone that has their handle as ridemyride69? Are people that ashamed of dating online that they feel compelled to give such a ridiculous username? Okay, yes. Yes, you do feel that compelled. I give myself the name of: Notlookingforloveyet81. I had to add the 81 because someone had already used that name. Really? No, seriously. Really?

My faith in humanity has crumbled a bit.

I have barely submitted my profile when I get a pop-up notification at the bottom of my screen. Shit. I am not ready for this.

Spacecatfree: Got a thing for M's, huh?

I cringe. It begins. Do I engage in a conversation with Mr. Spacecat, or do I ignore him and hope for others that may or may not ever come? I do the most logical thing and click on his profile. A series of 5 photos come across. He's not bad. Not gorgeous, but not bad. I instinctively know to avoid the drop-dead guys because those sorts of guys do not need dating sites. Those 'hunks' have scam written all over their six-pack abs. But this guy, he has got a little bit of a pooch, dark beard, deep-set eyes, and hair. He has a full head of hair. Yes, I am shallow even in my one-date-only dating logic.

I decide to jump in, headfirst, and hope I don't break my neck in the shallow end of the gene pool.

Notlookingforloveyet81: Just never dated an M before. Thought I should give it a whirl. Where are you from?

Spacecatfree: I am in uptown, you?
Notlookingforloveyet81: Lincoln Park

I lie. Like I'm gonna tell this guy where I live.

Spacecatfree: Well, since you're not looking for love yet, how about hot sex?
Notlookingforloveyet81: Not looking for that either. l8ter.

And, just like that, I create my first block. I shudder. Creepy. After I close his chat screen, two more appear. Good God, it is like vultures hovering over a freshly wounded dog.

Love2dance77: Hey there. My name doesn't start with M, but I can be whoever you want me to be, baby.

Ew. Close and block love2dance77. Too bad. I love2dance2.

farmvilleking43: My name is Mike. What's yours? Odd request on the name thing. Most women could care less. You have piqued my curiosity.

Hmm. Forms full sentence and didn't give a sexual innuendo and actually spelled piqued right. I hover over his profile name and click it. Mike seems like a basic nice guy. Nothing too threatening or attractive. Looks like he is mid 40's. Works for the Post Office. He has a job too. Hot damn. He's heavy set, but that doesn't bother me. I don't need looks, just the letter M. Well, that's not true. I don't need them to look like Brad Pitt, just someone who doesn't make me want to vomit. Yes. I have high standards.

Notlookingforloveyet81: How about I tell you the story over drinks? I'll be at Andy's Jazz Club downtown. Meet me at 8:00. If you're not there by 8:10, I walk. My name is Dee.

I don't wait to see if he answers. I shut the laptop and forget about it. I asked. If he shows, fine. If he doesn't, I still get to have a drink outside of the confines of my room.

"Deeeeeeeeeeeee."

I sigh.

That would be Gail. She has been particularly needy this week. She's only been home for 3 weeks and she's already sick to death of being bed ridden. She's been throwing darts at her goal calendar until it became so shredded I had to make a new one. The first goal is for her to make it to 24 weeks. The babies would still need to spend about 3 months in the NICU, but they could survive. 28 weeks is an even better goal. Still risky, but much more has developed. They doubt she'll make it to 37 weeks, which is ideal for twins, but for now, we just go day by day. I know this whole being stuck in one place is an adjustment for her, but it doesn't stop my tongue from its native sarcasm.

"Coming your High-Ass," I sing.

I walk into her room. Gail is lying on her side; magazines, a tablet, crumpled bits of food wrappers cover the vast expanse of her bed.

"Need another magazine? Or a book?" I offer, even though I know what the answer will be.

"What I need, is to get out of this bed! Will you help me get into the living room? My back is killing me from not moving. I am having my masseuse over today to help work the kinks out. She has this wonderful foam padding that allows for my belly to fit into the hollow of it, so I'll actually be able to lie on my stomach. My stomach, Dee!"

I smile. "That's great. I'll get to look at your backside all day."

"You're welcome," She says rolling herself over to the side of the bed.

I sit in the chair and wheel myself over to her. Gail raises an eyebrow. "What? I think the chair is fun." I get out and try to help her get in. I'd like to say that I gracefully lifted her and placed her daintily into the chair without grunting, but let's be honest, I'm not that coordinated, nor is Gail that dainty. When she finally is in, I wheel her out into the living room and position her in front of the TV.

"No, God, don't put me in front of the TV. I am sick of watching that thing!"

Cocking my head, I turn her around so that her back is facing the screen instead.

"Better, grouchy pants?" I ask.

Gail slumps her shoulders. "My mother is coming next month."

I roll my eyes. "Yes. I know. You've told me, at least, a hundred times now."

"Why is she coming to see me, Dee?" Gail's face is stricken with panic.

"Um, because it's Thanksgiving and she is your mother, and you are on bed-rest with her grandchildren."

Gail rubs her temples. "No. She wants to show me her disgust with me and this pregnancy in person. Apparently daily calls about how I've fucked up my life aren't enough. You'll be here for Thanksgiving, right?"

"I wouldn't miss it for the world." I beam. Gail glares at me in a most pathetic way. "Oh, calm down ya big baby. I'll be here to help counter any of her zingers and Rosetta will sedate her by making her favorite, roast quail. Which means I'll be downing Cheetos that night." I shiver. "Quail. Gross. Rich people have no taste buds."

"Because Cheetos are an acquired taste?" Gail blinks at me.

"You love Cheetos, and you know it."

She nods. "I do. And if you eat the whole bag, I will stab you to death with my salad fork."

I wave her threat away, "You can't kill me. Who would be left to amuse you?"

Gail scoffs. "To be honest, you're kind of sucking in that

department. Moving boxes in and out with Neil and the rest of the Village People was only mildly amusing. When do you start the dates-from-hell-athon again?"

I cross my arms. "You're pathetic, you know this, right?"

She sighs over dramatically. "I know, I know. I am so bored! I still have 5 more months of this shit!"

I rub my own temples this time. "This, I know."

"Seriously, Dee. When are you going to start dating again? I need something to think about. You're all moved in, there is no reason you can't go out—"

"I have a date tonight, thank you very much," I say calmly.

"You little bitch, when were you going to tell me?"

I plop down onto the leather couch. "Right after you shut your yapper."

She frowns. "Dish. Tell me everything."

I shrug, putting my feet up. "Nothing exciting, I'm afraid. I set up an online account—"

"Wait, you what?"

I roll my eyes. "I set up an online dating profile, Gail, it's not that shocking."

"Dee, the most exciting thing that has happened to me today is that I didn't pee when I sneezed. Now tell me everything."

I proceeded to tell Gail, in as much detail as possible, the four accounts that I set up and the horrid responses thus far.

"I don't think I'm doing that again, though. It was just ... sucky." I say.

Gail's eyes light up. "Let me do it for you!" she squeed. Yes, she squeed.

"Do what?"

She claps her hands. "Let me act like you online and set up dates for you!"

I cock my head. "Isn't the point of the bet that I have to ask them out?"

Gail crosses her arms. "I created the bet; I can modify it to where you just have to go out with them. Oh, please, oh please oh, pleeeeeeeease. I need something to do! I'll go crazy!"

I raise my hands up in defeat. "Fine! If you wanna talk to these douchebags, be my guest, but so help me, if you set me up with serial killers or wack jobs just to fuck with me, you will wake one morning to a buzz cut."

She places her hand over her heart. "I solemnly swear that I am up to no good," she says, giggling.

I glare at her. She's never read Harry Potter. Quoting from the movie is just cheating.

"Promise me."

"Dee, of course I won't! I'll find the most interestingly sane people I can manage," she says. "Now, for tonight? What are you going to wear?"

I glance down to the jeans and V-neck I am wearing. "This."

"Um, no. Get me the phone."

"Why?"

She gives me an exasperated sigh. "Just do it."

Shaking my head in defeat, I dig my cell out from my back pocket and give it to her. She starts pushing buttons.

"Neil, darling," she purrs, "I need your and Chad's cute little fannies over here. I have a fashion emergency and Chad is just who I need." She frowns listening to his reply. "No, this isn't for me, I am not going anywhere, I'm imprisoned by my own body, don't you remember?" she says with exasperation. "This is for Dee." She smiles listening to what I am sure is a snide comment at my expense.

I sit up and yell at her. "I don't need help to put on clothes to go for one drink!"

Without missing a beat, Gail says, "Yes, you do."

I throw my hands up in the air and stretch back out on the couch. I close my eyes and let them play. I'm just glad Gail is yakking to someone besides me for a change. Gail wheels herself into the other room, probably to talk about me some more, but I don't care. Her couch is too damn comfy, and I didn't sleep well last night. Of course, that could be because of the ho-ho I ate before bed.

I must have dozed off, because when I wake up, it's to the sound of Neil saying his hellos to 'the fat lady.' I smile as I hear his arm being smacked.

"This is what she was planning on wearing," I hear Gail whisper. Someone gasps. Probably Chad.

"I can hear you; you know?"

"Oh, good, now we can talk about you louder," Gail says. "Neil, will you wheel me into Dee's room so I can examine her closet?"

"No!" I shout, yanking myself upright. "That is my room, you don't get to go in there!" I say, thinking about shelves full of junk food I am currently shielding from Gail.

Gail narrows her eyes at me. "What are you hiding from me, little girl?"

"Nothing," I say, too fast.

"She's lying. Neil, quickly, push!"

Not hesitating even for a second, Neil starts racing her to my room. That fucker knows what I have in there because he helped me unload it. Chad just raises his hands in exasperation. He's learned to just stay out of our arguments. Smart man. I scramble off the couch to go after them, but it is a losing battle. They beat me there simply because their girth is too wide for me to get around.

When I step into my room, breathless, Gail is there, holding my opened box of Ho-Ho's "Deidre Margaret Harper, you wench. You have been hiding junk food. I knew I smelled chocolate!"

I cover my face with my hand. "I am sorry. I just didn't want to eat them in front of you because then you'd make me share and then you'd moan about how fat you were getting because of me, so—"

Gail scoffs, "Honey, please, the smell of chocolate makes my stomach turn these days, so your stash is safe. Of course, so does the smell of popcorn, Chinese, feta cheese, broccoli—oh you get the point. Eat away, just use some spray when you're done."

"I can do that," I say, relieved to not have to hide it anymore.

Chad walks in, and the look of horror at the state of my room is all over his face. I am a bit of a pig. Neil rubs his shoulder. "I know. I know," he says.

Ignoring them, I plop onto my bed. Gail wheels over to my bookcase lined with junk food (yes, I should be ashamed of myself). "You little bitch!" She says pointing at the 12 pack of Dr. Pepper on the bottom. "Oh, this is low, even for you," she says, glaring at me.

"You can't have caffeine…" I try. Dr. Pepper is Gail's

kryptonite. She'd never even had it until I introduced it to her in college. She's been trying to stop drinking it ever since. This has been, by far, the hardest thing for her to live without since becoming pregnant.

"But the Dr.?" she asks, wounded. "You had a plethora of sodas to choose from, and you pick the Dr.?"

I hang my head in shame. I too have a slight Dr. Pepper addiction.

"I know, I know, I am the world's worst friend."

Gail puts her finger in the air. "Just for this, I get to give you one creepy date, and I am not telling you which one it is going to be, either!"

"No way," I begin, but Gail holds up a box of Swedish Fish. Another of her favorites. Her lips press into a hard line. "Oh, fine, but nothing too scary!"

Gail smiles then pushes herself toward my closet, keeping the Swedish Fish on her lap. My limited wardrobe only fills up half of the space the gigantic closet allows for. "Boys, we have our work cut out for us."

Chad pushes away Neil's arm, as though ready for action, and walks into my closet. "Is this seriously, all of your clothes?" Chad asks, looking at each hanger of apparent fashion disasters.

"Neil, talk to him. You've known me forever. You've

frowned at and/or made fun of every article of clothing I have. Tell him this is it. I mean, do you think I have a backup closet with all the 'good' clothes somewhere?"

"You don't?" Chad deadpans.

I push past him and take out a red silk scoop neck shirt. "I will wear this shirt, the jeans I have on, and my black boots. I may or may not wear earrings, depending on how feisty I am feeling. Now please, all of you, out of my room. Go and find lives of your own to live."

Neil makes a cat call. "Whoooo, someone needs to get laid!".

"Yeah, me." Gail answers.

"Ew," I say.

"What? It's true." Gail sighs. "And these new hormones aren't making matters any better. I've had to send Rosetta out to the store three times now for AAA batteries.

"Oh, God! La, la, la, la, la," I say, covering my ears.

Gail smiles. "Just you wait until you open your Christmas present, chicky. You'll thank me."

"You better not have."

She smirks. "What do you think that big box is under the tree?"

I give her a look of absolute horror and she starts laughing.

Chad appears unfazed by our conversation as he continues to

paw through my clothes. "Where is that cute little black dress Neil got you for Christmas last year?"

I start to speak but hold my tongue to find a way to put this delicately. "Funny story."

Neil puts his hands on his hips. "That, I doubt."

"I tried it on, and, well, it didn't fit, so I tried to return it for a different size, but they didn't have one that fit, so I just exchanged it. For a toaster oven."

A gasp actually escapes Chad's lips. "You returned a Vera Wang for a toaster oven."

"I got some frying pans too," I say weakly.

"I know that dress fit you, I know measurements," Neil says. He does. He's a damn designer.

I didn't want to have to play this card, but he is not giving me any choice. I go for the truth.

"You knew my measurements when I had my uterus. Things shift when that's gone."

Neil blanches. "Oh, honey, I didn't realize."

I walk over and hug him. "I didn't either until I tried that dress on. It was actually quite depressing. I made a lot of toast that night," I say, remembering.

"You're gonna rock those mom jeans," Neil says, kissing the top of my head.

"Why yes, yes I am," I say, hugging him again.

"This Christmas I'm buying you wine instead of clothing, okay?" he whispers.

"I love you."

Neil laughs into my hair, "Yes, I know. I love you too, shmoopee."

***

Journal Entry: Say what you want about mom jeans, but they are the most comfortable thing in the world, aside from pajamas.

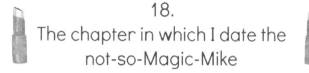

18.
The chapter in which I date the not-so-Magic-Mike

Neil and Chad stay for dinner. Chad insists on cooking a baked chicken marinated in beer. Gail got all excited until he told her the alcohol gets cooked out. While he cooked, the rest of us discussed the impending doom that is the arrival of Gail's mother and all the things that could possibly go wrong with the visit. We've managed to cover flash floods, flying midgets, and sandstorms. Gail worries far too much. The visit will be just fine. Horrible, mind you, but Gail will be fine. She's had a long time to swallow her mother's indignant nature. Besides, Rosetta knows how to do a Thanksgiving dinner. That woman can cook. Her gravy makes me want to switch teams and bat only for her. For real. It's that good.

As they moan and groan, I watch the clock, counting down to my fast-approaching date for tonight. I didn't think that one through at all. All I know is that his name is Mike, and he looks like every single 40-year-old, still single guy, I know looks like. Nondescript. How am I going to know who he is? I didn't even tell him where I would be sitting. I debate logging back on, to give him some more information, but I don't want to get sucked into that black hole of creepdom. It will be what it is.

When dinner is over, I push up from the table. "Well, as much fun as this is, I have to get ready for my date." I fluff up my hair. "There. I am ready."

Neil stands up and gives me a hug. "Knock the socks off him."

I laugh. "Will do."

"Just make sure he is wearing a hat," Chad says without looking up from his plate.

"Huh?" I ask.

Neil pats my head. "A condom. Make sure you use a condom."

I turn red. "Seriously? I'm not going to have sex with someone I just met," I say.

Gail coughs, loudly.

"Okay, fine, I'm not going to do it again."

Neil looks at me wide-eyed, waiting for an in-depth explanation. I shake my head. "Nope. Talk to Gail, she'll tell you all about it. I am off to mark 'M' off my list."

I turn around and head toward the door.

"Do you need me to have Harold take you somewhere?" Gail

asks. It dawns on me that she doesn't know anything about our... situation. I think I'd like to keep it that way. At least for now.

I stop in mid-stride at the mention of his name. "No. I can get a cab. Don't wait up," I say, telling myself that even if the date is a bust (and let's face it, it will be) I am not coming home until late. May hit a movie—or, gasp, go shopping. I know, I am a wild and crazy woman.

I arrive at the bar annoyed that I have to be here. I checked out what's playing at the theatre on my phone while in the cab, and there are a couple of good movies playing just down the block. They both start within the hour, so I'd really like this date to be a bust.

I picked Andy's cause the music isn't awful even if you don't like jazz, which I don't. The crowds are mellow, too, either because of the music or the golden lighting that floods the place. If I have to have a drink alone, this is the type of place to do it without feeling self-conscious about it.

The bartender sees me sit down near the end of the bar and tosses a small square white napkin in front of me. I order a glass of wine and take out my phone to feign interest in whatever is on the screen. My peripheral vision is on high alert, however. As I sip and scroll through status updates online, I am also keeping very close tabs on the time: 8:06, then 8:08, then 8:11. That's it.

I'm out of this place. I take a big chug off my wine. I plan on getting my 7 bucks a glass worth.

"What are ya drinking?" a voice asks from behind me. I turn and find a youngish guy, maybe late twenties, heavy set. I can't call him fat because that's not PC. I can say this: he's a husky human being.

"Nothing, actually. Just finishing up. It's 8:11 and my date didn't show, so I'm going home," I say, standing to put my phone in my pocket.

"Your name isn't Dee, by any chance, is it?"

My feet stop in mid step. How does he know my name? Fuck. This isn't Mike. He's way too young. And about 3 times heavier than his photo indicated.

"How do you know my name?"

He smiles, he holds out his hand. "I'm Mike."

I stare at his hand, then back at him. "No, you're not. The Mike I'm looking for is a good 10 years older than you," I say instead of what I'm thinking.

Mike scratches the back of his head. "That would be my brother. I may have used his picture as my profile pic."

"Dude, that's not cool." I down the few drops of wine I had left and walk away from the bar.

"Wait," he calls after me. "I showed up. You owe me a drink

at least."

I spin around and jab my finger at him. "Look, Mike, you don't get to have a drink with me. One, you're late. Two, you lied about who you were, so I don't owe you anything."

"Yes, I lied. But, come on. Look at me. No one would want to date this," he says gesturing to himself.

"Because you're fat? I've dated fat guys before. In fact, I almost married one. But you know what? Turns out he was a liar, too." I turn around and flip him the bird. "Nice meeting you, Mike."

Giving him the finger, I realize, was completely uncalled for. The gesture wasn't for him, it was for Dylan. The idiot I almost married. Man, that feels like a lifetime ago. I thought I'd come to terms with that, but my flippant finger seems to suggest otherwise. To this very day, he remains a thorn in my side. Every 6 months or so, he'll send me a text or an e-mail, comment on a post of mine—almost like he needs something to make sure he still has an 'in' with me. I never answer him, but damn it all, if it doesn't make me think of him when I see that message come up, which is, of course, why he does it. It's really a toxic relationship. I don't know why I don't just block him. I guess there is always that piece of me that's convinced that I need to hang onto him. Just in case. At the end of the day, at least, he'd take me if no one else did. I know. I have issues, but that's a story for another day.

Shoving my hand into my pockets, I head to the movie theatre. Alone. It's really not that pathetic. I go to the movies alone all the time. Okay, maybe that is pathetic. The only uncomfortable part is getting a ticket for one and that look that the ticket lady gives you. 'Just the one?' they always ask. After that, it is not such a bad way to spend a Friday night. Yes, I know, I am not helping my pathetic status.

The theatre is dimly lit, but not so dark that you can't tell I'm sitting alone. With my jumbo tub of popcorn with extra butter and flavored salt, I find the first empty seat on the aisle that I can. I need an aisle seat. I get claustrophobic otherwise. I shrug out of my coat and place it into the seat beside me, not only securing myself some personal space but also giving the impression that I am waiting for someone who has just gone out to get snacks.

As the obnoxious commercials repeat themselves with annoying frequency, I down the first fistfuls of the buttery popcorn in reverent silence. The first layer is always the best. It's still warm and has become all shriveled up with butter and has the heavy-handed helping of salt. That top layer makes having to eat the bland half-popped kernels at the bottom worth it.

I'm fishing around for the leftover buttery gods of the popcorn tub when I hear someone say my name from behind me.

226

A voice I did not want to be hearing.

I stop in mid-search, even though I'd spotted a really good looking one. I don't say anything. I freeze and actually shrink deep into my seat, pretending I didn't hear him.

"Are you seriously trying to pretend that you can't hear me?" Harold asks so close that he could nibble on my ear if he wanted to.

"What? Um, no. I was picking up some popcorn I'd dropped." I scramble.

"Please, tell me you don't plan on eating it."

I frown then glare at him. "What are you doing here?"

"Um, watching a movie," he laughs. "You here with a date?" He gestures over to my coat.

"No. I actually just finished with one." Take that.

Harold whistled. "That good, huh?"

"What's that supposed to mean?"

"Well," he says standing, then moving to my aisle and sitting in the chair where my coat used to live. "Hold this," he says giving me my coat. "It's 8:30 on a Friday night. The date couldn't have been that exciting if you are here now with only your coat to keep you company."

"I didn't say you could sit here," I sneer at him.

"Wow, it was really bad. Want to talk about it?" He holds out a limp Twizzler. I yank it off and bite off the tip.

"No."

Mercifully, the lights dim, and the previews come up. I chew my Twizzler in annoyed silence. This is not how I thought this night would go down. Of course, I suppose it could be worse. I could be here with Mike. As a peace offering, I hold out my tub of popcorn.

"So, help me God," I whisper, "if you eat all the buttery ones I will pelt you with the uncooked kernels at the bottom." My eyes are on the screen, but I don't miss the smile his face breaks out into.

When the tub is finished, the little bugger tries to hold my hand.

"Stop that," I hiss. "Friends don't hold hands."

I see him smile in the darkness. "Good friends do."

I cross my arms over my chest, locking my hands away. He's not playing fair. We have to stay neutral if we have any hope of this working. There would be jealousy, no matter how insignificant the dates may be, and jealousy can destroy relationships. I know this from experience. If I have to be the strong one, then so be it.

When the movie ends, I grab my coat and walk out. I don't even say goodbye. I ignore him calling after me. If I turn around,

I would end up letting my guard down, and I don't want to risk losing him. How ironic is that?

"Dee, slow down. I'm sorry. Let me, at least, take you home." I hear him laughing behind me.

I stick my hand out for a cab and for the first time in my life, one actually pulls up.

"I'm all set. Thanks, though," I say as I climb into the cab. I shut the door, but not in time to drown out his little chuckle. He's enjoying this 'friend' status far too much.

***

Journal Entry: Stop thinking about Harold.

19.
The chapter in which Neil tries to help. Tries.

Where the hell does time go? I swear, just yesterday it was September, and now here it is a few days 'til Thanksgiving! Tending to Gail's 'needs' has been a time suck. Well, that and redecorating her apartment. Gone are the red, white, and black, and in their place, soft sage green, and cream. She claims it is her 'nesting' color. Little did I know that helping her out was going to entail so much pillow placement.

So, when Neil called me last night to invite me over for dinner with him and Chad, I jumped at the chance to get out of the apartment. Gail wasn't feeling up for the fuss of going out, so she had one of her staff stay. I felt bad for leaving her, but she shooed me out the door, telling me to have fun for the both of us.

With a bottle of sweet red in my hands, I knock on their door. When Chad opens it, I instantly know something is wrong. He is way too excited to see me. Chad is never happy to see me.

"Oooh, look who's here, it's Dee," he sings, taking my jacket for me.

"Who were you expecting, Elmer Fudd?" I ask, raising my eyebrows. "You did invite me here, after all."

"Oh, aren't you funny," he says over his shoulder so his voice would carry into the living room.

"What's wrong with you?" I ask.

His smile vanishes and he pulls me down to whisper in my ear. "For the record, I was not on board with this plan." Before I can figure out what he's talking about, he drapes his arm around mine and pulls me into the living room where Neil is sitting on the couch. There's a huge ass Christmas tree sitting by the window that looks like Martha Stewart decorated it herself. Why do gay guys get all of the decoration sensibility? It's not fair.

That's when I spot Neil. He's sitting across from a woman in her late 40's. Short blond hair, business suit. Looks like large diamonds studs on her ears. I glance down at my own raggedy jeans and sweater and silently curse Neil for not telling me this was a party.

"Hey, Neil," I say, tentatively walking further into the living room, "What's going on?"

Neil clears his throat, the way he does when he's nervous.

"Dee, I'd like you to meet Natasha Petit. She works in publishing. Chad met her when she came to the site to gather notes about generating a non-fiction book on beer making."

Publishing. What is he up to?

I blink at him, then remember my manners and hold my hand out. "Nice to meet you."

"Likewise," she says, giving my hand a weak shake.

I suppress my frown. They've invited me over to get me writing again. This has Gail's interference written all over it. That's why she didn't want to come. I grit my teeth and smile, imagining all of the nice things I'm gonna say to Gail when I get home.

"Let me open that bottle, shall I," Chad says, taking the wine and leaving me standing there with nothing to do with my hands.

"Sit," Neil says. Not really seeing another option, I sit on the far end of the couch next to Natasha so that Chad and Neil can cuddle up together when he gets back.

"So. A beer book, huh? I'm more of a wine person myself."

Natasha gives me a small smile. "As am I. We have several wine books through our company, but we felt it might be nice to branch out to the working class."

I glance over to make sure Chad didn't hear that. He would have gone off on her about that comment.

"All ready for Christmas?" I ask. I hate it when people ask me that. All it really means is: 'Have you finished spending every dollar you own on gifts people won't like?' And no, I'm not ready.

It's not even December yet, people. Can we, at least, have Thanksgiving first? Oh, wait. I asked that question. Shit. I hate myself.

"I don't celebrate Christmas," Natasha says.

Of course not. Dee, can't you ever be tactful?

"Oh, sorry. Um, are you from the area?" I ask. I so want this night to be over. I hate small talk. Clearly, I suck at it.

"I am from New York, but I travel to the city for business on a fairly regular basis."

I nod like that is the most normal thing in the world to be a freaking nomad.

"Must be hard on your family to do that much traveling," God, why did I agree to this? I should have suspected something was fishy when Gail grinned just before the door closed.

Natasha uncrosses her legs and leans across the couch. "I'm currently unattached," her lips curl into a smile. No. Not just a smile. A seductive smile.

Ah.

I am going to kill all of them.

I turn and face Neil who has suddenly developed a very keen interest in the hem of his pants because he refuses to look at me.

"Who wants wine?" Chad says, bring out a tray of four large glasses.

I stand up and grab one, glare at Chad, then down half the glass.

"Neil, would you mind stepping into the kitchen with me?" I ask.

I don't wait for an answer but turn and march into the kitchen, taking another huge chug of wine as I walk.

"Now, Dee, before you say anything—" Neil tries.

"What sort of drugs are you on that you are trying to set me up with a woman?"

"Lower your voice," he hisses.

"Why? I'm not gay!" I shout over my shoulder so she can hear me.

Neil frowns. "Well, how do you know? Have you ever dated a girl? I mean, maybe that's the reason that you're still single at 40? Maybe it's not that you haven't found the right guy. Maybe it's that you haven't found the right woman."

I set my glass down, trying not to break it. With as level a voice as I can muster, I say, "I know that I'm not a lesbian because the idea of sucking a woman's boob doesn't turn me on."

"Have you ever tried it?"

"Have you ever tried sucking on a woman's tit?"

Neil makes a face. "Good God, no. Why would I want to do that?"

"Exactly."

He pouts. "Fine. I just wanted to help. Chad and I thought this might be a good idea."

I stick my finger at him. "No, you don't. You don't get to drag Chad into this, he ratted you out, boy. This is all on you."

Neil growls, or, at least, it sounds like a growl. "Traitor."

"I am not going to sit through an entire dinner with—oh God, her name is Natasha."

Neil squirms. "Gail said you were up to N."

"Gail said?" I shriek. "So she is in on this?"

Neil waves his hand at me. "Of course not. She just wanted to hear a good story when you got home."

I rub my chin. "So, there are now two murders I need to plan."

He takes my hands and gives me puppy dog eyes. "Do you hate me forever?"

"You'll be forgiven, as long as you never try this shit again." I let out a deep breath and stand a bit taller. Then, I walk back into the living room. "Well, it's been great meeting you, Natasha, but I'm afraid I must go. I have to go find some young guy's cock to suck."

I walk down the hall and snag my jacket to the sounds of Neil and Chad making their apologies for my language. I fight back a smile. Oh, to have seen the look on their faces. I know it was rude but I'm too old to do the nice thing anymore. Time is limited, and I don't want to spend it with Natasha.

Outside, I'm still beaming from the scene I just caused and decide to have a little fun with Gail as well. I pull out my phone and dial her number. She answers on the third ring.

"Gail, oh my god, Gail, you won't believe what happened," I say.

"Oh, honey, was it awful? I knew it was a bad idea—"

I smile. Caught red handed. "Wait, you knew about Natasha?"

"I did. I know it was cruel of me not to warn you, but—"

"No," I say, trying to hold it together. "I want to thank you."

"You do?"

"Yes! You and Neil were right."

There is a long pause. "We were?"

"Yes, I had no idea how much a woman could turn me on, but we've already snuck into Neil's bedroom and gone at it twice now."

"You what?"

"Don't wait up!" I giggle and hang up.

A huge smile spreads across my face. That was epic. I pat myself on the shoulder for that one. She'll figure it out of course, but until then, I'm going to let her stew on that.

I start buttoning my coat. I can feel my phone buzzing in my pocket. I dig around to end the call because I know it will just be Gail calling me back. By the time I get it out of my damn pocket, though, it slips through my fingers and falls to the ground. The back comes off, dumping my battery onto the ground with it.

"Fuck."

I bend down to start gathering the pieces.

"Wow, she warned me you might be hammered, but you've only been there like thirty minutes. What the hell did you drink?"

I stop in mid-reassembly. I look up to see Harold peering down at me.

"What are you doing here?" I say standing up and stuffing the bits of my phone into my purse.

He holds his hands up in surrender. "Waiting for you. But, I'm working." He hitches his thumb behind him to where his limo is parked. "Honest."

"Gail paid you to wait for me?"

He takes a cautious step back. Smart boy.

"She thought you might be either drunk or upset when you left, so she wanted to make sure you got home safe. What happened in there?"

I don't answer him.

"I am going to fucking kill her," I say, pushing past Harold and letting myself into the back of the limo. I am so cranky right now. I hear the front door open and close.

"Where to, Miss?"

"I don't know, just drive."

"As you wish."

I roll my eyes. "And stop quoting The Princess Bride. It won't earn you brownie points."

"Huh? I don't know that one. Is it a movie?" He asks. I see his eyes looking back at me through the rearview mirror. I'm shocked. He's serious. He doesn't know The Princess Bride.

"Take me to 8th and Lake."

He cocks his head to the side but does as instructed. I lean back in the car and jam my broken phone back into my pocket. "And turn on the radio," I bark. His lips form a tiny smile. It's kind of fun bossing him around.

He leaves me to my tunes as he drives. I don't really pay attention to the songs; I just like watching the back of his head bob up and down with the beat.

"Parking might be a bit of an issue, um, Miss Harper," he says, clearly trying to respect my boundaries. "I'm not seeing anything open."

I unbuckle and slide to the door. "That's fine, just stop and

I'll jump out. Circle around until you see me again."

I open the door as he slows. I don't even wait for a full stop when I jump out. I hear him yelling that I'm insane, but choose to ignore the jab and instead I skip towards the store. I smile as the welcome bells announce my arrival. I stop inside and smell the mustiness of the store.

"Hey, Dee, what are we renting today? Godzilla? Pretty in Pink? Please not Twilight again," says the little old man behind the counter. Methinks I may come here too much…

"No, Hank, today is an emergency. I have someone within my presence who has not seen The Princess Bride."

Hank gasps.

"I know. A crime." I lean on the counter that is set up like a movie candy display. He has the hard to find candy too, like Skye bars. I notice he's moved where he puts the Snow Caps. Bumped to the bottom glass shelf. Oh man. I do come here too much if I'm noticing that kind of stuff. "Think you can help me out?"

Hank takes his hat off his head and puts it over his heart. "It would be my honor."

He walks around the counter and walks over to the 'Must Watch Before You Die' rack. Sadly, Twilight is not on his list. I make a mental note to place a copy of it there one day when he's not looking.

"Ah," he says, reaching on his tip toes to reach the top shelf. Holding a well-loved copy close to his chest, he sighs. "It is a privilege to watch a person see this movie for the first time. You make sure to watch their expressions, no?" His thick Italian accent comes out when he talks about things he loves.

"Can do," I say, taking the movie from him. "Now, I need a big popcorn and two sodas to go with this, please." This is one of the main reasons I still rent DVDs from here. Sure, I could download this and watch it on my phone, but it wouldn't be the same experience. Downloads are for throw away movies. DVDs are for the movies to remember. It helps that the store is hella awesome too. I want to come in here. It feels like home. Rickety wooden shelves, well-loved floors, cheesy movie posters. They even have a curtained off porn section. You toss in his kick-ass collection and that concessions case, well, then you have movie magic, my friends.

Hank places two cans of Coke into the bag, the movie, and tucks the popcorn in oh so gently into a paper bag and wishes me well. I head back outside to wait for Harold. I bob my head down every now and again into the bag and lift up a piece of popcorn with my tongue. Eventually, I see him coming and I wave at him with my elbow as he pulls alongside a fire hydrant. I shift the bag and climb in.

"Okay, now take me to Home Depot," I say, putting the bag down between my legs.

"Home Depot?" he asks. "Hey, do I smell popcorn?"

"Drive, man," I say, pushing the button that will bring up the privacy screen.

He shall not know of my plan to educate his ass before I am ready to reveal it. As he drives, I prep the built-in DVD player. Yes, her limo has a DVD player. It has everything new and current, but I don't know how to use anything but this ancient technology. This rig also has a pull-down screen. I shit you not. It's fun to be Gail's friend some days.

I hide the movie case in the bottom of the bag and set up the rest of the goodies, humming as I do. I am positively giddy by the time he pulls into the Home Depot.

I let the privacy screen down and tell him to park in the end of the lot.

"Are you about to murder me?" he asks.

"Yes. Yes, I am. Now park it."

Once he's parked he kills the engine and turns around to look at me through the window. "Now what?"

"Now, come back here."

"Dee, this isn't really the place to make out," he winks.

"If you don't get back here in two seconds, I am going to

change my mind about showing you this."

His eyes light up. "Now, you've piqued my interest." He climbs out of the car.

"Pervert," I whisper with a smile.

When he opens the door, he looks a little taken aback. I've pulled up the movie onto the screen so it shows the opening title. I have his seat set up with a soda in a cup holder and a bucket of popcorn. I've kicked off my shoes and have curled up in the seat beside him, popcorn in my lap.

"Um, what's this?" he asks, taking his proffered seat.

I turn to face him. "You indicated earlier that you have not seen The Princess Bride. As a decent human being, I could not let this travesty go on any longer. I have taken it upon myself to educate you in the wonder of this epic tale."

Harold sighs. "It looks like a kids' movie."

"Blasphemy!" I shriek. "Behave or I'll kick you out of my movie theatre."

He raises his hands up in surrender.

"Now, I want you to rid your mind of any preconceived ideas about this movie and come on a ride with me." I reach across to hit play, "And not that kind of ride."

"I didn't say a thing!" he says.

"Mmm, I heard your brain checking out my ass, don't deny

it."

He laughs. "What? I can't admire a great view?"

I narrow my eyes at him. "No, friend, you can't. Now watch and learn."

The movie comes on, and as much as I want to keep my attention firmly on the screen, I can't help but glance over at Harold. His face is full of skepticism as the first shots come into view, but by the time the princess is captured, he is engaged. He doesn't even attempt to hold my hand or try anything funny at all because he is too invested in the movie. He laughs in all the right places, even has to wipe a tear away from a belly laugh at 'Anybody want a peanut?' I'm watching him fall in love with something he thought he would hate. There is some demented joy in that.

Just as they are about to storm the castle, he scoots forward in his seat, ready for justice. That's when the movie shuts off. Well, everything does.

"Shit. What did I do?" Harold says. "Did I hit the remote?"

"Um, no. I think we killed the battery." I say in the blackness.

"No! No, I need to know what happens!" He says scrambling to find the door handle.

I climb out of the car with him. He tries the engine a few times, but nothing happens. Getting back out, he puts his hands on his hips. "Well, good thing we're at Home Depot. We can just buy a new battery."

"You know how to change a battery?"

"Haven't a clue, but I bet they do, or at the very least sell us some jumper cables. No worries. We'll get the car started again and then we need to find a comfy place to finish this movie." He holds out his arm to me. "Shall we?"

I sigh but take his arm. "As you wish."

***

Journal Entry: The battery wasn't the only thing that got jumped that night...

20.
The chapter in which I get wet
(and not in the good way.)

In retrospect, going to his place to finish the movie was not the best idea I'd ever had. My plan had been to keep my distance from the boy, at least until after the bet was over, but we couldn't finish the movie at my place because Gail would be all over that in a heartbeat. The less she knows about me and Harold, the better. That left his place.

So here I lie on Harold's couch, in the middle of the night, naked as the day I was born, while he makes us some eggs. Yes. Eggs. We were hungry and that's all he had. Poor bachelor boy doesn't know how to take care of himself.

From where I'm sitting, I can see his naked butt as he works the frying pan. I can't help but grin, but then I curse myself. Dee, this is exactly what you didn't want to do!

Harold says coming back with two plates of eggs and wearing only his smile. "Stop trying to plan your escape, would ya?"

"I wasn't."

He frowns. "You are a horrid liar."

I drop my head. "Yes. Yes, I am."

He sits down and hands me my plate, the eggs are covered in cheesy goodness.

"These look so good," I say taking a deep inhalation.

"I'm a really good cook when I have stuff in my in the fridge. In case you were keeping tabs."

I smirk. "I wasn't."

He takes a bite, then points his fork at me. "I know what you're thinking."

I load my fork up. "I highly doubt that."

"You are thinking that what we did last night, what we did several times last night, was a mistake."

I blush. That is exactly what I was thinking. Damn it. Am I that transparent?

"I was not."

He shakes his head. "Didn't we just cover the whole not-good-at-lying thing?"

I sigh.

He gives me his killer smile. "I know it doesn't make any sense, but I think we might have something here and I'm not just going to give up on it because you think I can't handle you dating a few guys first."

"It's more than a few. A dozen to be accurate."

"Eleven after tonight," he says taking another mouthful of egg.

"Why, what's happening tonight?" My gut sinks.

Harold puts his plate down and scoots across the living room to grab his cell. He takes the blanket hanging off the back of a chair then comes back.

"This naked thing is for the birds. My boys are cold."

"So are my girls, share that thing," I say cuddling up beside him.

He opens his e-mail and scrolls till he finds what he's looking for. "Okay, so it looks like I am to drop you off at 8:00 tonight. You will be meeting a guy named Oscar. He'll have a table reserved and wearing a red rose in his lapel. Oh, sounds fancy. You may actually have to wear a dress for this one."

"What are you talking about," I ask snatching his phone away. The message he's reading is from Gail.

"Don't be mad at her." Harold tries. "Gail told me that you are letting her set up your dates now and that I am to be your transportation to ensure that: 1, you go through with the dates, and 2, you're safe. I'm not going to argue that there is an added bonus for me, but I just do as I'm told." His smile fades a bit. "I assume you haven't told her about us?"

"No. It's not her concern. She'd just butt in, even more so than now! I'm going to kill her," I say tossing his phone back at him.

"Why? I think what she's doing is really admirable. She wants to torture you, sure, but she also wants to make sure you aren't murdered. I think this is a perfect plan."

"You're just loving this, aren't you?" I say, stealing the blanket away from him.

I don't get to hear his answer because a tickle fight starts which ended all logical thought once he has me pinned.

"Date me, Dee. Now, not after the bet." He says peering down at me. "If you end up meeting someone better, than I'll bow down gracefully." He leans over and kisses the nape of my neck, bringing goosebumps to rise. "Please," he whispers hotly into my ear. I can feel how sincere he is against my thigh.

"Fine," I breathe, "but I want to go on record as this being the worst idea in the history of ideas."

"So noted." His lips find mine and suddenly the idea doesn't seem so bad anymore.

After two hours, yes two hours, of primping and stuffing my fat into Spanx I am finally ready for my 'date' with Oscar. Gail would only tell me that we both have writing in common. I'm starting to wonder if letting her find me dates is such a good idea… then again, the thought of going back to the online dating world doesn't leave me warm and fuzzy.

On the phone earlier, I told Harold the only way I would allow him to drive me on these dates is if he didn't say a word. Not one single word. If he did, I would find my own way there. I had to draw a line. He had to be my driver, not my boyfriend, while on these dates. This had to be a rule if I was going to be able to handle it.

I am mentally reminding myself of this rule as I approach the car. True to his word, Harold doesn't speak, he merely opens the door for me. I smile. Good boy. After a few minutes of nervous silence, he pulls up to a restaurant I've never been to though Gail tells me their dessert menu is to die for. I make a mental note not to get dessert. I tend to overdo it on the sugar thing. I'm not entirely sure I would be able to fit it in my stomach anyway. Gail made me wear one of her gowns that requires an undergarment that has somehow managed to push my fat into all the right places. I can't breathe, mind you, but it was totally worth it for that two seconds that Harold couldn't pull his eyes off me. So naturally, when he opens the door for me at the restaurant, I make sure to thrust my chest out a little further than really necessary. I see his mouth open for a moment before he pulls his lips into a hard line as though fighting back a naughty thought. Just for that, I throw a bit of hip into my walk as I pass by him. I know. I'm evil.

The restaurant is dark and noisy with conversation. My stomach starts to do flips. I don't like meeting people and I don't like fancy places. I'm going to need a lot of wine. In fact, I am debating hitting the bar first when the hostess lets me know that my party is waiting. Of course. Here goes nothing.

She walks me to a section in the back. Happy couples surround us, all cheerfully chatting about this venture or another. Gaudy jewels are draped on every woman in the joint. Pieces so big you'd swear they had to be fake. I finger the single diamond hanging from my necklace. So much for fitting in.

I scan the sea of black suits for a red rose in a lapel of a single guy. I don't trust the picture Gail's showed me of him. Not after the Magic Mike disaster. Then, I spot him. Mr. Red Rose himself. He's got a full head of dark hair. A goatee, which would have to go, and a nervous twitch. He's got a death grip on his menu and seems to be sweating. Aw, he's nervous too.

"Here we are," the hostess says.

Oscar looks up from his menu, awestruck. I can't help but blush—I don't get that sort of look often, but this dress has garnered me quite a few of those tonight. I can start to understand why women put themselves through this much torture.

"You're Dee?" he whispers.

"Yeah. Oscar, right?" I reach out to shake his hand which feels ridiculous and terribly low class for a joint like this. He starts to stand up, but I wave him down.

"No need for that. I'm not that much of a lady, I just clean up nice," I say.

Before the hostess gets a chance to run away, I snag her elbow. "Can I have a glass of one of your sweet reds, any brand will do."

"Of course, I'll let your waiter know." She doesn't ask for his drink order as it seems he's already downed a few glasses of what smells like bourbon.

"So, Oscar. You're a writer."

"More of a journalist," he says, patting his temples with his napkin. He's not a bad looking guy, aside from the goatee. It's cute that he's so nervous. I must intimidate him. I've never intimidated anyone before.

"A journalist," I say. "That's impressive."

A waiter appears with a glass of wine and a menu for me then dashes off to his next table, clearly determining that we won't be dishing out big tips. He's right. "What paper do you work for?"

"Um, it's a magazine, actually," Oscar says, putting down his menu to take a swig off his glass, finishing it in one gulp. Damn. I thought I could drink.

"Magazine? Now I'm really impressed. Which one?" I could be sitting across the table with a journalist for People, or Entertainment Weekly, or maybe something more educational like National Geographic.

"Cum For Me."

I blink at him. "Excuse me?"

"Oh, no. See, that's the name of the magazine." Oscar says rubbing the back of his neck. "It's a porn rag. I know, I know, but you have to start somewhere, right?"

I give an uncomfortable laugh. "I suppose. What sort of articles do you write?"

"Mostly about the girls, their likes, dislikes. How big a dildo they can take? I'm their go-to guy for all of the dish." He dabs his napkin on his temples again. He's gone a little white. Clearly, this isn't the sort of conversation he wanted to be having with a first date in a fancy place like this. Which leads me to think that it must pay well for him to afford this.

I take a large drink of my wine. "How long have you been there?"

"Only six months, but they may make me an editor."

"Oh. That's great. What did you do before this, then?"

He starts letting small breaths out of his mouth. "Um, nothing really. I live with my Ma, you know, helping her out and stuff, look, I think I need to use the restroom. I'm not feeling so hot. I think I may have had too much to drink."

"Oh, sure," I say, so much for that act of nerves being for me. He's just trying to hold onto his lunch.

He pushes his chair out, "I'll be right back."

When stands up, I'm flabbergasted. He's short. Like really short. If I stood up, I'd be a good 4 inches taller than him. Oh, hell no. I'm not dating a guy that only comes up to nipple level.

"I'm really sorry," he says, touching my shoulder.

"Hey, it's okay," I say, cause what else am I going to say? I'm totally leaving once he goes into the bathroom, though.

"I was just really nervous—" he stops. His eyes grow wide. His face goes green then, you guessed it, my wine, and I get hurled on. Vomited on, puked upon, upchucked on. Chunks in the hair sort of throw up.

The gasps around the restaurant begin echoing across the room, triggered by my scream. Everyone has frozen as though they don't know what to do. No one wants to volunteer to help in this situation. I swear I even see the waiter duck into the kitchen. Prick.

Oscar starts mumbling his apologies while continuing with his sickness on the floor beside me.

Stunned beyond belief, I stand up, walk over to the table next to me and steal a white cloth napkin right off a man's lap and wipe away the largest chunks, almost vomiting myself.

"I think it's fair to say that this date is over," I say between gags, tossing the napkin on Oscar's head.

In awed silence, I walk to the restroom in the collective horrified silence of the others. Holding my breath, I rush over to this sink, paying no attention to the woman ready to hold me a warm towel. She doesn't say anything, but buries her face in her shirt, probably to keep from gagging herself. I slop off what I can, but there is so much of it that the only way I'm getting this off is to shower, and in order to do that, I have to go home. Which means walking back out there where the waiting room of spectators lurk.

I rip a towel out of the woman's hands and drape it over my shoulders like a shawl. It doesn't hide the front of the gown or the dampness of my hair, but it's better than nothing.

I make a beeline to the exit, ignoring the whispers I hear trailing behind me. Outside, I take deep breaths. I want to scream. I want to cry. But mostly, I don't want Harold to see me like this.

From here, I can see that the limo is parked across the street, Harold is leaning against the hood, a book in his hands. I try to duck out of his line of sight, but as he turns a page he catches my eye. His expression goes from joy to confusion as he takes it all in. So much for Harold not finding out. Overcome with embarrassment, I plop myself onto a stone bench on the sidewalk, ignoring the bulge of fat that jabs out of its harness near my gut.

When I look up, Harold is running towards me, a look of panic on his face.

"What happened? Are you okay?"

I gesture to my once white gown. "I was used as a barf bag tonight. Ironically, it's not the first time. Gail can attest to that. Another story. A million years ago. Same horrific outcome."

"Oh. Ah. Um," he stands there, sort of shifting his weight on his feet.

I stand up and start walking—away from the limo.

"Thanks for hanging out, but you can go home. I want to be alone right now."

"What? Where are you going?"

"I can find my own way home. Trust me, you don't want this stench in the car. Gail would kill you. I'll call you tomorrow," I mumble.

Of course, the fool doesn't do as I ask, and instead starts following me. I try to ignore the fact he is there by keeping a few steps ahead of him. After about two blocks he's stopped asking what happened and just walks beside me. I'm not in the mood to talk about it yet. Maybe never. That's the sort of memory you want to forget, you know?

When we get to the next block, I stop. Millennium Park. And the fountain is still on. I smile.

"Oh, no, Dee. No, you're not gonna do that. The water is too cold, you'd freeze."

"Freezing to death would smell better than this," I say. Letting out a deep breath, I bolt. I can hear Harold's shouts of protest behind me, but I don't stop. This dried on vom must come off, like now. I don't even slow down as I get there, just dive headfirst into the geyser of water that comes out of the tower.

"Holy Fuck!" I scream as it smacks me in the face.

Another squeal comes as it lands on my back.

"Dee! Get out of there!" I hear Harold shout as I hunch my shoulders and brace myself for cold. Onlookers take my insanity in, then shake their heads and move on. Nothing weirds out city folks.

"Not yet. I still—Gah!—have some on me," I change positions so it can strike the front of me. That was a mistake. "God damn, that's cold," I screech, trying to rub away the goose bumps in a futile attempt to get warm.

"Okay, that's it," I hear him say. A moment later his arms are around mine, pulling me out. "You're clean enough," He lays his suit jacket over my shoulders and I try to speak through my chattering teeth.

"I'mmmm fffiiine."

"Sure you are. Now button that jacket so no one else gets the free show."

"The whhhaattt?'

"Your nips are showing. White gown and water don't mix. Now button up before I lose my mind."

I stop walking and look down at very prominent nips. The Spanx only covered my midsection and the cut of the dress had forced a no-bra situation. Well, fuck.

He stops and stands in front of me, buttoning the jacket. "I saw a guy leering at you as he passed by." He looks up at me and frowns. "I didn't care for it."

I know my feminist younger self should kick in and tell him that it's my body and I can show it off however I want, that he doesn't own me, yadda, yadda, yadda, but that's not what I feel. Instead, I feel—warm.

You may commence judging me now. I'm gonna go get me some limo nooky.

***

Journal Entry: I must have him volunteer to save me from myself more often.

21.
The chapter in which I make an ass out of myself.

I get home too late for Gail to grill me on the details of my midget-spew-a-thon date. I take yet another shower, (this time on my own) then shove down three oatmeal creme pies. I know I shouldn't be eating this kind of crap, but I was starving. I didn't get anything to eat at dinner, nor did I want anything for a good long time after, and then Harold and I—well, food wasn't on our minds. And, honestly, at this point in my life what's one more dimple on my ass?

After last night, I realize I need to take a good long look at how I want to define my relationship with Harold for the remainder of the alphabet, but I'm just too damn tired right now. I strip down to my undies and crawl into bed, not even having the energy to turn off the light. I'm out before I can even worry about being lucky to get four hours in before the sun comes up.

Just as I'm starting to have a really good dream, you know the kind, that pesky little beam of light that always manages to find the tiniest crack in my curtain and turn it into a spotlight on my eyeball wakes me up. I hate you, sun.

As much as I'd love to try and bury myself under the covers to escape the rising day, I can't. There is much to prep for Mommy Dearest's arrival later today. Gail is gonna need calming down to deal with that wench. She's probably dry heaving now, just thinking about it.

Yawning, I pad out into the kitchen. I didn't bother to put my pants on as the T-shirt I pulled off the floor is long enough to cover any offending bits, barely. The staff doesn't show 'til 9:00, so I have a good hour of half-naked time. Gail could care less what I walk around in. She's seen me in my skivvies more times than a friend probably should, but then, she and I have been through the wringer.

Although we were dorm neighbors, we didn't become really close until I broke up with the photographer, Jamie. I think she heard our fights. She used to knock on my door on those days after he left, and we'd just talk. Then came cancer—those were some really dark days. Days I didn't want to continue on with, that I didn't want to be sick one more fucking time. Then there was the whole cheating Dylan debacle, which left me a raving lunatic. But Gail stuck by me. Actually, refused to leave my side so I couldn't try anything, not that I was planning on it, well, not seriously, anyway. Her stubbornness was the only thing holding me together for a good many years. For that, I will be her friend to her dying days. That's the stuff most people don't understand about our very snarky relationship. We've both have been to hell, just at different times in our life, and we cling onto each other to keep from drifting back.

It is with that sense of thankfulness that I vow to make her visit with psycho mom the best it can be. Mrs. Morgan will see that her daughter does, in fact, have her shit together and, more importantly, can handle being a mom without unsolicited help from her mother. I can't stand that woman. Or this wedgie from hell stuck in my ass.

It is when I am in mid-removal that I hear a voice.

"Good Morning, Ms. Harper."

I stop dead in my tracks. My hand still on my undies. Leaving my left butt cheek exposed. I'd know that voice anywhere. Fuck.

"Mrs. Morgan," I say. Take your hand off your ass! I yank my hand away and try to pull my shirt down a bit, which only manages to tug the neckline dangerously low. "You aren't supposed to be here until this afternoon."

Mrs. Morgan purses her wrinkled lips together. Her silver hair is pushed back into a tight bun. She glares down at me from over the edge of her dark burgundy glasses. "I presume if I had arrived at that time, you would be wearing more appropriate attire?" She doesn't look down to my legs, no, she keeps her cold eyes locked right onto mine, so I can feel the full dose of her judgment. God, how the hell did Gail come out so normal? Wait… strike that. Gail is now forgiven for any of her insanity.

"I probably would have even showered," I say. Funny, she doesn't laugh. "I'm just gonna go get dressed and let Gail know you're here."

"Wise decision. Perhaps the next time I come for a visit you won't have to remind yourself that you don't live on a nudist colony."

I try to bite my tongue, but I can't. "Yet. I've applied for one," I say. "Just waiting on the acceptance letter." I beam. "Happy Thanksgiving!"

Mrs. Morgan doesn't flinch. Even her not saying a thing pisses me off. Exasperated, I march into Gail's room. She's still sound asleep, but I think the sound of the door slamming should fix that.

"Holy fuck," Gail screeches, ripping her sleeping mask off.

"Oh, did I wake you?" I say politely. "So sorry. I just thought you'd like to know that your mother is here." I flop on her bed face first.

She bolts upright. "My mother? Jesus, Dee, why didn't you wake me?"

I lift my head off the silk to glare at here. "I thought I just did."

She huffs and throws the blankets back, "I meant earlier." She scrambles to reach her wheelchair.

"Gail, she's four hours early. This is not on me."

Her head whips around. "She's early. She is never early. Being late is something she prides herself on."

"Well, now she can pride herself on seeing me in my underwear before I've even had my coffee."

Gail gasps looking down to see my Wonder Woman undies. (Shut up, they're awesome). "She will never let you live that down, you know?"

I roll over onto my back. "This, I know."

"Dee, how am I going to get through this?"

Propping myself up onto my elbows, I smile. "A lot of wine on my part. You, however, are fucked."

Gail takes off her robe to reveal that she's fully clothed underneath. Like a sweater and pregnancy trousers sort of dressed. I gape at her.

"What?" she says. "You're not the only one who has been caught with their pants down by my mother."

"Methinks, your mother is a bit of a perv."

At that, Gail laughs and relaxes a bit. "Go find something in my closet to wear. I don't want her to see you streaking the halls again."

I grumble because Gail will only have dressy pants or skirts, but it seems like the lesser of the two evils at the moment.

When I've managed to find something of hers that doesn't trip me because of the sheer length of pant, I wheel Gail out into the living room where I assume I would find Mrs. Morgan, but she's not there.

"Where the hell did she go?"

A voice calls from afar. "If you are referring to me, dear, I have yet to be invited in, so here I stand, old and weary, with nowhere to sit."

"I knew she was a vampire," I whisper to Gail.

Gail jabs my ribs with her elbow.

"Mother, don't be foolish, come and sit with us. Dee can bring us in some tea."

I glare down at Gail. "She can, can she?"

"Please? Rosetta should be in any second now." Her eyes are full of worry.

"You owe me."

I take my leave, happy to not have to endure the monster, and head into the kitchen and make the specialty tea that Mrs. Morgan insists on. No other tea is worthy of her palate. It takes all I have not to switch it out with Nestea just to prove her fancy-pants taste buds are wrong.

When I come back into the room with the tea tray, Gail is staring at her mother, sort of horrified. I'm used to this look because that is how I often look at her, but for Gail, it's a new thing.

"Everything okay?" I ask, setting the tea down on the glass table between them.

"Of course," Mrs. Morgan insists. "I've just informed Abigail that Jonathan will be around next week." I cringe. Gail hates being called Abigail. She's also not fond of her mom's attorney, Jonathan.

"Why is he coming here?" I turn to Mrs. Morgan. "Are you dying?" I blurt out. Yes, I am tactless.

Mrs. Morgan scoffs, "Dear child, I will likely outlive you. No, Jonathan is coming over to set up the trust fund for the twins."

"Oh." Well, that doesn't sound like a bad thing, so why does Gail look so shocked?

I sit down because I don't know what else I'm supposed to do.

"Just a few signatures and he'll be out of your hair, dear." Mrs. Morgan says, then begins sucking in air through her teeth at me. "I suppose, as a guest, I am supposed to serve my own tea as well?"

I look at Gail who is still staring, shell-shocked, at her mother. I bite down on the edge of my cheek but get up to start pouring her tea, but then stop. This is exactly why Gail is mute. She is at a loss for words at the gall her mother has. Setting up a trust fund isn't an act of charity, it's an act of control. She is trying to control the grandchildren before they are even born.

"Actually, you only need to serve yourself the tea if you want it," I say, standing fully up. "Not sure if you know this, but slavery has been abolished for a long damn time, Mrs. Morgan. Get your own damn tea."

At that Gail snaps out of her stupor. I hear her making apologies for me as I leave the room. I won't apologize, though. No way in hell.

"Sorry I can't stay, ladies, I have a date," I lie. Well, a date in which I will gorge myself on pancakes at The Original Pancake House. I'll hit the Lincoln Park one now that I'm at Gail's. I'm moving up in the fast-food chain world. And yes, it will be open on a holiday. This is Chicago, people. We don't close for anything.

"Oh," I add, popping my head back in. "In case I don't see you this afternoon, happy fucking Thanksgiving."

Frustrated, I grab my purse and head out the door. Of course, in my rush, I neglect to actually watch where I am going and run smack into Rosetta. She starts cursing at me in Spanish and I try to apologize but, I get distracted by the man that's next to her. Damn. He's too young to be her husband, so it must be her son. He has her same almond shaped eyes.

Rosetta sees me sizing him up.

"Dis is my son, Pedro. He is drop me off. It is start to rain too hard to wait for bus," she rattles off other things I don't understand because I get hypnotized by her rolling r's. That and the half-grin her son is giving me. She must have said some sort of farewell in there because she gives him two kisses on his cheeks before she goes inside. I don't bother to warn her about Mrs. Morgan. There is no real way to prepare for that.

"I am so sorry," I bumble, as though I trampled over him instead of his mother.

He laughs, it's deep and smoky. "No problemo." He smiles a subtle seductive grin, then turns to leave as in slow motion, as though he is waiting for me to stop him.

"Hey, Pedro." A perfect P name. "I was just about to stuff myself with pancakes and a pig's worth of sausage. You wanna join me?"

He turns to look at me over his shoulder. There is a wicked glint in his eyes. "Si," he whispers.

Si.

***

Journal Entry: P is for pancakes with Pedro piled high with a pound of pork.

22.

The chapter in which Gail throws a baby book at my head.

Breakfast with Pedro turned out to be a bust. It was obvious that he just said yes so he could get into my pants. Had it been a few weeks earlier, I may have indulged the idea, but now that I've been with Harold, I just—I don't know, it just doesn't appeal to me anymore. Harold has contaminated me against other men! When I told Pedro he wouldn't be getting any (he actually flat-out asked) he got up and left, sticking me with the bill. Jerk. I must remember to glare at Rosetta the next time I see her for raising a son with such low morals. Yes, I know the irony of that statement since I just asked him out because his name started with P. It doesn't mean a glare still isn't in order. Christ, Rosetta glares at me enough. At least now I have a legitimate reason to return the gesture.

After I pay for two breakfasts, I call Harold, but he doesn't pick up. Instead, I get his voicemail. I ask him to call me when he gets a chance and begrudgingly head back to the house. I so don't want to go back there, but at least now Rosetta is there to cater to the beast's every whim. Hell, I might be able to sneak into my room without her even noticing.

I get off the elevator and paused, waiting to hear sounds of shouting or, at the very least, the repetitive splattery sounds of a knife going into an elderly woman's chest, but alas, all is quiet. Still, as I tip-toe into the house, I have double check to see that I'm still wearing pants. Damn that woman.

The kitchen smells faintly of egg, so I'm guessing soft boiled eggs were demanded. I'm sure she insisted on the silver egg holder and hammer as well. Pretentious witch.

I'm about to sneak into my room when I notice something. It's quiet. Too quiet. Maybe I'm in luck, and they went out or something. I chuckle at the thought of Gail being trapped by the grip of her mother's hands on her wheelchair, controlling even where she goes. Hell, that's probably where Harold is now, driving their asses around.

I'm about to breathe a sigh of relief when I walk into the living room to watch some Netflix. The second I step foot onto the carpet; however, I am knocked clear across the forehead with something. Something hard.

"Fuck!" I shout.

"Oh, Dee! Shit, I'm sorry," I hear Gail say.

"Abigail, language." Mrs. Morgan tsks.

"Screw you, mother. You just made me hurt my friend."

I open my eyes through the sting along my forehead. Was Gail really talking back to her mother?

"Honestly, Abigail, can you not accept responsibility for anything? You are the one who threw the book, not me. This seems to be a theme for you. This whole situation is your fault. You are the one who disappointed your father by not taking a leadership role in his company and now have no earned income of your own, you are the one who wasted your youth with people of poor breeding," I don't miss the glance she shoves my way, "and you alone are the one got knocked up without knowing who the father is. Face it, Abigail, you are a failure and, therefore, have no choice but to accept my help."

Through my one opened eye, I see Gail's face go from white to deep red.

"The only thing I have to do is kick your ass out of my apartment! Rosetta!"

Mrs. Morgan doesn't even bat an eye. She just smirks at her daughter, almost daring her to try.

"Yes, Ms. Morgan?" Rosetta says, rushing into the living room, a dish towel has been thrown over her shoulder. There is a smudge of her cum-worthy gravy brushed along the bottom. I know it would be in bad form to get up and lick it off, so I stuff my hands in my pocket instead.

"Rosetta, please see my mother out. I'm sure she knows how to hail a cab, being so infinitely wise as she is."

Gail pushes out of the living room and wheels into herself into her bedroom, where the resounding slam of the door reverberates off the walls.

"Yikes," I say, looking at Mrs. Morgan. "Well. Always a pleasure. Good luck with that cab. It helps if you can whistle. Loud." I give her a wave then head to my room. I really want to go see Gail, but I also don't want her to hurl something sharper at me while she's this angry. Long time coming, I say. Her mother is vile. It's about time she got a taste of her own medicine.

Behind my closed door, I can hear Mrs. Morgan shouting at poor Rosetta. A good ten minutes of flabbergasted comments erupt from Mrs. Morgan, interrupted only by the occasional 'Si' from Rosetta. Smile and nod, that's the way to deal with the rich. I bet they are taught that early on in housekeeping school...Yes, I know there is no housekeeping school, but if there was... I'll stop now.

When I hear the front door slam, I wait a few minutes before accepting that the coast really is clear. I duck my head out and hear Rosetta mumbling in Spanish so I know the coast is clear. As fast as I can, I rush over to Gail's room and knock quietly.

"Gail, honey," I coo. "The mean old lady is gone. Can I come in, or do you have a stiletto in there you are gonna throw at me next?"

She doesn't answer, so I take that as a 'come in' sign. If she were ticked, I would have heard her reply. So would Canada. I open the door slowly, though, just in case. The soft sobs let me know her guard is down.

"Oh, sugar booger, what happened?"

Gail looks up at me from her chair, her eyes puffy. She has a tissue clenched in her hand.

"Why won't she just leave me alone? I am 41 years old. Why can't she just let her hatred of me go and leave me in peace?" Gail sniffs.

"Because she is a horrible, horrible woman who you had the misfortune of hatching from," I volunteer. It gets me a small smile.

"She's threatening to cut me off."

I stare at her for a moment, letting the weight of that sink in. Gail has never not had money. She wouldn't be able to function without it.

"What? How? Why?" Yes, I'm very eloquent when shocked. It's a gift.

She doesn't answer but instead wheels herself over to her

bed. I rush over to help her settle into her down. This much stress can't be good for the babies.

"Can you hand me my pills? I need to take them soon."

I turn around and snag the bottle that's on her bedside table and hand them to her.

"God, it feels like I just took one of these," she sighs.

"Four hours flies when you're battling the devil," I say, "which brings me back to the: What? How and Why?"

Gail ignores me for a moment as she pretends to be getting comfortable in bed. Her stomach is just large enough that the days of her sleeping on her back with any sort of success are over. I help her put a pillow between her legs and tuck the sheets under her chin. "Don't think I don't know that you're stalling."

"It's all so juvenile that it's embarrassing," she says playing with the edge of the sheets. "I know I should have told you this before, but for obvious reasons, I didn't." Another sigh. "When Daddy died, he didn't leave me money from his estate; instead, he put it in a trust fund that my mother was to oversee until I was 45. An age Daddy thought I may have grown up by." She snorts. "How sad is that?"

"What's sadder, is that he knew your mom would live so long."

Gail ignores the joke. "She was a ripe old bitch about her

new-found power at first. Only giving me chunks of money if I did things she wanted. Like, join the board, become one of her women's group—"

"I always wondered why you did that. Here I thought it was so you could embarrass the living snot out of her."

Gail smiles. "Well, naturally I did that, which is why she lightened up on her demands. She found it easier to pay me to shut up then to try and keep me in line, but now… now she knows how much I am going to need that money, so she pulls this shit."

"Ah yes, the shit that forced you to throw a book at my head?"

She frowns. "Yeah. Sorry about that." She shifts onto her elbows. "She is insisting I name the twins 'family names.'"

"That warranted a book to the head?" I ask, rubbing it again.

Gail rolls her eyes at my theatrics. "The girl's names are fine. Either Valerie or Jaclyn after my Great Aunts."

Not a fan, but not my kids.

"Okay…" I say.

"It's the boys that I won't budge on. Ernest or Whitman," she growls. "Grandfather's names. Old names. Names that will win them no friends. I won't do it. I won't. I won't let her micromanage my life like this!"

"Ah. Well, yes. I can see your point. Not really much you can do with those names except get them a nice walker."

She glares at me.

"Look, it's easy," I say. "You give them cool middle names and call them by that," I say.

Gail balls up the tissue in her hand and chucks it at me. Like a fool, I attempt to dodge it. A tissue. Yeah, I'm pretty bad ass.

"That's not the point! The issue is her even demanding such a ridiculous thing in the first place."

I sit down on the bed beside her, trying to phrase what I am about to say carefully since I am now within pummeling reach.

"So, you're going to give up the money, then? Good for you. You don't need to live in a penthouse or have any staff." Eek. What about Harold? He'd be out of a job. What did he do before driving? It's odd that I don't know this. Isn't it? Then again, how much do we really know about each other? I mean, it's not like we're an actual thing or anything. It would be weird if I did know his whole life story. Why does it feel wrong not to know? Too many thoughts. Focus now. Gail is upset. Focus on Gail.

Beside me, she rolls onto her side. "Oh, I'm not going to give this all up. Don't be daft. I'll have to give in, but she can, at least, sweat my rebellion for a few days before I go crawling back to her."

I put my hand on the lump that is her leg. "You don't have

to, you know. You could kiss it all goodbye. Start fresh, get a job—" Gail throws her head over her shoulder to glare at me. "Right, scratch that. No one would hire you."

"I'm not qualified for anything but being a bitch," she says with a sadness that makes my heart hurt.

"Gail, that's not what I meant—"

She holds her hand up. "I know. Doesn't mean it's still not the truth. I am my mother's daughter, after all." She rubs the swell of her belly. "They won't be like me, though. I promise you. I will not let them turn out like me."

I frown.

"You better let them be like you, or I'll be pissed," I say. Gail rolls back over, clearly a bit taken aback by the hostility in my voice. "Those kids better have a solid dose of my best friend in them, because there is no one else like her on the planet and the world needs more kick-ass people like her." My bottom lip starts quivering, even though I don't mean it to. Damn stupid emotions.

Tears well in Gail's eyes too.

"Thanks, Dee."

I crack a small smile. "You're welcome, you dumb bitch."

We start laughing until the tears turn from sorrow to joy.

***

Journal Entry: Thanksgiving was just Gail and me, drowning every piece of food in gravy. Best. Thanksgiving. Ever.

23.
The chapter in which discover rapid-fire dating.

Two weeks have passed since the Great Book Incident. Christmas is knocking on our doorstep, which has made Gail a tad more sentimental and giving. She's simmered her anger down and agreed to meet her mother halfway. She gets to choose one of the twin's names, and Gail will choose the other. It's not ideal for either one of them, which, is probably why they agreed to it. At least, they would be equally miserable. It's the little things that keep families close.

I've finally got my Christmas shopping out of the way. Gail insisted she go with me when I shopped for her. Since she is, by her own admission, the world's hardest person to buy for, I thought taking her with me might prove easier. It was. Sort of. Gail told me what she wanted, and I told her what I'm willing to pay. Compromises were made.

I kept dragging her toward the baby stores on our outing, but she refused to buy anything else for them yet. She thinks she's already jinxed herself by getting the cribs and car seats. She won't buy anything more until week 27 when the babies will be at a safer gestational age. I shake my head at her superstitions, but buy gifts for her, Neil, Chad, and my mom instead. Yes, perhaps Harold has a gift too, but I'm not telling you what. He hasn't called me since that night with Oscar. I'm starting to think something is wrong. Or maybe he's finally respecting my 'wait until the bet is over' mantra. Whatever the reason, it's kind of bumming me out. I'm trying really hard not keep checking my phone for missed calls.

In dating news, Gail has introduced me to the world of Rapid-Fire-Dating. Apparently, this is a thing. She found out about it through the message boards on one of the dating sites. She is so excited about the concept that she's tagging along. Get this: she's going to pretend she's had foot surgery to explain why she's in a wheelchair. I know. I'm rolling my eyes too. She has already found the perfect baggy top that manages to hide the baby bulge, but not her chest. Gail figures if the girls look good, they won't even notice the rest of her, which is, sadly, probably true.

She won't listen to me when I tell her the doctor doesn't want her that active, to which she tells me she will be in her chair the whole time and to stop nagging. She has her mind set, so it's better to let her go. She's giddy about getting out of the house for something other than a doctor's appointment. The way Gail tells it, all we need to do is show up at the place listed and for the next two hours, 'date' the men that show up. My definition of Hell.

There will, supposedly, be tables set up around the room and you have 5 minutes with each person. A buzzer sounds and the men move to the next waiting woman. Sounds more like a cattle call than a date to me, but if I can get a good chunk of letters off my list in one night, I'm in.

I've tried to reach Harold all day to moan about my upcoming evening, but I keep getting voice mail. Again. A not-so-great feeling has been sinking its claws deeper into my self-confidence with every day that slips by. Of course, Gail has no idea what's going on, or so I think. She hasn't used him at all since that night either if I am remembering right. When her mom was visiting, they used Mrs. Morgan's driver because she didn't trust anyone else but her Vincent to drive her in the big bad city. The only times I went out with Gail were on the weekend, which isn't Harold's shift, so I'm probably just being paranoid. It's the holidays, people get busy.

Or change their minds.

"Okay, so I have our list of questions for tonight," Gail says, wheeling into my room breaking me out of my downward spiral. I really need to install a speed bump or pothole or something. That woman is too damn quiet in that chair.

"We need to have questions?" I ask. "We're barely gonna get out: 'What do you do for work?' before they move on."

Gail rolls her eyes at me and tosses me a set of index cards (neon pink, mind you) that are hole punched in the top right-hand corner and have a small metal ring connecting the ¼ inch stack.

"Um…" I say, flipping to one of the first cards. "This seems excessive." I flip to one of the cards and read the question printed there. "'Which Kardashian would you rather fuck?' Seriously? This is a question on which you base an opinion of someone's date-ability?"

She crosses her arms. "What if they say Kim?"

I gag.

"You see the relevance, then?"

I ignore her and flip to the next one.

"'If you were a serial killer, how would you kill me?'" I look up at her. "Really? Really?"

"That's basic Psychology 101," Gail counters. "How fucked up is his mind? That's the first question I'm asking." I refuse to tell her she has a valid point, because, well, that would just be creepy to actually admit out loud.

"So, you're suggesting that asking them what they do for a living, is irrelevant," I begin, "but what wine they would serve while carving up your body to eat, is not?

"Ooh, that's a great question!" She grabs the cards back and flips to a blank one in the back. "The type of wine they selected would say a lot about what they thought of me and volumes about their taste."

I shake my head. "And I thought I was the insane one."

Without looking up from her cards, she says, "This is not the first time I have proven you wrong on that very topic. I win the crazy vote every single time." She laughs, then looks over her shoulder at me. "Please tell me you're not wearing that?" I glance down at my jeans.

"Don't be silly. Why would I wear comfortable jeans to meet men I don't want to date when I can wear whatever torture device you call fashion which you surely have all planned for me?"

"Good girl. Follow me."

Sighing up towards the ceiling tiles, I do as instructed. To do otherwise would be futile. It hurts my head less to just do what she wants. I'm starting to understand her relationship with her mother on a whole new level.

On her bed is a black mini skirt and a silver sparkly top that looks like the girls would have to struggle to stay inside of.

"Um, no. I am not wearing that." I say, crossing my arms over my chest.

"No, you're not. I am."

"But—"

She copies my arms across her own chest. "But what? Just because I'm 23 weeks pregnant, doesn't mean I can't still dress sexy. It's a maternity mini, so clearly, the pregnancy fashion world agrees with me. I'm pregnant, Dee, not dead."

I hold my hands up in protest. I'm not touching that.

"Fine, what am I wearing?"

Gail smiles. "This." She spins around and wheels herself over to her dresser. Pulling open the second drawer, she holds out a soft pink cashmere sweater. "This would look cute with your sexy butt jeans and my black knee boots…"

"Wow. I—I actually like this. It isn't like see through or something and will show my nipples, is it?"

Gail laughs. "No. But it will make men want to reach out and touch it. Cashmere has that effect on people. Makes you instantly approachable."

I reach out and take the sweater in my hands. It is the softest thing I've ever felt. This must be what a cloud feels like. "I've never seen you in this. Is it new?" I bring the sweater to my face and rub it against my cheek, closing my eyes against the delicate fibers.

Gail doesn't answer. When I open my eyes, I see her reflection in her vanity mirror. She has her lost in thought look

The ABCs of Dee   Danielle Bannister

on.

"Gail?"

She blinks a few times. "What? Oh, no. It's not new. Daddy gave me that. Before he died, obviously. It was just another attempt of his to make me into the good little girl he so wanted." She lowers her head. "I was such a bitch. I told him I'd wear it to his funeral." A single tear spills from the corner of her eye. "I didn't think he would die so soon after I'd said that. It was a mean, hateful comment, and I never got to take it back. He died thinking his daughter hated him. Oh, Dee. I was a horrible daughter. What makes me think I'll be any better as a mother?"

"Gail, stop and think about your own mother and what a shitty job she did, and you still turned-out pretty kick ass," I say, trying to lift the mood.

"Ugh. Mother." She grabs a tissue and angrily wipes at her nose. "I met with Jonathan yesterday to finalize the trust paperwork." She blows her nose. "I had him draw up a will, too. I am not going to let my kids fall into her hands if I bite it before her. No way in hell."

"Yeah. I can't see your mom tending to children." I start laughing at the mental image of Mrs. Morgan running after toddlers.

"Exactly. Now go put that on. I want to see how fuzzy you

284

look in it."

"Are you sure?" I say.

She nods emphatically.

An hour later, we are primped and ready to speed date. I'm not really sure what I was expecting for this event, but it definitely wasn't the normal looking restaurant that we pulled up to. "Be back in two hours, unless I call," Gail tells the driver.

"Two hours is a long time," I say. "Why do we need that long?"

"Darling, it's going to fly by. Besides, think of how many names you'll be able to check off tonight alone. I am doing you a huge favor by allowing this night to even count," Gail says, adjusting her breasts.

"What do you mean, a huge favor? I still have to ask them all out. Odds are, none of these guys will be letters I need anyway. That will just be my luck."

She stops me just before we enter the restaurant. "Dee, your job is to tick off, at least, five letters off your alphabet. Any less, and I will disown you."

"Promise?" I snicker.

Gail laughs as the driver opens up the door with her wheelchair at the ready. She's been in that thing more often than she probably should be, but Gail is a spirit that just won't sit still.

"Lighten up," she grins. "This is going to be great."

Taking a strengthening breath, I wheel her inside. The noise once the doors close behind me is unexpected and a tad overwhelming. There are a plethora of excited women standing in small clusters chatting nervously. I frown. I'm in a sea of divorced moms hungry to get laid, retired women with a last-dash-for-love mindset, and the women who were always chosen last in gym class. Is this what women of a certain age have been forced to subject ourselves to? Are we all that desperate to find companionship? Then I notice something.

"Gail, where are all the men? Did 50 women just get collectively stood up?"

She scoffs. "No, silly. The men are already inside at tables waiting to be dazzled by us."

"Great. No pressure then," I say.

The event coordinator, a thirty-something woman dressed in an olive-green pantsuit walks into the center of the room and clears her throat a few times to gather our attention. She's about to explain the rules. Oh goodie. I listen in silent agony as I learn that first, we each are to wear a name badge placed where it can easily be seen. The woman beside me sticks it over one of her DDD boobs. "Let's see if he misses that," she chuckles.

The pants suit lady ignores the laughter and continues.

"You'll have five minutes at each table, ladies, no more. When the alarm sounds, the men will stand and move to their right until the two-hour mark is reached or the number of matches is maxed, whichever comes first, so if you like a guy, make sure to mark him off on your ballot. If he checks your name off as well, we can provide you with their contact information at the end of the evening, but only if you've both selected each other. Got it?"

I look around the room.

I quietly pray that there are only two guys in the room so we can get the hell out of here. I debate just telling Gail I'm not gonna do it when the women in the suit opens the doors and the room is rushed. Seriously. Rushed. It's like these women have never seen men before! Gail is no better than the lot of them because she's at the front, ready to wheel anyone down who gets in her way.

Cowering, I stand back and let the mad dash thin a bit before entering. Once I find Gail in the darkened restaurant, she hands me a card that has the number 10 on it.

"Oh, does this mean there are only ten guys?" I ask, full of hope.

She frowns and holds up her number 13. "No. It's the table number at which you will start.

"Oh." I crane my neck to see over the heads of the waiting women and into the room beyond. Just from their husky voices alone, I know this is gonna be a long night. Great.

"See you in two hours," she winks and wheels herself to her table.

Around me, women are fleeing to their tables, but I hold back. I really don't want to do this. Maybe if I just hide in the bathroom for a few hours, she'd never know?

"Need help finding your table?" the pant-suit woman asks. Damn it. My escape plan has been thwarted. "Oh, number 10," she coos. "That's right over here, Sweetie." She essentially pushes me towards the table, no doubt sensing my reluctance.

I am officially in hell.

I no sooner sit down and say hello when the evening starts. The first three guys are a blur. I never even think to look at their name tags. There are too many 'Have you ever done this sort of thing before?' 'Me, no. You?' sort of questions that I never stop to think to check for their name. On the fourth pass, I actually notice his name, not just because the name is… unique, but also next on my list to check off.

"You name is Q? Like from James Bond?" I ask, taking a swig off the unlimited drinks they provide as part of your dating fee.

Q doesn't laugh or even smile. He is all business. He narrows his dark eyes at me. His shiny bald head reflects the light from above. He looks like a cross between Pee Wee Herman and Daddy Warbucks.

"Time is short, so I'll get to the point," he says, folding his hands on the table.

"Oh, sure, please," I say, laughing nervously flagging down the waitress. I need a drink just for this guy.

"I am a Dom. I am looking for my next submissive. Are you submissive?'

I snort. Yup. A good old-fashioned snort.

"I didn't think so." He takes his hands off the table and places them in his lap and looks to the next table as though he's officially done with me.

"Wanna go out?" I say, grinning like an idiot. This one is in the bag.

"No."

"Awesome. Thanks for saying no!"

Laughing, dig out my phone and wait for the nice lady with the drink cart to help me make this creep disappear from my memory.

After Q comes Aaron, Justin, Frank, Hal, and Bob, who I don't pay much attention to because they aren't letters I need, nor are they in the least bit attractive. I do my best to try and seem interested when I meet Shawn, a salesman from Nebraska who tries this rapid-fire dating every time he's in Chicago. I asked him out, to which he said yes, then I mentioned that I needed to go into the doc soon to see if my crabs clear up. He called it off. Win. I also played a similar card with a guy named 'Red.' A red head with wildly curly hair. I asked him out, he said yes but when he started talking about his job as a taxidermist, I started talking about my job at PETA and he too backed out of the date. Oh well. Toyo seemed like a nice guy except he didn't speak English. It came in handy when I asked him out, though. He didn't answer, so that counts as a 'no' in my book. You'd think that speaking English would, at least, be a requirement for something like this, but then again, there doesn't seem to be much requirement other than your ability to pay the fee and have a pulse. A string of Steve's, Dans, and Phil's round out the rest of the evening. I asked one of the Steve's out, but I can't remember which one. Couldn't get that one to back down. May have to ask Gail for a freebie on that one. He was weird. He kept talking about his niece and how much I reminded him of her. There shouldn't be that level of horniness in a guy talking about his niece. Just saying.

Before I know it, they are bringing up the dimmed lights, making all those people who got sloshed have to squint. (Yes, I'm squinting, too.)

"All right, Ladies, to the front where you came in. Men,

please stay seated. We'll collect your clipboards and give you any matches."

Since I can't see Gail as we file out, I merge with the herd of pathetics out of the restaurant and into the lobby that's doubling as our holding pen. I really want to 'baah,' but I have a feeling I'd get smacked.

I spot Gail easy enough. She's near the back. She has her hand over her head. No doubt disgusted that she put us through this. I'm about to gloat about my letters when she glances up at me as I walk toward her. Something is wrong. Very wrong. Her skin looks blue.

"Gail?" I run over to her, pushing women away as I do. "Gail!"

When her head rolls back onto the chair and her arms fall limp to her side, my pulse begins to quicken.

"Someone call an ambulance!"

***

Journal Entry: The sound of sirens doesn't stop. Not even after you're in the hospital and all the lights are off. The noise stays with you, refusing to let you hope.

24.
 # The chapter where the world stops moving.

The waiting room hasn't changed since the last time I was here. Just the people in it. They wear the same nervous expressions, talk in hushed voices and text non-stop to worry wishers. Even in the dead of night, there are people pacing the halls praying to Gods too far away to hear. I've whispered my prayers so many times these last few hours that my voice feels hoarse.

I am completely wigging out. I've tried to reach Harold a half a dozen times. No answer. I've called Neil, and he actually picked up on the first ring. He and Chad are on their way. I forced myself to call Gail's mom. She tried to be all snooty with me on the phone until I told her that her daughter was in the ER. Never heard another nasty remark. She too will arrive soon, but for now, I'm on my own in a room filled with crying strangers. It's not that I'm not relieved people are coming. I'm just upset that the one I want here the most isn't talking to me. Why isn't he talking to me? What did I do, or say, to make him just stop talking to me? Gail is in the hospital—why can't I reach him? Then, panic hits. What if he's not avoiding me? What if he got hurt, or sick or— Bile rises in my throat.

Not knowing what else to do, I begin a desperate search on the web for the limo service he works for. I remember the name: Leno's Limos. I always joke with Gail that they named it that because their stretch limos were so large they could fit the size of Jay Leno's chin.

I call the number and hold my breath while it rings.

"Leno's Limos," a man with a thick Italian accent says.

"Um, yeah. I am calling on behalf of Gail Morgan. She's a client of yours."

"Yes, yes, of course. Do you need a car?" he asks.

I fight to keep from crying. "Um, no. Um. Actually, I was calling to speak to her driver, Harold. Is he there? See, there has been an accident—"

"Oh, my. Is Ms. Morgan all right?" he asks, clearly concerned more with the cut in the paycheck versus Gail's actual well-being.

My voice catches. "I'm not sure yet. She's in the emergency room. That's why I wanted to talk to Harold, to let him—"

"I'm sorry, ma'am, but we don't have any Harold's that work for us. Are you sure you have the name right?"

Chills run up my spine. Has he been lying about working here? Impossible. How would he get the limo? You can't steal those things. There has to another answer "Um, yes. Well, that's what Gail—Ms. Morgan calls him. He's tall. Dark hair, young, part Native American…"

"Oh, you mean Yona," the man says.

"Yona?" I begin.

"Yes, Yona was the driver for Ms. Morgan," he says. "Do you have a complaint?"

My head starts to spin. His name is Yona? Then it picks up on something else he just said. "What do you mean Yona was Ms. Morgan's driver?" Nothing about this call is making sense.

The man clears his throat. "We have a strict policy that we do not employ those with criminal records. Surely, you can understand. Our clients are more comfortable that way. Please let Ms. Morgan know that we have a new driver already lined up at her disposal for Monday morning."

"Criminal record? What are you talking about? Harold—Yona isn't a criminal," I say. Is he?

"Ma'am, I am not at liberty to discuss this with you. I'm sorry, did you say that Ms. Morgan needed a car?" The confusion on his voice is clear.

"Um, no." I hang up more discombobulated than I've ever

been. What the hell is going on?

"Ms. Harper?" A voice calls from behind me. Spinning around, I see one of the doctors that met me in the ER. He is covered sweat and… and blood.

My knees go weak. "What's going on?"

"Deidre!" Gail's mom comes into the waiting room, causing the tension to rise. "Where is Gail? Where is my baby girl?"

The doctor turns to Mrs. Morgan and stretches out his hand. "I'm Dr. Stewart. I have been working on your daughter. She came in with low vitals and some vaginal bleeding."

Mrs. Morgan goes white. "The babies," she whispers.

"Please, sit," he asks us. I do as instructed, vaguely aware of my movements.

"Where is Gail? What's going on?" she demands in the enraged tone only scared mothers are forgiven for using. Little does he know this is her normal tone.

"I've had a chance to look over your daughter's chart. She's a high-risk pregnancy, as I'm sure you were aware. But her pregnancy is risky, not just because of her age, or medical history or even because she's carrying twins, although those all present higher complication risks, but your daughter has the added condition of monochorionic-diamniotic. Were you aware of this?"

I shake my head along with her mother. Mono-what?

The doctor pauses. "What that means is that both babies are connected to one placenta instead of one separate one for each of them. Now, in most cases, there are no complications; however, it appears as though the placenta has separated from the uterine wall. That caused the internal bleeding that we've been able to stop, for the moment, but we need to act fast."

"What does that mean?" I hear myself ask.

The doc lowers his head a bit. "We are preparing her for C-section."

"What? It's too early! She isn't due until March! They'll die!" I can hear the hysteria in my voice, but I am unable to control it.

"I am aware of the risks. However, all three of them are in danger if we don't perform the C-section. We have the NICU on call ready to incubate the babies. The odds aren't great if they are delivered now, but they are zero if we don't get them out. We have to try. It's their only shot."

My vision starts to blur behind a wave of tears.

Gail's mother raises her hand slowly as though guilty of something. "She has a DNR." Her voice is barely above a whisper.

I swallow the lump in my throat.

"She has A-Do-Not-Resuscitate order? Jesus! Wait, is it that bad? Is she at risk too?"

"It's too soon to tell. I will let you know after the delivery. Until then, all you can do is pray."

After he leaves, I don't move. I just sit and stare at a coffee stain on the floor. I can hear the sound of my heart thrumming in my ears and the dull hum of chatter coming from out in the hall. My vision narrows. It feels like what one might feel like after an explosion: shell-shocked.

"Deidre." I feel Mrs. Morgan pulling on my sleeve, but I don't move. I can't. "Deidre. Come now. Snap out of it. Gail needs us." I blink a few times trying to see through my tears. "Come," she says again. "We need to find a chapel. We need to do as the Doctor instructed. We need to pray for Gail."

Despite my best intentions, I scoff. "God doesn't exist. Surely tonight would prove that for you."

"He exists for us all today. And when He brings them all of them out of this unscathed, we will rejoice in His glory." Her lips press into a hard line but they quake a bit. There is something she doesn't have control over, and it's destroying her.

Reluctant, I stand and follow her as she guides me down the hall, not because I want to, but because I don't know what else I should be doing.

Hours pass. Could be days for all I know. I haven't moved from this spot since we left the chapel. Gail's mom has been pacing, yelling at people on her phone and demanding answers from anyone that remotely looks like a doctor. Her attorney arrived bearing her living will to give to the doctors. Harold called, or whoever he is, but I didn't pick up. It doesn't matter anymore. Nothing matters except making sure they are all okay.

I'm not sure how, or even when, I fell asleep. I think my body just gave out. The sound of a kid running down the hall jerks me awake. I sit up from where I must have laid down and try to work out a kink in my neck. When I get up to stretch, I see Mrs. Morgan talking with a doctor. When she collapses, wailing into his arms, my heart drops. I move on autopilot.

"What's going on? Are the babies okay?" My voice sounds scratchy from disuse. Over the chaos of Mrs. Morgan's wails I learn that one of the babies didn't make it.

It was a girl.

My entire body goes numb.

"I'm so sorry. We tried everything we could," I hear the doctor say. "Her lungs just weren't developed enough. The boy, though, he's larger. Stronger. And so far his vital signs are good. He's in the NICU. If everything remains stable, he'll still need to be there for at least three months."

My mouth is dry. There is very little air suddenly. "How is Gail? Does she know?"

In my mind, the doctor rests his hand on my shoulder and tells me that she is fine and focused only on the speedy recovery of her son, but when he says nothing, my heart begins to hammer. "What about Gail?"

Mrs. Morgan stops her sniveling long enough to hear his answer.

"She lost too much blood. We couldn't save her. I am so very sorry."

I don't feel my knees give out, or the feeling of the floor as I fall. All I feel are the gasps of breath as they try to fill me and the stab of disbelief as the world that I once knew crumbles to the ground beside with me.

***

Journal Entry: She's gone...my best friend, and her baby girl... they're both just...gone.

25.
The chapter where I give up.

I am the last to leave the hospital waiting room that night. Neil and Chad were here for hours, helping me use up the last of the hospital tissues. I shoo them away, letting them think I want to go home and pull myself together, but I don't leave. I can't. I can't seem to motivate myself to.

After the tears, the anger, the dual funeral discussion, and prayers for her son still in the NICU, I finally stand up. I've run out of excuses to stay here. Gail's mother will be staying up in the NICU for the duration of his stay. The nurses direct their attention toward her. No one talks to me. Gail's gone. They needn't bother with the best friend anymore. There is no use for me now.

Sadder than I've ever felt in my life, I exit the hospital. The chill of the night would normally make me shiver, but tonight I could care less about the discomfort. There is nothing left to get upset over anymore. I scan the parking lot, searching for my car, only to realize I didn't come in one. We came in the ambulance. Never again. I am done with ambulance rides. Even if it's for me.

Just leave me to die on the side of the road. Don't put me in one of those rigs and fill me with false hope that I might actually survive.

Tears that I thought had long dried up, start to fill in the corners of my eyes. I dig into my purse to find a tissue and notice that Harold has tried to call yet again. Now he calls. Fuck him. Fuck everyone. I don't need him. I just need—a drink. Ten of them.

I stick my hands into my pockets to warm them, bury my head into my jacket, and walk to the closest place that has booze and a place for me to just sit down and make the world stop spinning. A knock off Olive Garden three blocks away does the job nicely.

I don't taste the first two shots, but on the third, my mood is slightly lifted. The two guys at the bar flirt with me and I let them. I don't even ask them their names. I don't want to know.

When the bar closes, I plant sloppy kisses on the boys I've deemed Hottie 1 and Hottie 2. I think we exchanged numbers, but I will have to check in the morning. For now, I just want to go home and crash.

Home. Gail's apartment was my home.

"I don't have a home anymore." I hear my drunk self say. "I don't have a home!" I shout it out to the street around me, garnering the attention of a woman passing by. She just clutches her purse tighter to her body and picks up her pace.

"Gail's dead, which means my apartment isn't mine anymore," I yell after her. She turns the corner and leaves me alone again. "Where the fuck do I go?" I ask a streetlamp. I blink slowly. I drank so much that I can't even think straight. I don't have a home. This seems like a big problem. I hiccup. I dig out my phone and dial 9-1-1.

"This is an emergency," I say, wobbling over to a bench. "I need help. My friend is dead, and I can't go home."

The last things that I remember are curling up on the very hard floor and the very loud echo of cell doors closing.

***

A roll of nausea rockets through me like a tidal wave. I sit up and find a toilet not two feet from my head. Perfect. As I yak the alcohol away, the shattered pieces of the night start to come back. Gail, her daughter, the booze. The dry heaves quickly turn into sobbing chest heaves.

"Gail," I cry between gasps of air.

"Hey," a loud thunk on the cell door pulls my attention. "Simmer down. Your bail has been posted. Go cry somewhere else," a large, uniformed man says, unlocking the cell. There are a few snide comments from my 'cell mates' but they don't register. I just want to stop the shaking of my insides.

"Jesus. What happened to you?"

The sound of Harold's voice is not one that I was wishing to hear.

I look up at him, and instead of giving him an answer, I just push past him. He is the last person I want to deal with. How dare he post my bail? How dare he show up now? He makes me sick.

Fuck, my head hurts.

Of course, he can't just leave me be, he has to follow after me. Fine. If he wants a scene, I'll give him a scene. I stop just outside of the jailhouse. The look of surprise on his face when I spin around on him confirms that he is wishing he had left me in that cell to rot.

"You want to know what happened to me? Maybe if you picked up your phone the last few weeks you would know what happened to me, Yona." The look on his face is one of shock. Yeah, busted, asshole. "I don't even know who you are. Why do you deserve to know anything about me?" My head is throbbing, and I feel like I'm going to be sick again. Damn him for coming to bail me out. "How did you even know where I was?" I spit. "Were you following me again? Because I know for damn sure Gail didn't hire you to do it this time. You've been fired!" I laugh a twisted and hurtful laugh. "Guess we're both criminals now."

I am being a bitch, I know it, but right now the hurt inside is too much. I can't deal with this right now. I can't deal with another loss. Better to just run from more hurt.

I whip around and march full speed ahead. I have no idea where I'm going, but maybe now he'll leave me alone. I don't hear his footsteps behind me. Good. Good riddance.

"The cops called me," I hear him say. I stop but don't turn around. "I was the first person on your cell contact list." Now come the footsteps. "And as for the criminal record? I admit, that was dumb. I had a few words with a friend of yours. It didn't end very well."

At that, I turn. "A friend of mine?"

Harold looks at me, steel in his gaze. "Pedro."

"Pedro... how did you know about Pedro?"

"Certainly not from you," he says. His words are laced with venom. "Gail called me that morning to let me know she and her mother needed a ride to Macy's. Steve was still on vacation, so I came in to cover for him. On my way, I see you and Pedro going into a restaurant."

I look at him, dumbfounded, not sure if I believe him or not.

"I watched you with him from the car. You were laughing, batting your eyelashes. Doing everything but screwing him right there on the table." There is a layer of hate carved in his face. "When he came out alone, I wanted to make sure he hadn't upset you. Apparently, he didn't like what I had to say. A few fists were thrown, the cops got involved and well, my job was too."

He is blaming me for his getting fired.

"Not that this is any of your business, but I was only dating him to finish my letter P. He's Rosetta's son. Yeah, I probably flirted. So what? It's not like you were answering my calls. Did he want to fuck me? Yes, he even asked me back to his place, but do you know what? I said no! God! This is why I told you we wouldn't work while I was finishing the bet. I told you I needed to do this on my own. I didn't want you to get hurt! You were the one who said you could handle it."

Snow starts falling gently from the sky. Flakes land on my cheeks. Their chill lasts for a second before they melt away on me. "Not that any of that matters now," I say to the ground.

Harold scoffs. "Why? Did you find your true love with the letter Z in jail?"

I look up at him. There is so much pain in his eyes that it's hard to speak.

"Because the bet is off. Gail died last night, you asshole. So did one of her babies. If you hadn't been such a prick and answered your phone, when I needed you to, you would have known that by now."

My words drain him of color. I hate to admit it, but I wanted them to hurt. I wanted him to hurt as badly as I was. I wanted someone else to feel their loss as deeply as I felt them.

I don't say anything else. I turn and leave. I don't want to hear his 'I'm so sorry for your loss' comments. I just want to be left alone.

When he doesn't follow me, I can tell that my mission to hurt him was achieved.

***

Journal Entry: Grief makes you do awful, horrible things that you can never take back.

26.
The chapter where the shit
hits the proverbial fan.

After yelling at Harold, shit, Yona, I feel empty. Not knowing
what else to do, my feet find their way back to Gail's. All I know
is that I need to sleep and get this gross feeling (which may or
may not be urine) off me. What happens next is anybody's guess.

When I get to the apartment, there is a bright yellow
NOTICE posted. Basically, informing Gail's staff they are no
longer required. Well, fewer people I have to explain what
happened to, I suppose.

I dig around in my purse trying to find my keys. They are
never in the pocket that I first look. When I try the lock, though,
it doesn't budge. It's locked firm.

"What the hell?"

I double check to make sure I have the right key. After the
night I've had it wouldn't surprise me to be using my mailbox key
instead. Nope. Right key. I look at the handle. It's gold. It was
silver before. The locks have been changed. I press my ear against
the door and hear people talking.

"Hey!" I yell, pounding on the door. "My stuff is in there you stupid old bitch," I say, knowing full well, the only person who could have done this would have been Gail's mother.

To my surprise, the door opens. I am ready to scream some more, but it's not Mrs. Morgan that answers, but her lawyer, Jonathan.

"Where is she?" I hiss.

"Ms. Harper! Delighted to see you," he says as though nothing is amiss. British snot. I push past him.

"Never mind, I'll find her myself."

Around me, there are packing boxes all taped up and holding Gail's belongings. White sheets have been placed over her artwork, artwork her mother always hated.

"What the hell is going on?" I ask as she comes into the room, alerted, presumably, by my not-so-subtle entrance. "What are you doing? She's not even in the ground, and already you are taking her shit away?"

"Oh, Ms. Harper. Always a treat to speak with you. However, this," she gestures around the room, "is none of your concern. Now, I must ask you to leave."

I laugh. "Leave? I live here."

She frowns. "You lived here while my daughter was alive." Her gray beady eyes pinch into an evil slit. "Consider this your eviction notice."

Bile rises in my throat at how callous she is being so soon after Gail's death.

"No. We had an arrangement. I quit my job to come and live here to—"

Ms. Morgan blinks at me. "To what? Sink your claws deeper into my family's fortune? I know exactly your sort, Ms. Harper. You were only interested in my daughter's money." She raises her head to look down at me. "That's the downside of being wealthy. We are not privileged enough to get true friends."

My mouth drops. I want to hit her. Hard. Till she bleeds.

"You heartless bitch. That may be true for you, but Gail, wasn't just my friend, she was my *best* friend. I didn't give a shit about her money."

She smiles, as though waiting for me to say that. "Really? Jonathan?" she calls over her shoulder without breaking eye contact.

Her attorney walks into the room like a hungry lap dog. "Yes, Ma'am?"

"The envelope, please."

"Of course." He reaches into his dark blue suit and takes out a thick manila envelope and hands it to the wench. "If I might have a word," he begins.

"Later. I need to talk to Ms. Harper." Jonathan stands at attention. "Alone," she says. Jonathan looks at me as though embarrassed to be spoken to this way, but he obeys her, just like they all do, and walks into the other room. After he leaves Mrs. Morgan walks over to me, practically nose to nose. "I believe this is yours." She hands me the envelope.

"What is it?" I ask.

"Open it."

Reluctantly, I break the seal and look inside. It's money. A lot of it. Thick, bound bundles of hundred-dollar bills. "What's this for?"

"Settlement of past debt. I understand you two had a bet going on. $50,000 was the amount, correct? Now, friend of Gail's that didn't care for her money, your payment has been made. Now please, remove yourself from this house and don't ever return. Our movers will deliver your items to any address you provide on your way out. Good day." She turns and walks away.

The room starts to feel exceedingly small, and the envelope, very heavy. I know what this looks like to her, and I can't stand it. "But I never finished the bet…" I whisper at the envelope.

"That hardly matters. After all, it was a bet amongst friends."

That's it. My blood starts to boil. I want nothing more than to throw that money right in her face, but who am I kidding? I have no job now, no apartment. Nothing. No. Not nothing. I have my savings. I could use what I'd saved for adoption fees and get by for at least a month or two. Maybe. I clutch the envelope in my hand. As much as it would help me start over, I'm not taking this. Before I give it back, though, I have to do something first. In front of that wench.

"Hey!" I yell. "Don't walk away from me. I have something to say." I follow her into the kitchen where the look of exasperation on her face makes me want to haul off and smack her.

She just puts her hands on her light pink pencil skirt and drums her jeweled fingers on the edge of her hip, waiting.

Instead of speaking, I reach into my purse and dig out my phone. "White pages, Chicago, IL," I say into my microphone. After it brings up the link, I type the letter U in the search box. It brings up a few names. I look for men and find two: Uriah Quanano, and Uhan Jones. "Ooh, Uriah Quanano. He sounds cute. Let's ask him out, shall we?" I start punching the number listed.

"What are you doing?" Mrs. Morgan asks, bored.

"Finishing the bet. I had to ask out 26 men. One for each letter of the alphabet. I still need U, V, W, X, Y and Z." The phone starts to ring. "Scratch that. I've dated a Y. Yona. He's a lying asshole."

"Honestly, have you no manners," Mrs. Morgan sighs.

"Hello?" An older man's voice answers. Like really old. Scratchy voice, probably a chain smoker.

"Hey, is this Uriah?" I say, staring right at the witch.

"Who's calling, please?"

"My name is Dee. Wanna go out?"

"Excuse me? Who are you looking for?" A confused voice replies.

"I'll take that as a no. Oh, oh well, thanks anyway." I hang up. "Four to go." I press the microphone on my cell again. "What is the number for Victor, Chicago, IL?"

"This is ridiculous." Mrs. Morgan says, walking away.

I follow after her as I dial the first Victor I see. "Hey, Victor. It's Dee, wanna fuck?" Ms. Morgan gasps. I hang up.

"Another no. Three more." I do the same for a Will, who actually says maybe, but I hang up too fast. Xavier actually says he might be willing if I'd be willing to—I hang up before he can finish.

"This has gone on quite enough!" she yells. "I don't know what you think you are trying to do, but—"

I stop her cold by throwing the envelope of cash at her. It comes flying out in all directions. The perfect money shot, pun intended. In a million years I could never get that to fly out like that again but thank you karma gods for getting that throw right. "What I'm trying to prove to you, is that I am a woman of my word. I'm not the money grabbing whore that you seem to think I am. Gail was my best friend! I don't want her money. I just want her back!"

Traitorous tears start clouding my vision. I won't let her see me cry. I won't. I'll figure out what to do about my stuff later. I just—I don't want to see her anymore. I spin around and practically plow over Jonathan who was on his way into the kitchen.

"I don't ever want to see you again!" Mrs. Morgan shouts after me.

"Not a problem," I say without looking back.

"Um, if I may, Mrs. Morgan, you may want to rethink that statement," he says. "That is, if you want to see your grandson again."

"What on earth are you talking about, Jonathan?" she huffs.

"Please, Ms. Harper," Jonathan urges. "Don't leave yet. I would like to show you something first." He walks over to his briefcase; pops open the locks and pulls out a white folded sheet of paper.

"What is this?" Mrs. Morgan barks.

Jonathan clears his throat. "It's your daughter's Last Will & Testament."

Her eyes grow wide. Shit, that's right. Gail told me she'd made up a will. I totally forgot. My stomach turns. Did she know she wouldn't make it? Did the doctors tell her about the placenta issue earlier and she just decided not to worry us? My heart aches at the thought of her having to deal with that prognosis on her own, but that would have been just like Gail, to suffer in silence.

"When did she write a will?" Mrs. Morgan scoffs.

"The same day she signed the trust document."

Her face grows pale. "Why didn't you tell me about it?" The accusation in her tone is crystal clear.

Jonathan stands tall. "That's attorney-client privilege, Ma'am."

"You are my attorney!" she wails.

He holds up one finger. "Actually, Mr. Morgan hired me as the family's attorney, so technically, I was hers as well," he smiles almost as though he's been wanting to stick it to her for years. Probably has, the poor guy. Jonathan has just gone up a rung in my book. He walks over to her and holds out the paper.

"She mentions you in this section, here." He points to the middle of the page.

Mrs. Morgan glares at Jonathan for a moment but then

snatches the paper out of his hand. She adjusts her glasses.

"I remember my mother, Vivian Elizabeth Morgan, but leave her nothing in this, my Last Will & Testament."

I can't help but smile.

Mrs. Morgan flares her nostrils. "As though the child had anything to give."

"Actually, that's not true. She had some assets you were unaware of." He stands up straighter and points to the paper. "Keep reading. Paragraph three," Jonathan advises.

Frowning, she starts scanning the page, choosing not to read out loud anymore.

The frown on her face turns from a hard-set scowl to a slow, open look of horror. "No. No. This can't be right. Surely, there is a mistake, a loophole somewhere."

"The document is perfectly legal, Mrs. Morgan. I drew it up myself."

My curiosity has gotten the better of me. "What does it say?"

Jonathan smiles. "She left the custody of her children, well, now just her son, to you, Ms. Harper."

My mouth goes dry. "What?"

"You are to be the legal guardian of Gail's remaining heir."

Jonathan walks over to me and gestures to the table to sit, which I do.

"This is outrageous!" Mrs. Morgan screams. "No! No. Whitman shall not go home with that skank!" Mrs. Morgan shouts, storming toward me.

"Whitman?" I say standing up. "Gail's son will not be called Whitman. I don't care how much money you threaten to keep from him. I don't want a single cent of your money. Not one cent! And neither does—" Think Dee. Think of a name that would piss her off and please Gail at the same time.

A sudden warmth spreads over me. "Zac." I smile. Gail would be pleased just by the look of shock on her mother's face. "I'm naming him Zac, as in Efron!" I say down my nose at her. She looks confused. She has no idea who that is. I wish I could see the look on her face when she finds out. "And he and I will find our own way, without your 'support.'"

Jonathan clears his throat. "I feel I should also advise you that Gail has left her estate to you."

"Her what?" I say.

He chuckles. "Her fortune. Her house, her bank accounts. All of it. It's now yours."

I cock my head to the side, making sure to look at Mrs. Morgan. "But Gail didn't have anything. It was all trust fund money," I say. Surely he must know that.

He nods, "True, but her life insurance policy was left in your name. As was a secret account she had me set up some years ago. She's been building it ever since college." He looks down at Mrs. Morgan. "She told me she got some good advice from a friend to start saving for a rainy day and not rely on her parents for everything." He smiles. "I can only presume that friend was you?"

I nod slowly.

"Well, she took your advice and bought some very good stock. It has served her far better than I imagine she ever realized."

"That doesn't surprise me. That woman never did understand a thing about finance," her mother says under her breath.

"You know what? That's it. That is the last time you insult my friend's memory. You disgust me."

I stand up and get up in her face. "Now, if you don't mind. Get out of my house."

Jonathan stands as though to leave. "Jon, you can stay. I'm gonna need some help looking over that will of Gail's. If you don't mind."

"But, of course," he smiles.

Mrs. Morgan turns beet red.

"You are fired!" she shrieks at Jonathan.

"Oh good, you can come work for me, now," I tell him.

He smiles wider. "It would be my honor, Ms. Harper.

"Oh, Dee, please. I'm too young for Ms. Harper."

He nods in agreement.

"You will be hearing from my new attorney," Mrs. Morgan spits before she slams the door on her way out.

"Don't worry. The will is airtight," he says. "She never gets to lay a hand on that boy if you don't want her to."

My head is spinning with everything that just happened. My mouth feels dry and my legs feel heavy. I practically collapse back on the chair.

"Okay. I need to breathe." I say, holding my head in my hands. "I need—I need to try and get my old job back." My head flies up. "I need to find some better medical coverage, I need to call the hospital, I need to come up with a plan—where's my journal?"

Jonathan clears his throat. He folds his hands together; the glint of his gold watch catches in the overhead light. "With all due respect, Ms. Harp—Dee," he says, struggling with the first name basis. "Mrs. Morgan left you a very large sum of money." I glance up at him. "You and your son will never want for anything."

"Nothing?" I whisper. "Wait, are you telling me that I'm—"

"Filthy rich, yes," he smiles. "And a mother."

I let out a huge breath. "Holy shit."

Jonathan chuckles. "Yes, Holy shit, indeed."

After Jon and I talk about everything legal under the sun, I politely kick him out. I tell him I need to rest, which is a lie. He gives me an attested copy of the will so I can show it to the hospital, which is, of course, where I am headed now. I had planned on going to try and see if they'd let me visit Zac in the morning before I found out I had custody, but somehow, it seems much more urgent to see him now.

I'm actually shaking with tears when the nurse takes me from the waiting room, bringing me up to speed on how he's doing.

"So far he seems to be thriving," a nurse in purple scrubs tells me. "His lungs are strong for his age." She smiles. "Technically, I probably shouldn't let you see him until the probate court officially grants you custody, but given the situation, I think it's best you be here."

I just nod, scared out of my mind. We turn into an unattended birthing room and she gestures for me to sit.

"Put these on, Honey." She hands me a hospital gown and a hair net. "Put the johnny on backward for me. I'll be back in a second."

I hold up the gown, confused. "Oh, I'm not his biological mother, I can't, like, nurse him," I say.

She laughs lightly. "I know, but you're his mom now. We need to start the bonding process."

"Oh," I say like that's the most rational reason for putting on a johnny backward.

After she's gone, I stuff my hair under the hair cap willingly to ensure less exposure to germs before I see him. I also have to scrub my arms and elbows for three minutes, too. We have to be careful. He's still so little. I just want to make sure he's still breathing and to let him know that he is not alone in this world. That I am going to take care of him. I want to tell him not to be scared. I want to tell him he is loved. I want to tell him all the things I wish someone would say to me.

Not knowing what else to do once I'm changed, I have a seat in the rocker.

A moment later there is a knock on the door. It opens and the nurse wheels Zac in. He's in this little cocoon of a NASA-worthy concoction of plastic and rolling monitors. From where I'm sitting, I can see the tubes coming out of his nose. Wires are connected to just about every section of exposed skin. His flesh is so red it almost looks burned. They have placed a small blue hat on him that is so big he's almost swimming in it.

"He looks so tiny," I whisper, stepping up to the glass. There are round holes on either side for human interaction. "I am afraid to break him," I say. "Do I need to put a glove on first?" I ask, gesturing to the hole nearest his head.

"Oh, you're not gonna just touch him, Mom. You're gonna hold him." The nurse says, opening up the plastic bubble keeping him warm.

"What?" I ask, backing up. "How? He's all hooked up, he's too little, he needs to stay in there and cook some more, it's okay. I can just look at him."

The nurse is kind and smiles. "He needs skin to skin contact. He needs to bond with you. He needs to know someone is there for him, to protect him, to keep his spirits up. Babies who have this sort of therapy are much more likely to beat the odds than ones who feel left to fend for themselves."

Sure, that makes sense. Am I ready for this?

She picks up Zac, being careful of his wires, and brings him over to me. I just watch her, transfixed. "That's why I had you put the gown on backward. I am going to lay him on your chest. Skin to skin," she says. "We call it Kangaroo Care."

"Oh," I say, fumbling to unbutton the fabric. I don't care that I'm flashing her a bra that really needs to be thrown out. She's going to let me hold him. I would let her see anything for that.

"Okay, Mom. Here's your son."

My eyes start welling up. She places his tiny little body on my chest. My hands instantly close around him. He's so warm! His little head is laying gently against my neck. I can feel his stomach rising and falling. He weighs no more than a kitten. How can something so tiny be alive?

"If you need anything, just press this call button." She places a white cord with a red button next to me.

"Wait, you're leaving? I mean, you're leaving me alone? With him? What if he starts to cry, or—"

The nurse laughs a small, knowing laugh. "You're his mom. If he cries, comfort him. If he needs medical care, the monitors will let us know," she motions to the bank of monitors that rode in along with his buggy. "Don't worry. Just hold him. Talk to him. Rock him. Reassure him he's loved. You'll do just fine." She gives me a kind smile.

"Thank you,—" I say, fishing for her name.

"Beth. I'm Zac's night-shift nurse. I'll be seeing a lot of you the next few months." With a small nod, she leaves me in peace.

For the first few minutes, I'm in tears. I am just so in awe of this boy on my chest. His little feet squirm on me, tickling my skin. I'm afraid to move, afraid I might unplug something vital.

He shifts again, not as though he's upset, more that he's getting comfortable. My heart swells with the idea that he might be settling in a little bit to me as his mom, too.

"I know I didn't carry you in my belly, little man, but I am gonna love you and take care of you for the rest of my life," I whisper close to his ears.

As I rock, I start to have faith that those really loud noises the monitors make are normal since no one is rushing in. In fact, after a few minutes the beeps of the monitors seems to move in time with my rocking motions, or perhaps I have attuned myself to them. It feels nice to feel the rhythm. It's as though things finally are the way they should be.

"I know this was a rough start, buddy," I say softly, "but from this point out, we'll have the time of our lives, okay? I'm going to tell you so many wonderful things about your birth mom. She was amazing. Her name was Gail." My eyes well up. "She was the bravest and strongest and kindest person you would ever meet. You're gonna grow up knowing everything about her. I promise. I won't let you forget her." I kiss his little forehead, amazed at how soft his skin is. Gail would have never believed that a child's skin could feel softer than cashmere. "I promise you, buddy, you will know who your mother was," I vow. "In fact," I say, a light bulb going on in my brain, "I'm going to write a book about her life. Oh, the stories I will tell you," I say. "Your mom was something else. A force of nature." I laugh softly. "A Gail Force Friend. Ha. That's what I'm gonna call it, just because she would have hated it." I sigh, contented, then realize that I'm smiling. Maybe I would be okay. Maybe we both would.

"You would have loved her, little man. I'll do the best I can to honor her by bringing you up the way she could have if she were here to do it."

**

Journal Entry: I'm a mom.

EPILOGUE

The next three months blur in my mind like one big, bizarre dream. The days were a mix of joy and sorrow, of course. Early on, I had to deal with the body of Gail's first born. The cremation had been arranged but somehow they hadn't signed off on what they were calling 'baby girl Morgan.' They didn't even have a name to call her in the morgue. It was like she never existed. I made damn sure to change that the second I found out.

Her name was Abigail. After her mother.

I arranged for her ashes to be mixed in along with her mother's. A joint service was held in late January. Not gonna lie. That was hard.

Having Harold show up didn't make things better. I dodged him the whole time and blocked his number from my phone once I got in the car. I don't have the energy to deal with his lies anymore. I have more important things to focus on.

My son.

After that day, I vowed to be strong for Zac. I came in every day to the NICU. Seven days a week, I was there. I held my son, sang to him, read to him (Harry Potter, of course) and quickly became an extended member of the NICU family. I went home only to sleep and shower. I had to forget about anything else and put every ounce of focus into making sure Zac got stronger; and little by little, he did.

The feeding tube came out last week and I've been able to feed him a bottle for the first time. I thought it would be hard for him to learn how to nurse, but the little bugger took right to it.

His time in the NICU progressed so fast that when the day shift nurse, Ms. Jasmine, came into his room this morning with a cupcake with blue frosting, I was confused.

"What's that for?" I ask, giving Zac's cradle another soft push.

"Zac's going home present," she says. Her white teeth pop against her dark skin.

"His what?"

She laughs a deep belly laugh that makes her soft middle jiggle a little bit. "You heard me, honey. You get to take your son home today."

My eyes grow wide. My hand freezes on the cradle. "Oh my god. Oh my god," I say, jumping up. I rush over and give her the biggest hug I can muster but stop when I feel something wet on my chest. Oh, please tell me I didn't do what I think I just did.

I peel myself off of Ms. Jasmine to find the smushed cupcake flattened to smithereens on both of our chests. It looks like we've just committed a smurf double murder.

"I've killed the cupcake," I whisper in horror.

"Good thing it wasn't the baby?" she laughs.

After a few more chuckles we clean up, and I rush home to get his coming-home-outfit and his car seat. I've had the outfit picked out forever now, a gray, long-sleeved onesie with a picture of Zac Efron on it (because it's funny) and jeans. Yes. They make jeans that tiny. I know!

Once I have the diaper bag and car seat in hand, I take a breath and only then start to panic. I want to call Neil and Chad to and ask them to tag along with me on the ride from the hospital and back to the apartment today, but I also know I can't rely on them for strength. I have to do this on my own. I have to get used to being able to take care of him. Regardless of how scary that idea is. I'll invite them over next week once the two of us have settled in.

They call my driver for me as I sign the last bit of paperwork. I swear, trying to take home your son is worse than buying a house—well, I assume it is, as I've never owned one, but you get the point. Not one, but two nurses follow me outside and watch as I place the car seat in the car. Apparently, I need that much help. Fortunately, they are kind and give me patient instructions on how to do it as I fumble with the latches. My newest driver, Steven, doesn't seem bothered by how long I'm taking. He doesn't seem to be bothered by much. At his age, he's set in his ways. He's quiet. He only speaks when spoken to, so the car ride back is blissful. Zac sleeps the entire way, regardless of how many times I check to make sure he's alive.

The elevator ride up to the apartment makes my stomach roll a bit. What do I do with him when I get inside? Do I have enough diapers? What if I bought the wrong formula? What if he gets sick?

I don't have time to go into the full panic attack that I'm headed for because when the elevator doors open I find an uninvited guest waiting for me. He's sitting on the floor in light blue jeans and that damned leather jacket, all leaned up against my door looking like every 80's rom com you've ever seen. I hate that he looks so good.

"This is not a good time," I say, trying to ignore Harold, who scrambles up to his feet. I put the car seat down. Why are those things so heavy?

I adjust the diaper bag and dig out my keys. I pause when I get the key in the lock. "What the hell do I even call you? Aside from lying asshole?"

"Dee, please, let me explain."

I cross my arms and glare at him.

"Look, my legal Native name is Yona, but I don't go by it. I haven't since I was a kid. My dad hated it, so he nicknamed me Harold. It was his dad's name. Over time, it stuck. It's my legal name but I don't use it. I should have changed it years ago. I had to give them my real name at the limo place because it's on my driver's license. Okay? Now, I am not going to leave this spot until you talk to me."

"Let's test that theory, shall we?" I open the door to my apartment and dead bolt it behind me. Take that. My nostrils flare as I march into the kitchen and toss the diaper bag on the table. The diaper bag. Zac is still in the hall.

Fuck.

The sound of Zac crying out in the hall makes me stomp my foot. "Damn it!"

Unlocking the door, I fling it open to find Harold bent down and unbuckling a now-calm Zac.

"Give me my son," I say.

Harold looks at me. "Your son?" He pulls him up from the seat and hands him to me, confusion all over his face.

I take Zac and cradle him against my chest. "Yes, my son.

Gail left him to me, now would you please leave? This is our first day home and you're fucking it up!"

"Oh, language. Mom." He winks at me.

"Ugh!" I try to slam the door, but the car seat catches in it.

"Two minutes," Harold says, picking up the seat. "Just give me two minutes and I'll walk out of here and you'll never have to see me again."

Zac starts to fuss. This is not how this day was supposed to go. "Fine." I march Zac into his room and lay him in his crib. Harold follows me into the nursery. "Look, stay here. I'm going to make him a bottle." Zac gets a little louder with his cries. Fucky, fuck, fuck. Rushing out of the room, I dig through the diaper bag to find the formula they gave me. Never before have I felt so inept at anything, then I do right now. I pry open the metal safety lid and end up spilling a bunch of it on the counter. Awesome. The little scoop has gotten itself buried in the powder, so I have to fish around to find the handle. As I measure out the powder, I wonder if I've just contaminated the whole damn thing by putting my unwashed hand in it to find the scoop.

I stick my wrist under the running water like I've seen the nurses do. I've read all the books. This is how you tell the right temperature for a bottle, but how the hell do you know if it's too hot just by sticking your wrist under the—Fuck! That's hot! Guess that's how you tell.

Frustrated, I turn down the water until it doesn't feel too hot or too cold, but instead, Goldilocks warm and hope for the best. I dump the mix in and shake it, forgetting to cover the nipple and thereby sending formula onto the ceiling. I let out a slow breath.

Don't worry. You'll get better.

I cover the top with my thumb this time and shake, and again curse myself for not washing my hands first. I'm gonna kill my kid on the first day home. Sighing, I dump out the bottle, wash it and my hands, and start over.

I rush back into the nursery expecting to find a very annoyed baby, but instead, I find Harold, rocking a sleeping Zac in the corner.

I cross my arms in frustration. The gesture causes me to fling milk across the room. Of course.

"Shh," he says. "Don't yell, you'll wake him up. You wouldn't want to do that now, would you?"

I let out a deep, slow breath. "Talk fast. Your two minutes has begun."

His playful face turns serious. "I know you think that the reason I stopped calling you was because I got cold feet or something, but that's not what happened. I was asked to stop calling you."

I narrow my eyes. "By whom?"

He drops his eyes to the floor. "Gail."

I scoff. "Right. And why would my best friend tell the guy I am getting serious about to stop seeing me? Don't do this. Don't drag her name through the mud when you are just too scared to tell me the real reason."

Harold cocks his head to the side. "And what reason was that?"

I sigh. The bastard is going to make me say it out loud. "That you made a mistake. I mean, maybe you thought, at first, we could be a thing, but then, after a few dates, the novelty of dating me wears off and the rough patches start to show. I get it. I've been here enough times in my life to know the signs of withdrawal."

Harold stands up, carefully, so as to not wake Zac. I force myself not to notice how natural he looks doing it. Like he's done it a million times before. He's not at all clumsy like I am.

"You're right. I did make a mistake."

My teeth clench together. I will not cry. I will not cry. I will not cry.

"I made the biggest mistake of my life," he continues, but I can't look at him. It's hard enough to have to hear it. "I let you slip away. And I won't do it again."

At that, I have to look up. I have to see the expression on his face because I can't seem to compute the words. I need visual confirmation that I've just heard him right.

"When Gail told me I wasn't good enough for you, that I should just walk away and let you find someone who could actually support you financially, I—I should have told her to go to hell." He whispers the last word and covers Zac's ear with his hand. "But then," his eyebrows pinch together, "then she told me you said we didn't have any chemistry."

My eyes grow wide. She told him that?

"Oh, she said a lot of things. What stuck out, though, was when she told me she wouldn't allow her friend to settle for a man who didn't drive her wild in bed." I can hear the shame in his voice. "Guess I couldn't argue with that one."

"I-I," I babble.

"So, it's true. You said that?" His shoulders slump ever so slightly.

"No. Yes, but I only told her that to get her off my ass about you. I didn't want her butting in. She would have ruined this for me. She would have made this into something it wasn't yet. I only told her about us not having chemistry to convince her I wasn't falling for you." This is such a messed up conversation.

"So, I'm not bad in bed?"

My cheeks redden against my will. "No. You are not." I look

at my shoes, feeling the blush run down my neck. "Not bad at all, actually."

"That's good to hear." I can hear the smirk in his voice, but I keep my eyes on the ground. "Even so, she was still right. What do I have to offer? I'm a limo driver. I'm almost forty-five and I have nothing to show for it." He shakes his head. "I never thought I'd end up here. This was a summer job, right after college. It was supposed to be temporary. But the days turned into months, the months into years, and before I knew it, I was too old to actually pursue the vet degree I'd started on so many years ago."

I look up at him in time to see him lower his gaze.

"I'm a failure, Dee. You deserve better than what I can give you. That's the real reason why I stopped answering your calls. I hoped maybe you'd find someone worthy of you during the course of the bet."

I clench my teeth against the emotions threatening to boil over. "I did, actually." Harold looks up at me. "Toward the end of the alphabet, ironically. After I'd given up hope on just about everything."

Harold's face hardens, the pain is clear in his eyes.

"Oh? Good," he says, barely audible. "I'm glad you found someone."

He shifts Zac in his arms to give him back to me.

I take my son from him and then reach for Harold's arm. "It's you, Yona. You, dumbass," I say, choking back tears.

"What?" The look of shock is evident.

"It's always been you," I whimper.

His bottom lip does a little quiver but then turns itself into the biggest smile I've ever seen from him. He folds Zac and me into his arms for an embrace and I let him hold me. Hold us both.

Finally.

***

Journal Entry: Now, I would love to say that what followed the loving warm and tender embrace was the kind of kiss that lasted until the final credits rolled. However, this is my story. Zac woke up just as we were about to kiss, sending us into a laugh-cry, sloppy sort of emotional wreckage. It wasn't pretty. But it was ours. Ours. Huh? I like the sound of that.

Harold moved in the following week and the days have turned into blissful months. My novel about Gail has been started, Harold started vet school again, and Zac is now pleasantly plump and learning to roll over. Help us all!

It may have taken 40 years, but my life is now complete, from A to Z.

DON'T MISS OUT on the next story from Danielle Bannister! Stay up to date on all of Danielle Bannister's release information, cover reveals, sales, and giveaways by joining her newsletter at http://bit.ly/DanielleBannisterNewsletter

ALSO, KEEP READING for a sneak peak of another great book by Danielle Bannister.

SNEAK PEEK

Please enjoy a sneak peak of a steamy contemporary romance, The First 100 Kisses by Danielle Bannister.

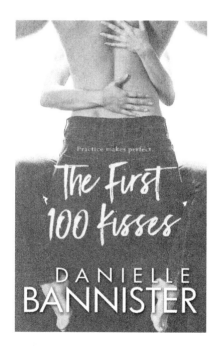

Chapter 1

"Chloe, I have a huge favor to ask," my bestie, Liam, said just as the theme song for Outlander started. The side-eye glare he got in response should have been all the answer required, but Liam didn't pick up the meaning.

"The answer is 'yes' to whatever you need but shut it now. The show's about to start." If my glare were actual daggers, Liam would be as bloody as the men were about to become in the Battle of Culloden. Seriously, what the hell was he doing speaking right now? He knew this was a no-talk-hour. Gasp or squeal, sure, but no conversations, boy! This was sacred time. If our years of friendships taught him anything, it was to never cross me when my shows were on.

I took this stuff seriously. Just like take out Tuesdays and longest fry Fridays. I always won and thereby got to use the ketchup first. We had our rituals that we'd developed over the years –well, I had developed and drug him along, and tonight was movies and munchies. You don't just abandon dedicated viewing time to ask favors. You do that nonsense after the post-show discussion with wine and whiskey. It's like he was new here.

He opened his mouth to speak but I hucked a piece of popcorn at him.

"Not another word, mister. Or the M & M's are next." I lifted a red one for good measure. Liam hated the red ones. He thought they had deadly dyes in them or some shit.

"Fine," he huffed as he settled into the couch.

Satisfied I had won that argument, I swung my legs over, flopping my feet unceremoniously in his lap. Liam looked at my feet, then at me, and shook his head. Still, he took my feet in his hands to massage them. It was heaven. I smiled at him, then diverted my eyes back onto the screen.

As he worked my feet, I couldn't help realizing that nights like this never happened when I dated a guy. I was never as chill as I am with Liam. On the rare times I went on a repeat date with someone, I could never fully relax into myself. I was too busy pretending to be a version of the woman that the guy wanted me to be. I was a chameleon. I'm sure a therapist would say I had issues with abandonment or was just trying to be loved or some shit, but we all had our neurosis and mine was knowing I'd never really be good enough for someone. I didn't need to pay a shrink to tell me that. I already knew it.

When I was with Liam, though, I didn't have to pretend to

be anyone other than me because we're just friends. Perfectly platonic. Seriously. We'd been friends *forever*. Well, not forever, forever, but a long freaking time. He was the only guy friend that I had that I hadn't screwed. Not that Liam wasn't screwable. The man was delish, and he knew it. Normally, that was a turn off for me, but Liam seemed truly annoyed that he had good looks. I often felt like he wished he were more common, like us peasants.

Liam was like me when I went on dates. Uncomfortable in his own skin, but he was like this anytime he was out in public. Liam liked routines, and schedules, hence why he liked my weekly themed events. He liked knowing when and how things were going to happen and when they didn't go as planned, he got anxious.

Unfortunately, this was one of the many reasons he was probably still single. He was a handful, that one. But he was my crazy friend, and I had no problem keeping him in check when he crossed a line (not that he did all that often).

Sometimes he'd blurt something inappropriate, not out of spite but out of not stopping to think first. And there was zero danger of him crossing a physical line with me. He had drawn that line in the sand years ago. A really deep line.

And I got the message. Loud and clear. After a few years, that is. What? He's pretty! Can you really blame a girl for lusting even if it was a dead end?

Liam warmed my cold feet with his long fingers and I moaned in content. He knew I loved having my feet rubbed. Couple that massage with the drool-worthy kilt action on the screen, and I couldn't be happier. This was why I busted my ass each week as a lowly waitress in a city of a thousand restaurants: This end of week bliss. Scottish men, foot rubs, and wine. Nothing could be finer.

As the show progressed, I couldn't help but see Liam out of the corner of my eye each time I grabbed more popcorn, which, I noticed, he hadn't eaten any of it yet. It was clear that he was frustrated. Probably a costume was wrong or one of the weapons wasn't quite period. Liam was a bit anal retentive about that sort of thing. He was a bit anal about everything, truth be told. Most people couldn't stand Liam once they got to know him. I got it, he was a gigantic know-it-all, and no one likes a braggart. It wasn't his fault. It's just how his brain was programmed.

Liam made a low grumble and I shushed him.

"It's almost over. Cool your jets."

When the end credits rolled, I really wanted to discuss what happened in the show, because *Holy Hell* what an episode, but it was clear we were going to be talking about other things ˒ ˑt. Liam shoved my feet off his lap and began to pace ˒

small living room floor.

That couldn't be good. Liam paced when he was having a hard time figuring something out. He hated when there was a problem he couldn't solve, or if there was something he didn't know at least the basic information on. He became obsessed. Frantic. When he got like this, it made him hard to be around, which meant I needed to help him solve whatever was on his mind or I'd be the one ultimately suffering.

"Okay. You may speak now. What's crawling up your ass?" I asked, putting my feet on the coffee table instead. It wasn't nearly as nice as his warm lap.

He stopped pacing, "How long have we been friends, Chloe?" he asked.

I cocked my head and thought. "Well, you moved into the building about seven years ago. I helped you move your boxes. You lectured me on the right way to lift a box, I thought you were flirting. I tried, unsuccessfully, to hit on you. We didn't speak for months after because I was mortified of how epically bad I'd read you. Then, you got locked out of your apartment one day. The super was out of town. I crawled out on the fire escape because you are a chicken who can't deal with heights, and I shimmed my ass into your apartment and saved the day, and we sort have been friends ever since."

He nodded along, validating my word-vomited list of events leading to our friendship. "And in that time, how many women have you seen me bring home?"

I shrugged. "I don't know. A few."

He narrowed his eyes at me because he knew I was lying. I totally checked his dates out through my peep hole. He knew 'cause I told him. I'm a moron.

"Okay, fine, I know you brought home a few, like, five or six maybe? I can tell you this: they were all blonde and big boobed. You, sir, are a cliché," I said, looking down at my very opposite body type. Rail thin, smallish boobs, no real hips. Tack on basic brown hair and eyes and you had an amalgamation of all the qualities guys didn't want.

"They haven't all been blonde," he said, affronted. "One had dark hair."

I stood up and dusted the bits of popcorn off my oversized Sassenach sweatshirt. "Please, she was dirty blonde and easily had double D's."

He didn't argue with me because he knew I was right.

I'll admit, I was jealous the first time he brought one of the bimbos back to his place. Mostly because I realized that he had a 'type' and I would never be it. A bootylicious Barbie I wasn't. I finally got over crushing on Liam by pretending he was g' that he had the male anatomy of a Ken doll. Seeing Liam as untouchable in that intimate viewpoint helped me. Seeing Liam as asexual helped our friendship flourish.

He let out a breath and began pacing again. I headed over to turn off the TV by hand, because who knew where the remote was anymore.

"Liam, help a girl out. What is bugging you? Let's figure it out so we can have ice cream and talk about the show."

He turned and ran his hands through his own dirty blonde hair. I frowned. He had that perfect beach hair that no one from New England should be blessed with. And his eyes. Good gravy. Gorgeous eyes. That's what I'd first noticed about him, and quite honestly, why I offered to help a perfect stranger move boxes. They were the lightest shade of blue I'd ever seen on anyone before or since.

His eyes made him stand out, which I think he knew. He tended to keep his gaze down in public, though it could also be that people, in general, made him uncomfortable. And eye contact, when you thought about it, was really something intimate. Maybe that's why you had to know Liam for a long time before he would maintain eye contact with you for longer than two seconds. We'd advanced to the normal level of eye contact, but it took years to get him there.

Even though we are not involved in a sexual way, nor would we ever be, my heart still did a little flip when he looked into my eyes sometimes. There was just something so captivating about them. I called them his voodoo eyes. Women were powerless against them. Men, too, for that matter. It was his curse. Poor baby. Must be hard to be beautiful.

"Okay," Liam asked, "In the time that we've been friends, how many gentlemen callers have you had over?"

"Um…I don't know." I said, trying to dodge this bullet by pretending I had no idea. 27. I might be a Plain Jane but that didn't mean I didn't like me some booty. The number wasn't skank high, but it wasn't prudish either.

Liam's lips pressed together. He was agitated by my uninformative answer. "Can you ballpark it? It's important. I'm trying to collect the data before I ask the favor."

Good old socially awkward Liam. The things that came out of his mouth, sometimes. He came off as a normal guy, until he opens his mouth and says crap like that. "Collecting data," I mumbled. "You mean in the last seven years?"

"Yes, please," he said.

"I don't know, Liam…A few dozen or so. It's not like I keep a journal of the guys I have over," I huffed. At least, not since I got out of high school. After that, it was just a mental list.

The ABCs of Dee   Danielle Bannister

He nodded again. "And of those *scores* of men, how many of them stayed over?"

Did he just call me a whore?

"Scores of men?" I hissed.

"That's not what I meant," he sighed, "I'm sorry. I realize this is none of my business. I am merely trying to assess if you are the appropriate person to ask this favor of."

I looked at him, my mouth agape. "By asking me how many guys I've slept with?"

Sure, we were best friends, but we don't talk about this kind of thing. We have discussed, in detail, what we had for dinner, or what the homeless guy in front of our building peed on today, or, my personal favorite, who ticked us off at work, but never about the people we were dating. If he was bringing up a clearly uncomfortable topic, it must be something huge he was struggling with.

"Yes. The number of men is essential for the data I am trying to compute."

Jesus, sometimes he sounded more like a robot than he did a man. "Not that it's any of your business, but like 99% of them. Now, can you tell me what the hell is going on in that head of yours?"

Liam sat down on the couch and started to bounce his leg up

and down. A nervous twitch he got in socially uncomfortable situations. I knew from being one of his only friends that this meant he was feeling overwhelmed by something.

I sat down beside him and put firm pressure on his knee with my hand to quiet his nerves, knowing that heavy touch was soothing to him in times of anxiety.

Liam looked down at my hand and quickly stood up. "See. That, right there," he said. "What do I do if…" He broke off his thought and went to the window, looking out at the night sky.

"What? Liam? What is going on? You're kind of freaking me out."

"Angel is moving back to town."

"Oh?"

Angel was his ex. They were serious high school sweethearts. I didn't like her. Why, I had no idea, as I'd never met or even seen a photo of her. I just knew that she'd done a number on my friend. Well, that and he's been hung up on her ever since. He'd mentioned her name maybe five times since we met, but every time he said her name, there was a lingering hurt in his eyes. I'm taking a shot in the dark that she's blonde with big boobs.

"How is she doing?" I asked.

"She's well. I think. She's staying with her mother until she finds a place." He turned around. A pained expression was on his face. "She wants to get together in a few weeks."

"Ah." That explained it.

It was one thing to catch up with an old flame on the phone. A whole different scenario when they wanted a face to face. He must be freaking out.

"Okay…" I said gently, as though approaching a wounded animal. "Dinner is good."

"Chloe, I haven't seen her since she broke off our relationship. We were kids then. So much time has passed. I don't know what to say to her. How to act. I don't know anything, especially what she wants from me."

"She probably just wants to see how you're doing. You know, catch up. I wouldn't stress about it."

He looked at me. "She said, and I quote verbatim, 'She missed me.'"

"Ha! Well, in that case, she wants to bang ya, buddy." I said, hoping that would clear up his confusion and we could start our ice cream. Liam wasn't great at reading people's body language and worse at understanding subtext. Now that he understood her intentions, I thought we'd be able to move on to dessert, but my translation seemed to upset him even more.

"I was afraid you were going to say that." His eyes were drawn tight with worry.

"Dude, it's okay. I got you. No stressing out allowed. I'll help make sure the evening is perfect. I can hook you up with a good restaurant. Maybe get you in to a fancy-pants place." Being a waitress had very few perks but knowing other waiters and hostesses from other restaurants helped bump you up the reservation lists. It also came in handy knowing which places were worth the money and which ones were dodging the health inspector. "Whatever you need," I continued. "I can help with your outfit, picking out the right flowers, where to go after. Whatever you need, just ask."

Liam turned around and put his hands in his pockets. His shoulders slumped. His eyes hid on the floor.

"Sex," he whispered so low I barely heard him.

"Come again," I replied. He didn't get the innuendo. I was used to that. He never got them—part of that sub-text block.

"You heard me," he said, still looking at the floor.

"Actually, I don't think I did."

"Chloe...I...sex, okay? I need help with a sex thing," he repeated. He looked up at me, with his intense eyes.

"Whoa, buddy, I know you wanna make a good impression with the ex, but is a threesome really the right play here?" I laughed, trying to ease his tension. Why did guys get so uncomfortable talking about sex? They loved doing it but God forbid you talk about what the other person wants.

Liam's eyes grew wide for a moment then he vehemently shook his head.

"No. Not that. God. No. Not that." He was blushing, something he did quite a lot. Especially on *Outlander* nights. Not that I could blame him— Those sex scenes were *hot*.

"Okay then, what do you need help with, lube, condoms, toy recommendations?" I wiggled my eyebrows. I could recommend some great things for him to try. I might be single, but I wasn't dead.

"No. Nothing like that." His face was beet-red now. This was getting fun. It was amusing seeing Liam so out of sorts. It didn't happen often. He liked to be in control of his environment, and this was a new situation to navigate. Whatever that might be.

"Then what is it, Liam?" I laughed, feeling totally clueless. "Help me help you. What *exactly* do you need help with around sex?"

Liam let out a slow measured breath, then locked his crystal blue eyes with me to make sure I was listening.

"I need to know *how* to do it."

Download The First 100 Kisses
to continue the ride!

HUG AN AUTHOR

Wait! Before you go can I ask a favor? If you liked this book can you leave a quick rate or review? Even a simple sentence like 'I enjoyed this book' helps the books visibility. Like it or not, people judge a book by how many reviews it has, so one of the best ways to help an indie is to leave a review. Thank you!

You can also follow her newsletter for updates:

http://bit.ly/DanielleBannisterNewsletter

ABOUT THE AUTHOR

Danielle Bannister lives with her two children in Midcoast Maine along with her precious coffee pot and peppermint mocha creamer. She holds a BA in Theatre from the University of Southern Maine and her Masters in Literary Education from the University of Orono. When she's not on the stage, or on the page, you'll find her binge-watching all the Netflix. As one does.

You can visit her website at: http://daniellebannister.wordpress.com/
or
You can also join her newsletter at: http://bit.ly/DanielleBannisterNewsletter

ALSO BY

The Twin Flames Trilogy:

Pulled, Pulled Back, and Pulled Back Again

The ABC's of Dee

The   Hallowed   Realms   Trilogy   with   Amy   Miles
Netherworld, Hollow Earth, Isle of Glass

Short Shorts

Doppelganger

Must Love Coffee

Taking Stock

The Lurkers Within: A Havenwood Falls Novella

The First 100 Kisses

What Moons Do

CONNECT

Newsletter	http://bit.ly/DanielleBannisterNewsletter
Website	https://daniellebannister.wordpress.com/
Facebook:	https://www.facebook.com/DanielleBannisterBooks
Reader Group	http://bit.ly/WriteAllTheWordsDanielle
Twitter	https://twitter.com/dbannisterbooks
Pinterest	https://www.pinterest.com/bannisterbooks/pins/
Amazon	http://bit.ly/DanielleBannister
Instagram:	https://www.instagram.com/daniellebannisterbooks
BookBub	http://bit.ly/BookBubAuthorPage

Made in the USA
Middletown, DE
26 September 2021